DARKNESS DESCENDING

A Mimi Patterson/Gianna Maglione Mystery
Lambda Award Finalist

Penny Mickelbury

MiGi Books
Atlanta and Los Angeles

ISBN: 13: 9781544169231
        10: 154416923X

DEDICATION

This book is dedicated to the memories of:

FannyAnn Eddy, 30
Murdered for being a lesbian
28 September 2006, Sierra Leone, Africa

Sakia Gunn, 15
Murdered for being a lesbian
12 May 2003, Newark, NJ, USA

Shani Baraka, 31 and Rashon Holmes, 30
Murdered for being lesbians
12 August, 2003, Piscataway, NJ, USA

And to all people who are hated for
Looking how they look
Loving whom they love
Worshipping their god their way
Being born where they were born
RESIST

"The world is a dangerous place to live, not because of the people who are evil, but because of the people who don't do anything about it."
— **Albert Einstein**

CHAPTER ONE

It was too damn hot for there not to be any air conditioning in the club. True, it was located in a piece-of-shit building in an ugly-ass part of town, but just because it looked like the third world didn't mean it had to act like the third world. The cheap bitch who owned the joint sure as hell made enough money to pay for air conditioning. The three nights it was open— Thursday, Friday and Saturday— the place was packed to the rafters and the line to get in stretched around the corner, even in winter. The fire department sign held the club's capacity to 250 at a time, but twice that number was the norm. Figure that maybe a thousand people routinely rotate through between its opening at 10:00 p.m. and closing at 4:00 a.m., at ten bucks a head, three nights a week: that's thirty grand a week, not counting the three-to-five bucks a pop for water, soda, beer or wine. Yet, on a mid-September night in Washington, D.C.—which is still the middle of summer in this part of the South—two fans are supposed to keep a thousand bumpin' bitches cool? Granted, they were industrial fans the size of jet engines and with that much power. Still.

Tosh shook herself like her dog did after a swim in the Potomac, hoping to slough off the wave of negativity that all of a sudden enveloped her. Why was she trippin' about some damn fans? She knew better than to allow external shit to affect her, yet here she was, tripping, not because Dee Fucking Phillips didn't have enough class to install air conditioning in her night club but because Dee Fucking Phillips had her night club in such shitty part of town. Tosh got pissed off every time she came over here, which, in truth, was really what was chewing on her ass: That she was coming so here frequently because of Lili. It was easier to be mad that she couldn't park her

Benz in this neighborhood than to admit that some bitch had got her nose wide open enough to drive the thing through.

She stopped walking down the dark, litter-strewn sidewalk, took a deep breath, and lit a joint. She always felt better when she got down to the real truth of a thing, and the truth was, in this case, two different and separate things: Where she was, and what she was feeling. She hated having to come to this part of town in order to be who and what she was, but her Tosh self didn't fit in across town where she lived and work. And neither of her selves was ready to be in love with Lili— or with anybody, for that matter. Talk about unexpected complications! Tosh hit the joint hard and deep and held the hot smoke in her lungs for a long, long moment, shutting off her senses to her surroundings. It wouldn't take much to induce her to turn around and backtrack the three blocks she'd just walked, get back on the damn subway, ride back to where her car was parked, get in it, and go home— but she'd promised Lili that she'd come tonight. Well, she promised she'd come either Friday or Saturday and Tosh had other plans for tomorrow. Anyway, The Snatch was as good a place to release the pressures of the week as any. She felt the buzz, exhaled the smoke, and resumed her trek.

As usual, the line to get into The Snatch snaked around the corner, the people in it too hot to fidget and shift from foot to foot. They just stood there, waiting for the door to open. Hot and heavy night air hung over this part of D.C. like dirty sheets. Funny, Tosh thought, how much difference environment made. Just a few miles away, in Georgetown, say, or DuPont Circle or Foggy Bottom, the same air would feel lazy or languid, but here, far enough south and east from upscale to be considered ghetto, it was just nasty hot. Even the moon looked bedraggled. Did they know, the night air and the moon, that they weren't overlooking stately town houses and boutiques and bistros?

Tosh ran her eyes over the scenery as she walked: Tight, sagging row houses and past-their-use warehouses lined the block on one side of the street, The Snatch anchoring the northwest corner. Opposite, a snaggle-tooth array of weedy vacant lots alternated with a liquor store, a Chinese fried chicken carry-out, a store front Holy Roller church, and a no-name gas station that doubled as a betting parlor. Yet, a mere three blocks away, the Green Line Metro station was a beacon of light and a ready escape into any other reality. "Don't even think about it," she said to herself. Think about Lili...

"Whattup, Dog?"

Tosh shook hands with Darlene the Dangerous, the bouncer at The Snatch, surprised, as always, at the sweet gentleness of her voice. Darlene was a massive woman, six feet tall and built like a boxer— not much fat and whole lot of power. She had a pretty face, surprisingly light brown eyes, and a deceptively mild demeanor. She always wore Washington Redskins warm-ups with Kobe Bryant Adidas high tops, and alternated professional sports team hats— baseball caps in warm weather, knit skull caps in cold. Tonight she wore a Los Angeles Lakers cap turned sideways. "You got 'em lined up early tonight, Darlene."

"Yeah, but least it ain't rainin' yet. How come you here so early?"

"I'm right on time," Tosh said, checking her watch. "Show starts in less than five minutes."

"Yeah," Darlene said, "it does, but it ain't the show you want. Lili dances the second show tonight."

"Bullshit!"

"For real," Darlene said. "Dee made the change this morning. You didn't get the word, I guess."

"Fuck that!" All the irritation Tosh had worked to banish resurfaced in an instant. "Ain't that a bitch! And it's supposed to rain, too?"

"Be cool, Dog. Don't let this shit disturb your peace. Besides, we need the rain," Darlene said peacefully, and inched aside so Tosh could enter— Lili's orders despite Dee Phillips's orders to the contrary.

"Hey! How come she gets to go in ahead of us?" somebody in the line yelled, sounding more hot than heated, but still instigating a chorus of complaint.

"'Cause it's my fuckin' door," Darlene replied sweetly, coolly, silencing the complainants. Tosh gave Darlene the half-smoked joint as thanks, promised to bring her a beer, and slipped inside.

Reality looked different inside The Snatch. It was industrial space without pretensions toward anything else, but there was nothing raggedy and dirty about it. The walls were shellacked brick, the floor smooth concrete. The furnishings were stainless steel, including suspended pole lamps and the sixty-foot bar. One end of the room had a raised ceiling. A steel spiral staircase led up to a cozy loft-like space above the main floor, and a pole fed down directly to the bar. From midnight to one, and again from two to three, The Snatch Dancers slid up and down the pole and danced on the bar and generally made it worth the trip to this shitty-ass neighborhood, because these were no beat up, broke-down junkie hos shaking their asses for a fix. The Snatch Dancers were some super-fine bitches who were professional dancers. Eight of them, two each Black, white, Latina and Asian, alternated shifts. Something for everybody. Tosh had to give it up to Dee on that tip: she knew how to attract a crowd. Bar dancers for women, in a women's bar, no men allowed, not even queens. Dee didn't like men, period. And something else she did really right was that there were six bathrooms in the place. No standing in line to pee. There was a bathroom in each corner of the room and two upstairs, and they were clean. No shooting up and no fucking allowed. That's what the upstairs loft was for. You could almost forgive the lack of air conditioning, if not the neighborhood.

Tosh gave up the ten dollar entry fee to the Moms Mabley look-alike just inside the door then stood against the wall, watching and listening— and calming down. Darlene was right; she was here now. Might as well enjoy herself. The place was jam-packed, the music was heavy and pulsing and writhing bodies blended with the beat. Jade, the DJ, was on the mark early tonight. Just then, the music and the lights and the mood shifted and the bar became the focus. Or, more accurately, the pole from the bar to the ceiling became the focus as the pin-point spotlight followed the first dancer down. Tosh moved in the opposite direction of the crowd, to the other end of the bar. No point in watching if Lili wasn't dancing.

"'S up, Dog?" she heard in her ear, and turned to find Tree Davis towering over her, grinning like she was trying to introduce her lips to her eyebrows. "It's all about you, TD," Tosh said, shaking hands with the collegiate hoop star, "but it won't be for long, you keep blowing off curfew. Kinda late for you to be out hanging, isn't it?"

"Fuck that shit! It's a night for celebrating! You know my homies just won the championship, right? I ain't sittin' up in no dorm, not tonight. No, sir buddy."

"Then have a brew on me, TD," Tosh said, high-fiving the baby-faced six-and-a-half foot WNBA-star to be. She'd forgotten that the women's championship game was played earlier in the evening but she knew that Tree was from somewhere in the mid-West, ergo, the women's basketball team from out there must have won the championship— Tosh had zero interest in basketball. She turned toward the bar and raised her hand. Four of the bartenders now worked the other end, busy because of the crowd attracted by dancers, but two still worked the back end, including Tosh's favorite. "Hey, Aimee. You get any finer, I'm gon' have to marry you."

"You talk any more shit, I'm gon' have to let you," Aimee said, and leaned across the bar into the kiss Tosh offered her. "And I don't mind if Lili joins us," she said, licking her lips.

Tosh licked her own at the thought. Two of the finest femmes she knew getting it on together? Yeah, she could get down with that even if most of her AG pals couldn't. Their loss. "You need to get me four brews and quit fucking with my head," she said to the bartender.

Aimee licked her lips again and reached behind her to get the beers, two in each hand. Tosh gave her a twenty, told her to keep the change, got another kiss, and began to enjoy herself. She gave Tree a beer and picked up two of them. "Be right back. Gotta take these to Darlene."

"Tell Darlene to give me my motherfuckin' money!"

Tosh shook her head. Darlene was a notoriously unlucky gambler, the kind who'd bet on whether or not the sun would rise in the east and set in the west on a particular day, and still people bet with her. She pushed through the throng at the bar to the front door. The crowd outside surged forward when she opened the door, and retreated when Darlene told them back the fuck up.

"Thanks, bro," Darlene said, then scowled when Tosh delivered Tree's message. "Tell that overgrown bitch I said suck my dick."

Tosh was still laughing when she got back to Tree and her beer, and laughed even harder at the girl's reaction. "It's not that she won't pay you, it's just that she owes a lot of people ahead of you."

"So, what're you sayin'?" Tree demanded.

"That you either shouldn't take bets with Darlene, or you shouldn't need the money," Tosh said, digging her cell phone out of her pocket. She flipped it open and punched a number. She squeezed the phone to her ear and held her other hand over the other ear so she could hear. "I'm here," she said when Lili answered on the other end, and shut the phone, angry at herself for sounding angry on the phone. She hadn't wanted to do that, blame Lili for Dee's actions.

"Hey! Look at that! I love that shit!" Tree was punching her on the shoulder and pointing to the menage a trois taking place on top of the bar under the fierce control of a Lady Gaga look-alike with a whip. "How much you think it'd cost me to get that Asian bitch to wrap her legs around my face like that? Plus Lady G and her whip?"

"They're not hookers, Tree, they're dancers."

"Bullshit. For the right dollars, I betcha any of 'em could be had."

Tosh looked up at her to be certain she was serious. "You need to stop making bad bets, Bro. I'm telling you, those bitches are dancers. Actors. That's just a job, what they're doing up there. They get paid to do it and y'all stick twenty dollar bills in their snatches, so they earn more in an hour that most folks do in a week."

"Bullshit," Tree said again, sounding a little less convinced.

But Tosh knew what she was talking about and in that moment, her proof appeared. Lili wrapped her arms around Tosh's neck, pressed into her body, and kissed her. Long, slow, deep. Tosh was subliminally aware of the buzz going on around them. She heard Tree's awed, "Damn, Dog!" Heard several other voices identify Lili as one of the dancers. Heard Renee offer "to get up in the middle of that!" But her focus was on how Lili felt that close to her. Then the spell was broken.

"You know I don't want you on the floor until after your set."

They broke apart to see Dee Phillips standing in front of them, dressed to kill, disapproval etched in her face, and even at five-eight, Tosh wasn't looking at her eye-to- eye. This was her first up-close-and-personal encounter with the club owner, and she now understood Lili's expressed dislike of the woman. "Whattup, Dee?" Tosh said, trying for polite, and pretending she didn't have to look up to do it.

Dee ignored her. "You need to get back upstairs, Lili,"

Tosh felt Lili stiffen in her arms. "In a minute, Dee. I need to talk to Tosh for a moment."

Dee squared her shoulders. "Maybe you didn't hear me," she said, and it wasn't a question. Tosh let Lili go and squared off herself, assessing whether the larger woman's bulk connoted strength or weakness. She needn't have worried.

"Maybe you didn't hear me," Lili said evenly, and Tosh realized how little she knew about this woman. "I said I need a minute. Either I get it or you get another dancer for the next set because I'm out the door. Your choice."

Dee's eyes narrowed slightly and shifted from Lili to Tosh. Then she turned and stalked away, solid and square, a concrete block in motion. Tosh realized that she'd been holding her breath and let it out in a whoosh. "Damn, Baby. You backed her up pretty good."

Lili flicked her hand. Dee already was a memory. "Tosh, I'm really sorry about tonight. Everything's a mess. Dee changed the schedule and I didn't know it until I got home from shopping, plus, I can't see you tonight. My sister called just before I left home. They had to rush my Mama to the hospital. I'm going over there soon as my set's over, and I don't know what time I'll get home."

Irritation surged. Tosh tamped it back down. "What happened?"

Lili shivered. "She was having trouble breathing."

"What hospital's she in?" Tosh asked.

"Georgetown," Lili said, eyes widening in surprise. "Why?"

"'Cause maybe I'll see you there later on," Tosh said.

Lili gave her a strange look, then kissed her again before hurrying away. Tosh struggled to settle and clarify her emotions as she watched Lili disappear into the crowd. She'd surprised herself with the hospital question, shocked herself with the reason for it, and stunned herself with the knowledge that she'd meant it. She really did want to be with Lili at such a crucial time and that really did worry her. Scared her, too. This was dangerous territory. Much too dangerous...

"What?" Tosh said. Tree was talking to her. "Say what?"

"Can you get your bitch to hook me up with that Asian bitch?"

The flash of irritation that had arisen a moment ago was back and Tosh opened her mouth to tear into the big girl, but on the heels of the irritation was the realization that anything she said to Tree would be a waste of breath. She was a nineteen-year-old kid from somewhere deep in Illinois or Michigan. What did she know? "No, Dude, Lili don't know the Asian bitch. They just work together, they ain't homies," Tosh said, and turned away without a trace of remorse for the lie she'd just told.

"Where you goin'?" Tree asked.

"To pee," Tosh said, draining her beer and heading for the toilet in the corner, back near Dee's office. That one never was crowded, probably because of the well-known danger of dropping drawers so close to Dee Phillips, who, despite her external panache, had a major reputation as a pussy pouncer, and who scored more often than not. She dressed full designer and got her hair styled every week, had plenty of money, not to mention a new Bentley— yeah, she got all the pussy she could handle. But not much love.

That's the thing that Lili had put on Tosh's mind that she didn't want there: the difference between love and lust and how one felt so much better than the other. And not the one Tosh always had preferred.

She pushed open the bathroom door and realized why she was here, and it wasn't to pee. The bathrooms in The Snatch were soundproofed. You went in and closed the door and the only music was some quiet jazz coming from speakers concealed in the ceiling along with the lighting. Like Dee thought that using the toilet should be a peaceful experience. Tosh sighed as the bathroom door shut out the din from the club and, with the deafening silence, a week's worth of fatigue settled down on her as she realized she could have stayed at home this evening; that she'd rather be at home she could be in bed, asleep. As the silence enfolded her, she realized that's where her other self wanted to be— at home, where it was clean and peaceful and quiet, inside and outside. "Shit."

"What'd you say?"

Tosh looked up, startled, and realized that three other women were in the bathroom, two at the sinks and one, in military fatigues, just emerging from one of the stalls.

"Just talking to myself," Tosh said. "Sorry."

"You don't dig the dancing girls?" one of the women asked Tosh, and the way she asked, along with the look she gave, made Tosh bristle.

"I've got to pee if that's all right with you," Tosh said, brushing past the women and into a stall.

"Fine by me," one of them said. The same one who'd asked the question, a cute little butch in tight jeans, a tight tee shirt, and some low cut, suede Kenneth Cole mocs with the wavy crepe soles Tosh liked. And the kind of haircut Tosh was considering— damn near bald. Too bad she had on that ugly ass, tacky waist-pouch. Nobody wore that shit any more.

A whoosh of blaring sound followed by instant silence told Tosh the women had left the bathroom and she was glad. Alone was good for right now. She wished she were home alone. There was no point in staying here if going home with Lili wasn't an option. And truth be told, no, she didn't really care about the dancers, and quite frankly, didn't understand the fascination with them. After the first time, what was there to see? Sure, they were beautiful, but it was the same women performing the same routines, every Thursday, Friday and Saturday nights. And some of the same people showed up to watch them every Thursday, Friday and Saturday.

She sat on the toilet much longer than necessary, then, finally, washed and dried her hands and left the peaceful silence of the bathroom for the whooping and hollering that meant the first set was reaching its climax— literally. She stopped and watched the crowd watch the dancers, their eyes bright and their mouths slack and wet, looking it at them like it was a good damn thing the dancers were up on that bar, out of reach. Maybe, Tosh thought as she watched the watchers, she didn't have a well-enough developed fantasy life. On the other hand, she really was fucking one of the dancers and didn't need to fantasize about it. She thought about her Lili, a Halle Berry look-alike, and the routine she did with a white girl who was a dead ringer for Angelina Jolie. Damn! Yeah, that was enough to make the Trees of the world talk and act crazy.

She pushed her way through the crowd to the door and out into the night. The dense, muggy air slapped her, making her realize how cool it actually was inside the club. OK, so maybe air con-D wasn't such a big problem. This shitty neighborhood was, though. She looked up and down the block. Carload of fucking gang bangers cruising by but no taxi cruising for a fare, not here, like there would be outside that trendy dyke bar across town. She could eat dinner there and get a taxi. Hell, she wouldn't need a taxi over there! She could have parked her car over there!

"Hey! I said, where you goin'?"

Tosh looked around. Darlene was talking to her. "Home," she said, and started walking toward the subway, giving a backward wave of her hand to Darlene's admonition to watch her back. She was so tired that lifting her feet to walk was an effort. Fuckin' heavy ass shoes. She wished right then that she had on those low cut Kenneth Coles. She kicked an empty 40 ounce bottle and it sailed, crashed and shattered, the sound following her as she loped across the street. As soon as she stepped up on the sidewalk she remembered that she'd planned not to cross the street until the next block because this one smelled like a piss factory. Every drunk mother fucker in town must come to this block just to piss on the sidewalk. Damn, men were disgusting. Pull it out and piss any damn where.

Suddenly she was on her knees. There was pain! In her back! But she couldn't fall on this piss-nasty sidewalk! She put out her hands to catch herself. Broken glass down there. Then— more pain! Burning. Hot. All the way down she went, sprawled on the pissy sidewalk. Vomit. Hers. More piss. Hers. Get up! God, she hated being dirty. Worse than just about anything, she hated being dirty. But she was so very tired. Go to sleep. Sleep. Sleep's good.

CHAPTER TWO

"How about a change of scenery?" Mike Reese suggested to her two best friends. She stood between them, her arms draped around their shoulders, the three of them standing as close as they were in spirit, their heads almost touching as they struggled to communicate over the noise. They should have remained in the bathroom, where it was quiet, for this discussion.

"What've you got in mind?" Cassie asked, knowing the answer: Mike wanted to go to the Bayou, had preferred the Bayou over The Snatch from the beginning, but Marti had wanted to catch the first set. She still couldn't believe that women danced naked on the bar in a club called The Snatch, owned and operated by women, but mostly she couldn't believe that part of her liked what she saw. Though they all were D.C. natives, had grown up and gone to school together, Marti lived and worked a hundred miles south, in Richmond, Virginia, and no longer spent as much time with her friends as she'd like, and Mike was in the Army.

Marti answered for Mike. "I've scratched my itch so I suppose it's your turn. Besides, a catfish Po' Boy would go down nicely right about now."

"I know that sex makes some people hungry," Cassie said, "but I didn't know that watching naked women makes people hungry."

"Unless watching naked women is as close as you've been to sex recently," Mike said, and backed quickly out of their tight little circle to avoid the smack Marti aimed at the side of her head.

"It's as close as any of us have been to sex lately and there's no point in pretending otherwise," Cassie said as they inched their way through the boisterous crowd toward the front door.

"Speak for yourself, Ali," Mike said smugly.

"She means real sex with a real, live woman," Marti said, and they all giggled at the memory of Mike's explorations with some products brought back from her most recent overseas posting. "The kind where you're in the same bed at the same time with the real woman and you do her and then she does you. Remember that?"

They followed a crowd out of the front door into the muggy night and right away Cassandra Ali knew something was wrong. Shouts from up the block confirmed the feeling. She pushed through the crowd, toward the commotion. She saw a knot of people a in the next block. Then someone screamed. Cassie took off running. Marti and Mike followed.

"OhmyGodOhmyGodOhmyGod," Cassie heard someone moan as she approached the group, and when she broke through the crowd, she saw why. "Fuck a duck," she muttered in perfect imitation of her boss, looking down on what she was certain was the dead body of the very alive person she'd talked to in the restroom not fifteen minutes ago.

"Isn't that..." Marti began.

"Sure as shit is," Mike finished. "Damn!"

"Did somebody call the police?" Cassie asked.

"What the fuck good are they?" somebody in the crowd responded, which started an ugly buzz that made Cassie more than a little nervous.

"Ambulance?" she asked, and got no response. She unzipped her waist pouch and took out her cell phone.

"You think ain't nobody got no sense but you?" an angry voice queried, and Cassie shut her phone and stuck it into her pocket, the tightness of the jeans leaving little room, even for the tiny phone.

Mike leaned over the body, extended two fingers, and probed the victim's neck. Then she straightened up, looked at Cassie, and shook her head.

"Who the fuck you 'sposed to be?" demanded an angry voice,

"She's a medic," somebody else replied, obviously someone acquainted enough with the military to recognize the insignia on Mike's hat and shirt.

"That right?" asked the angry voice, still angry.

"That's right," Mike answered

"Here they come," somebody said at the same moment Cassie heard the sirens. Cops and EMTs. She sighed her relief and backed out of the crowd so she could see and hear without being seen and heard. She'd already snapped a mental picture of the body on the ground, the blood pooled beneath and around it and soaking the pale blue Wizards jersey, the bloody footprint beside the body. She'd remember the faces of the people closest to the body, especially the two who had spoken. And certainly she'd remember the anti-police sentiment that rippled through the crowd at the mere mention of the word. This obviously was not the time or place to announce herself as a member of the Metropolitan Police Department's Hate Crimes Unit.

The sirens screamed the arrival of officialdom. Three squads rolled to a stop a foot from the sidewalk where the body lay, and the paramedics rumbled their bus right up on to the sidewalk, scattering the crowd. They jumped out, two men, a salt-and-pepper team, fortyish, world weary, bags in hand. They knelt on either side of the body, both checking for a pulse. They looked at each other, then up at the cops who had formed a semi-circle around them.

"Call the ME. You don't need us," the Black one said, standing up.

"But it was supposed to be a female," the white one said.

"What?" said one of the cops, the sergeant.

"That's right, Sarge," said another of the cops. "The call came that a female was shot and laying on the sidewalk, and that ain't no female."

"Yes the fuck it is!" someone from the crowd shouted, and the ugly energy that had just been hanging in the heavy night air surged forward like a living thing. The cops felt it and moved back a step.

The Black paramedic pulled on a pair of latex gloves and knelt back down beside the body. He looked up at the faces looking down on him. "How 'bout everybody moves back?" he asked politely.

"You heard the man," the sergeant said. "Back! Back up! Everybody move on back!" He gestured to the other officers and they formed a blue line behind which the crowd now stood, too far back to witness the examination of the victim, but not so far back that they couldn't tell that something more than death afflicted the body on the ground.

"Goddamn! Look at this shit!" the EMT said. His partner and the police sergeant bent down over the body, and both backed up quickly.

"The detective ought to be here any minute," the sergeant said, and, on cue, the unmarked rolled up, lights flashing, siren silent. The sergeant hurried over to meet the person who'd be responsible for this mess and the two huddled for several seconds, long enough for Cassie to make her way around the periphery of the crowd, to rear of the squad cars. She was looking for a familiar face, while still debating with herself about the advisability of remaining undercover until she found out what was going on, since it was obvious that there definitely was something going on, something more than a DB on the sidewalk. Her decision was made for her when the detective spied her. His eyes held recognition and he walked toward her.

Cassie watched him approach. She didn't know him, didn't know how or why he thought he knew her. "Officer Ali," he said quietly. "If I'm blowing your cover I can fix it by ordering you and your friends to move back out of the way."

"Will it help you if I move back out of the way?"

"It'll probably help your boss," he said. And almost under his breath, added, "You better call her, get her over here, and fast. Tell her Jim Dudley said so." Then, like a shape shifter, he morphed. "Get back over there! Sergeant, get these people outta here!"

Cassie, Marti and Mike hustled themselves away from the cops but not all the way back into the crowd of spectators, which had grown to several dozen, most of them probably Snatch patrons. Dee wouldn't be pleased, Cassie thought, looking at her watch. "You all should go," she told her pals. "I'm probably going to be here for the duration."

"We'll keep you company until your boss gets here," Mike said.

"Yeah," Marti added. "I wouldn't mind a glimpse of her. I swear, you two make me sick!"

"What did we do?" Mike asked.

"You've got that fine colonel for a boss is what, and Cassie's got that fine lieutenant for a boss, and what have I got for a boss? A bald, fat Arab who hates women and dykes and Black people and is convinced the government's spying on him because his last name is Hussein."

"He's probably right," Cassie said, passing up the opportunity to comment on her boss's physical attributes.

"I'm sure my fine colonel is in bed with the fine head nurse," Mike said wistfully. "I wonder if your fine lieutenant is in bed with her equally fine reporter?"

Lieutenant Gianna Maglione, head of the D.C. Police Department's Hate Crimes Unit, was not in bed with her reporter, which she very much regretted. Mimi Patterson was on the red eye, on her way back to D.C. from a three-week assignment in California. So, in bed alone, Lt. Maglione had read herself to sleep before eleven o'clock. When the phone rang a few minutes before two, she awoke immediately and fully, a habit honed by a twenty-year career as a cop. In all those years on the job, a middle-of-the-night phone call had never been a wrong number.

"This is Cassie, Boss. I'm sorry to wake you."

Gianna sat up and switched on the light. "What is it, Cassie?"

"I'm on the scene of what appears to be a homicide. The detective in charge, a guy named Jim Dudley, told me call you and tell you to get over here."

Gianna already was out of bed and halfway to the bathroom when she said, "Get over where?"

She was vaguely familiar with the general area of the address Cassie gave her. Shitty neighborhood, as she recalled. "Are you all right, Cassie?"

"Yes, Ma'am. I'm fine."

"Then I'll see you in twenty minutes." Gianna tossed the phone on to the bed, turned on the shower, and stepped in. She'd perfected the art of the two minute shower. The hot, stinging spray would finish waking her up and wash away any residual sleepiness fogging her brain. She needed a clear head to process the fact of Cassie's presence at the scene of a homicide in the middle of the night in one of D.C.'s worst neighborhoods, a homicide that a detective she trusted thought belonged to her Hate Crimes Unit.

She had underestimated the drive time to the scene. Despite the hour, there was plenty of traffic, especially on the major thoroughfares. She remembered when D.C. was practically a ghost town at this time of night. Now it was like

New York or Los Angeles— people out and about at all hours. No doubt good for the restaurant and night club business, nothing but trouble for the cops. The fact that she was heading across town at two in the morning was proof of that. And what about Cassie? She was a good cop, one of the best, but she also was excitable, and, recently, hell bent on proving her job worthiness following a medical leave of absence. Here she was on the scene of a homicide in a very iffy part of town, in the middle of the night. She had sounded... urgent. Not quite panicked and not exactly frightened but it was clear that she wanted her boss on the scene ASAP. Gianna used the solitude to indulge the weak spot she had for Cassandra Ali, the youngest member of the Hate Crimes Unit and the one Gianna thought of as most like herself at that age. A year ago, Cassie had suffered a brutal beating at the hands of neo-Nazi skinheads, angered because a Black female cop put a stop to their harassment of an elderly Holocaust survivor. The beating severely damaged her eye and caused severe emotional and psychological trauma, but Cassie had fought back, rehabilitated herself, and proved herself worthy of a return to full time active duty. Proved herself over and over again, at every opportunity.

Gianna knew she'd arrived at the crime scene as soon as she turned the corner. The area was lit up like a Hollywood movie set and half a dozen squad cars, lights flashing, parked at crazy angles in the middle of the street. An EMT bus was on the sidewalk. Several dozen people shifted and shuffled behind yellow crime scene tape, enough of them familiar with the appearance of an unmarked that the crowd parted as Gianna drove closer. She hung her ID on her jacket pocket as she climbed out of her car. Her hazel eyes scanned the scene, taking in as much as possible while looking for Cassie and Jim Dudley. Many pairs of eyes scanned her, some of them wary, many of them appreciative. At five-seven, lean and physically fit, and dressed in the black jeans, cowboy boots and silk shirt that had become her uniform, she made an appealing sight, even at a murder scene in the middle of the night. Her thick, dark mane of hair was corralled in a ponytail and brushed her shoulders as she walked.

"Am I glad to see you," she heard from behind her, and turned to find Dudley grinning at her.

"Jim. How've you been?" Her greeting was as warm as his had been.

"No worse for the wear."

She backed up a step and scrutinized him. "You've lost weight, bulked up some, let your hair grow longer..."

He gave her one of those head-shakes that didn't need words but he said them anyway: "I don't ever intend to let you meet my wife. You might decide to teach her some of the finer points of observation and then I'd be in deep kimchee."

"Um, morning, Boss."

Gianna stepped away from Jim Dudley, noticing the look Cassie gave him and the look Dudley was flashing her— a warning. He took her arm and there was real pressure in his grip. "Looks like you might have a first class mess on your hands here, Maglione," he said, and led Gianna toward the crime scene.

She followed, instantly and acutely aware of the reason for his warning, and grateful. Dudley was the lead investigator in the assault on Cassie, who still had no memory of that event or its immediate aftermath. She didn't know Jim Dudley from Adam and certainly wouldn't know that the credit for the collar in that case went to him. She looked over at Cassie who was walking beside her and noticed how she was dressed. Then she turned her full attention to the crime scene. She recognized one of the paramedics, two of the crime scene investigators, and the assistant medical examiner, and raised her hand in greeting to all of them. The MEs eyes met hers and Gianna's stomach jumped. She'd shared enough looks with MEs to understand the telegraphed message: What was waiting for her was more than just a dead body.

As she reached the make-shift barrier the ME had constructed around the body— as much to protect the crime scene as keep the victim from being a public spectacle— Gianna inhaled deeply, then looked down. She closed her eyes briefly, opened them, and looked again. Before she could fully process all she saw, Cassie leaned in close and whispered, "She's a girl, Boss."

"What?"

"The vic," Cassie said. "She's a girl."

Gianna was looking at a young male dressed in Philadelphia Seventy-Sixers attire— Allen Iverson's jersey number— and a pair of those too expensive high top sneakers. He wore a gold watch and ring on his left hand. His hair was corn-rowed. His eyes and mouth were open. The teeth were white and perfect. Gianna looked at Cassie, who was watching her closely. Then Cassie looked at Jim Dudley, who also was watching Gianna. He looked at the people nearest him— cops, paramedics, the medical examiner— and waved his hand at them, making a circle. And that's what they did— made a circle around Gianna, Jim, Cassie and the vic, making sure nobody could see that they saw. Then Dudley knelt down and raised the Sixers jersey. The first thing Gianna registered was that the torso had been cut— hacked to shreds. Then the real horror registered: This boy had breasts, small ones, and they'd been all but excised from the torso. "Good God."

"You see some shit like this and you wonder if He is," Jim Dudley said.

Gianna looked at the ME and Dr. Wanda Oland stepped over to her. "Lieutenant. I would say it's good to see you again, but..." The doctor shrugged off the need to add further commentary.

"Is this anatomically a woman, Wanda?" Gianna asked, speaking directly into the doctor's ear, making certain she wasn't overheard.

The doctor replied in the same fashion. "If you're asking me whether there's a vagina, there is. Fully and naturally formed. If you're asking me whether this is a hate crime, it is. Did you get a good look at what's carved on her body?"

"That's not just hacking?" Gianna asked.

She shook her head. "I'll save you having to look again. 'Die Dyke' is what's cut into her."

Gianna's stomach heaved. She didn't trust herself to speak, so she didn't. Instead she turned away to look for Cassie.

"Hey, Lieutenant." The ME called her and she turned back. "Thanks for not asking me a lot of those stupid television cop questions. I appreciate it," she said, and dug into her pocket for her cigarettes, holding the pack between her hands as if deriving pleasure from just the thought of the nicotine rush, though she'd no more light one than kick dirt on the corpse. "I'll call you when I have something to tell you," she said, and looked up at the sky, better scenery than down where they were. "And I'll be as quick about it as I can."

Gianna walked back to the doctor. "Well, maybe one question."

"Fuckin' cops," Wanda Oland said wearily. "What?"

"It's an easy one," Gianna said. "How old do you think she is?"

Oland nodded. "That is an easy one: Barely thirty, if that."

That's what Gianna thought. Actually, what she'd thought was that the victim was about Cassie's age. That's what she was thinking when Cassie appeared at her side. "Boss," she said, they walked away from the crowd, away from the official crime scene, and into the weeds and broken glass of a vacant lot. The smell of urine rose up around them. The night was becoming windy, courtesy of a hurricane that was tracking slowly up the eastern seaboard, bringing the promise of wind and rain and possibly cooler weather and an end to summer in D.C. Right now, though, the wind only blew the putrid urine scent back and forth.

"Tell me everything, Cassie, starting with who she is. If you know."

"I don't know. I do know that she was in the club earlier and that she left about one o'clock..."

"In what club?" Gianna looked all around. "There's a club around here?"

Cassie nodded, turned and pointed. "In the next block. That two story brick building on the corner there? That's the place. Thursday, Friday and Saturday nights only, though."

"And you know she was there because you were there?"

Cassie nodded again. "I left about fifteen minutes after she did. When I came out, I heard people yelling, shouting, and I saw a crowd up here, so I checked it out. I found her like you saw her."

Gianna looked around again, assessing the distance from the corner to where the body lay. "Where was she going? Would she have parked this far away?"

"She was probably headed for the subway. That's where we were going—"

"What we?"

"I was with two friends."

"Did you recognize any of the people near the body when you got there? Had you seen any of them in the club?"

Cassie shook her head. "I really wasn't looking at the crowd, not at first. I was concerned about the vic, and whether anybody had called it in. And whether or not she was still alive, though I didn't think so. But Mike checked for a pulse anyway—"

"Who? What? Somebody touched the body?"

"My friend, Mike. She's a medic in the Army. She just got back from the Middle East, so she knows dead when she sees it, and she said there was no pulse."

"Mike's a woman?"

Cassie smiled. "Her name's Mary Lynne but it's such a girly-girl name and she always hated it, so she started calling herself Mike in junior high and now everybody calls her that."

"OK, I'm sorry. Go ahead."

"The first squad arrived at one twenty-six, and that's when things got nasty. So I circled around to the rear, to see if I knew any of the cops, and that's when Dudley saw me and told me to call you."

"Nasty why?"

"Have you taken a good look at the people out here?" Cassie asked.

Gianna took a good look at Cassie. "Why do you ask?"

"You asked if I recognized anybody from the club and I don't, not specifically, but I'm sure that most of the spectators were there and they're hanging around not just being nosey, but to make sure nothing gets swept under the rug. And I guess that's why I stayed around, too."

Gianna let her surprise show, then her anger. "You know better than that. If this is a hate crime— and it certainly looks like it may be— then you know nothing will get swept under the rug."

"You thought the vic was a boy, right, Boss?"

"So what?" Gianna was more than a little irritated, and the Boss irritated was more than a little unnerving to Cassie.

"How many of those people over there you think are males?"

Gianna looked where Cassie looked, thought about the question, and looked closer, looked beyond the surface at the faces of all the boys in the crowd. Then she looked hard at Cassie. "What are you saying, Cassie?"

"Thinking about what's happened up in New Jersey, and thinking about some of the things that've happened around here—"

"What the hell are you talking about? What happened in New Jersey? What things have happened around here?"

"Saskia Gunn, Boss, and Shani Baraka. And just last month, a couple of Doms were denied entry to the Bayou."

"A couple of wha...you mean...what do you call them?'

"Doms, Ags— for Dominants and Aggressives. They couldn't get in. Just because of who and how they are."

Gianna recalled the mutilated body lying not ten yards away and felt an overwhelming sadness. No matter how much progress was achieved, it still was never enough. Somebody would always find a reason to hate something or somebody.

"I think we've been made," Cassie said, breaking into her ruminations.

Gianna perused the crowd and saw what Cassie had seen, and realized what the crowd was seeing: Cassie in her skin tight jeans and tee shirt, Gianna in her black jeans and boots, her shoulder holster visible beneath her jacket to anybody looking closely enough. Their own attire was as definitive as that of the, what did Cassie call them? Doms and Ags. "Well, you'd better come all the way out," Gianna said. "We've got a lot of work to do."

Cassie took her ID and weapon from her waist pouch and clipped them on her belt, aware that the crowd noticed. "Now what?"

"Go see if you can learn anything officially, now that they know who you are, while I call Eric. Then we'll organize a canvass and hope that somebody saw something and will tell us about it."

Cassie nodded. "OK, Boss." She turned away, then came back. "Who's Detective Dudley? Should I know him?"

Gianna hesitated briefly, then answered. "He was the lead on your assault investigation. He made the collar and the case that bought your attackers twenty-five to life in the Federal pen in Virginia."

"Damn," Cassie said, for once at a loss for her customary stream of words, and she sauntered off.

"Hey! You! Cop!"

Gianna looked toward the group of people that had been watching her and Cassie. One of them beckoned and she walked over. "Can I help you?"

"Where you send her? That other cop? The Black one?"

"Y'all ain't gon' let her find out who killed this dude, are you?"

"She's going to help find out," Gianna said.

"Why she got to 'help.' Why she can't be in charge?"

"Because I'm in charge. She works for me." She reached into her pocket and retrieved a handful of the cards she kept at the ready and passed them around to anybody who'd take one. Several people would not; this was not the crowd from which the police auxiliary drew its members. "You have anything to say, call. You can talk to her or to me or to whoever answers the phone."

"'Hate Crimes.' You think that's what happened to her? A hate crime?" somebody asked.

"It wasn't no love crime, Dog, that's for sure," somebody else answered, and a hot wave of angry emotion wafted through the crowd, and muggy night air seemed to hang even heavier.

Gianna noticed that the body now was bagged and that evidence cones now were in place along the sidewalk and into the vacant lot. Crime scene investigators and evidence techs were on their knees with cameras and tweezers and envelopes, picking up bits and pieces and scraps. The assistant ME was leaning against the EMT bus smoking a cigarette, waiting for the coroner's van so she could take the body. It was an odd, eerie scene: a narrow area hot with artificial light, surrounded by the blackness of night. Gianna made eye contact with Dudley and he broke away from a knot of people he was huddled with and came toward her.   "I'm sorry to have to say it, Maglione, but I don't envy you this one. This is some ugly shit."

"Hate's an ugly thing, Jim. I'm just glad you recognized it for what it was as soon as you did. Nothing worse than playing catch-up on one of these. I appreciate the heads up and I won't forget it."

He lit a cigarette, inhaled deeply, and blew smoke out of the side of his mouth, away from Gianna. "So, Officer Ali just happened to be on the scene?"

"Any ID on the vic?" Gianna asked, ignoring the question.

Dudley accepted the unspoken rebuke with a slight shrug. "Nope. We got a Metro fare card, a hundred sixty dollars in cash— crisp, new twenties— two joints in a plastic bag, a cell phone, and a car key. A Mercedes Benz car key."

Gianna followed Dudley to his car. She held up one of tagged evidence bags to the light and scrutinized the Metro fare card. It was a new one— a twenty dollar buy with one trip on it. If the victim had indeed taken the train, they could tell where she boarded by the amount remaining on the fare card. Thank goodness the Metropolitan Transit Authority operated on a distance-based fare system and not on a flat rate. "A fare card and a single car key. She parked at a Metro station and rode over here."

"Her ID's in the trunk of her car," Dudley said, following Gianna's train of thought. "Hey, Wilson!" he shouted, and rotated his hand in the air like a royal giving a wave. A patrol officer trotted over. "Find me a subway map." The uniform nodded and trotted off.

Gianna looked at her watch. Eric would arrive at any moment with the rest of her Unit. She looked around for Cassie, saw her talking to a group of people across the street, and walked back over to the crime scene. The coroner's wagon had arrived and Wanda Oland was overseeing the moving of the body. "You want something, Lieutenant?"

"If you don't mind, Doc, I'd like to take another look at her."

"No problem." The ME waved her techs aside. Gianna was grateful that the body now was on a gurney so she could see without having to kneel down. Oland unzipped the bag, pulled back the sheet, and Gianna leaned in close. The victim's skin was flawlessly clear— not the caliber of complexion obtained from drug store soap and lotion. Her nails were short but perfectly and professionally manicured. Her teeth were an advertisement for an orthodontist: Perfectly aligned, not a cavity to be seen. Gianna peered into the open, vacant eyes: Contact lenses. "Looking for anything in particular?" Oland asked, close enough that Gianna could smell the nicotine on her.

"Did you notice her watch and ring?"

Wanda Oland lifted and dropped her shoulders as if she expected some of the weight of her job to roll off. "Not beyond the fact of their existence. Why?"

"A Movado and a Penn class ring."

"So," the doctor said, the word carrying no hint of dismissiveness or disregard. Nor was it a question, really, and unless Gianna told her, the doctor would have no way of knowing that the cop remarked on the University of Pennsylvania class ring because, along with the Seventy-Sixers jersey, it struck a familiar chord. The cop was a Philadelphia native. And as the doctor said, So?

"Not typical jewelry for the victim of a street crime," Gianna said.

The doctor shrugged again. "But not unprecedented," she said.

"Really?"

"I can't tell you the number of upscale johns I've processed— pillars of their various communities— found in alleys, flop houses, crack houses, dumpsters, shitty neighborhoods like this one. Fruit from the forbidden tree and all that. So many of 'em I've lost track."

Gianna looked down at the brutalized, lifeless young body stretched out before her. Is that what this was, pursuit of a bite of forbidden fruit gone wrong? Or was this something else entirely? It wasn't no love crime, that's for sure. The words played themselves over in Gianna's head. A crime of passion, perhaps? Or, as it seemed, a crime of hate? She looked up and saw Detective Eric Ashby headed toward her, followed by Cassie, Tim McCreedy, Linda Lopez, Bobby Gilliam and Kenny Chang. The Hate Crimes Unit. Her team, her people. Time to get busy.

CHAPTER THREE

Cassie had convinced Gianna to let her handle things at The Snatch and now she was regretting her insistence. Dee Phillips flat out refused to discuss the murder of a patron a block and a half from her door, so expecting her co-operation was out of the question. "No law was broken in my establishment, therefore I have no interest in the matter," was her response. When Cassie kept talking, Phillips took her by the arm and ushered her out of her office and literally pushed her toward the front door. The woman was tall, square, and solid, more than strong enough to propel Cassie forward against her will, and certain enough of her legal standing not to be the least bit intimidated by Cassie's various attempts at intimidation.

"Are you certain you didn't see the victim tonight? She was back here, in the ladies room, just before she left," Cassie said.

"There are no 'ladies' rooms in this establishment," Dee Phillips said coldly. "There are rest rooms, or bathrooms, or toilets. But no ladies rooms. That's because no men are permitted on these premises."

"Whatever," Cassie said, now annoyed as well as frustrated. "I'm asking whether you saw the victim," and she described her again, down to and including the watch and ring she wore. And Cassie would have sworn an oath that Dee Phillips was lying when she said "That description means nothing to me. Now, go away and please don't bother me with this foolishness again."

"Foolishness? A woman is dead, murdered out there on the sidewalk. You think that's foolishness?"

"I think your attempt to involve me and my establishment is foolishness," Dee Phillips said. And something about the way she checked her watch and stole a glance at the dancers on the bar added dimension to the earlier lie.

She knows something, Cassie thought as she snaked her way through the crowd clustered at the bar. She pushed for the front door so she could exit before the show ended; she didn't want to get stuck inside here for an extra twenty minutes.

"You just made it," Darlene said, turning the key in the door.

"I think that's probably illegal," Cassie said, eyeing the locked door. Darlene scrutinized her. "You were in here earlier with that Army dude. I didn't know you were a cop."

"I wasn't," Cassie said, then, "I mean, I wasn't working then. I was just hanging out with some friends. The dead body up the block changed all that."

"Damn! That's some shit, ain't it?" Darlene's face turned sad and her voice became even lower and softer. She looked over Cassie's head toward the two dozen people still in line, turned her back on them, and leaned in close. "Hey, tell me somethin'? Was it really Tosh?"

"Was it really what?"

"Who got smoked up the street. Somebody said it was Tosh. Was it?"

"She didn't have any ID so we don't know her name, but maybe you could describe this Tosh for me?" And Darlene did, right down to the model of the sneakers on her feet and the description of her Mercedes Benz. "So, is it her?"

"Sounds like, but you understand that we have to obtain a positive ID, a confirmation, and then we have to notify the next of kin—"

"Oh fuck!" Darlene's eyes widened and she pounded the sides of her head with her fists. "Oh fuck! She got up from her stool and walked a tight circle.

"What? What's wrong? You know something else? What is it?"

"Lili," Darlene said, her whole face turned downward in sadness. "Lili don't know. Oh, this shit's fucked, Man."

"Who's Lili?" Cassie asked, knowing better than to push but needing to convey a sense of urgency to the big bouncer.

"Tosh's bitch. She just finished her set. Somebody better tell her."

"You mean one of the dancers? Lili is one of the dancers? And she's..she was the girlfriend of the dea...the victim? Which one is Lili?"

Darlene nodded. "The one looks like Halle Berry."

Cassie whipped out her phone and punched a button. "Boss, can you come here to the front door of the club? Right now? Just you and Linda? Not the guys." Cassie closed the phone to avoid having to explain her request in front of Darlene, to whom she did explain herself. "My boss is coming. Will you tell her what you told me? About Tosh and about Lili?"

Darlene looked at her watch. "She better hurry up."

Gianna did hurry. In less than a minute, she and Linda pulled up to the curb going the wrong way up the one way street. Darlene whistled through her teeth when Gianna stepped out of the car. "If that's the Boss, can you get me a job?"

"Boss, this is Darlene. She runs the door here. Darlene, this is Lieutenant Maglione and she runs the Hate Crimes Unit. And this is Officer Linda Lopez. Darlene thinks our vic's name is Tosh, and her girlfriend, Lili, is one of the dancers."

"Is she here now?"

"She just finished her set about ten minutes ago."

Cassie spoke up, loudly and quickly. "The owner, Miss Dee Phillips, has forbidden us to enter her establishment again."

Gianna paused for a single beat. "Has she?"

"Yes, Ma'am. She said since no crime was committed on her property, she's got nothing to do with it." Cassie waited for the reaction she knew was coming.

Gianna gave Darlene the Dangerous a full wattage smile of thanks and the big woman melted like ice cream under the summer sun. "Thank you. We appreciate your help, Darlene." Then she turned toward to door, which Darlene unlocked and opened. "Let's find Miss Phillips."

There were easily five hundred bodies packed inside the club, two-thirds of them on the dance floor. The music was so loud that Gianna felt her blood pounding in her veins. She looked around to get her bearings and stopped short at the images projected on the screen behind the bar.

"That one right there...I think that's Lili," Cassie yelled into Gianna's ear as she pointed to one of the gyrating images on the screen.

"What?"

"Third one from the left, Halle Berry look-alike? That's Lili."

"I thought they were real," Linda said, finally collecting her wits.

"This is a video of tonight's shows. They were very real on top of that bar until a few minutes ago," Cassie assured them.

Gianna looked from the women projected against the screen to the women on the dance floor to Cassie. "Where's Dee Phillips?"

Striding toward them, eyes snapping, dark skin glistening, hands opening and closing at her sides, was where she was. "I told you to get out of here," she snarled at Cassie, ignoring Gianna and Linda.

"I can have the Fire Marshall here in fifteen minutes and this place shut down, the doors barred, in thirty," Gianna said.

Gianna won and held the other woman's gaze. Neither blinked for several long seconds.

"What do you want?" Dee Phillips finally asked, gaze unwavering.

"Lili," Gianna said.

"She's gone. Left right after her show."

"Not out the front door, she didn't," Cassie said.

"Private door for the dancers. Exits directly to the parking lot so they can avoid the crowd." Dee Phillips sounded proud of the arrangement.

"Did you tell her about Tosh?" Cassie asked, and the other woman's gaze finally wavered. "What a shitty thing to do. Lili's girlfriend is laying dead out on the sidewalk and you wouldn't do her the kindness, the courtesy, to tell her."

"I told you, that's got nothing to do with me. It didn't happen here and I'm not responsible and you can't hold me responsible."

"But I can make your life miserable," Gianna said in a tone so matter of fact it was scary. "And I'm sure the Fire Marshall and the ABC Board and the building inspector would help me out."

"What do you want?" Dee asked again.

"Lili. What kind of car does she drive and where does she live?"

"One of those little PT Cruisers, red, Maryland license plates, and she lives in Silver Spring, but she didn't go home. Her mother's in the hospital. She went there."

"Linda, get a copy of Miss Phillips's personnel records. Names, address and phone numbers of all her employees—"

"I'm not giving you that information. I don't have to."

"I guarantee will shut you down, Miss Phillips, if you give me reason to," Gianna said, locking eyes with the enraged bar owner. Dee blinked first and stalked away, Linda Lopez trailing with obvious reluctance. Cassie followed her boss through the crowd, to the front door and out.

Darlene was sitting on her stool, smoking a cigarette and drinking a beer, looking relaxed. Nobody was in line. She leaned over and put out her cigarette in bucket of sand at her feet and expelled smoke through her nose. "Dee is 'bout ready to chew nails."

"How do you know that?" Cassie asked, then nodded when Darlene patted the cell phone in her shirt pocket.

"I hope we haven't caused you any trouble," Gianna said.

Darlene's reaction, a head-thrown-back belly laugh, surprised them both. She shook her head, then sobered, and looked directly at Cassie. "Would you let me know what happens? About Tosh? I mean, about a funeral or memorial service or anything like that?"

Surprised, Cassie nodded. "I'll do that."

"We haven't had any real trouble around here since the beginning of the summer, and I guess I was stupid enough to think that maybe they'd leave us alone," Darlene said softly and sadly. "So much for wishful thinking."

"Who'd leave you alone?" Gianna asked, on alert.

"Our friendly neighborhood dyke bashers. They usually just drive up and down the street giving us dirty looks, maybe some name-calling. But before, it was worse. Throwing stuff—"

"Stuff like what?"

"If we were lucky, just scalding hot water or urine and ugly words. If not, lye, rat poison. Bullets."

"Why didn't you ever report this?" Gianna was coldly angry.

Darlene was, too. "You think we didn't? Hell, we had to buy a weapon scanner 'cause some of our people were ready to fight back." She reached down behind her stool and retrieved a metal detecting wand. "I don't check much anymore, but used to be, I waved this thing over everybody going in that door." She looked hard at Cassie, then down at the Glock clipped to her belt. "I might start again, too."

"You said you reported the harassment? To whom? And when?"

Darlene looked at Gianna. "What difference does it make? Didn't nobody do nothin', as usual."

Gianna reached in her pocket for a card and gave it to Darlene. "I would have done something had I been notified. Now. Who did you tell?"

"That asshole Mid-Town commander. O'Connell's his name and he's one nasty bastard. We went to see him, me and Dee. He wouldn't even let us sit down in his office, made us stand in the hallway. He said there wasn't nothing he could do long as our 'clientele' was 'inciting' hostilities. And he had the preachers and church people on his side. Between the cops ignoring us and the holy rollers sending us to hell on a weekly basis, we didn't stand a chance, in this world or the next. Maybe now that somebody's dead we can catch a break."

Gianna was too angry to speak, so Cassie attempted to broach the silence. "He was flat out wrong, Darlene. O'Connell or whatever his name is—"

Darlene cut her off, waving Gianna's card in her face. She'd read it and was looking at them in wide-eyed amazement. "Where did y'all come from? All the hate people been throwin' at us since the day we opened, where the hell were you?"

"We would have been here helping you if we'd known you needed help," Gianna said. "And if you'd known to call us. Frankly, I don't know why you didn't."

"I know why," Darlene said darkly, her voice even lower and softer than usual, and Gianna braced herself for what she knew was coming. "I bet the white gay folks in Georgetown and DuPont Circle and Capitol Hill know to call you. We're probably the only ones who don't know." She fixed her gaze on Cassie. "How come you didn't tell us? This ain't the first time you been here."

"I didn't know anything about the trouble you've had, Darlene, I swear I didn't. If I'd known, I'd have told my boss and we'd have done something. That's for real. Please believe that, I don't care what O'Connell said."

Darlene looked from one to the other of them. "Well. Now you know," she said, stifling a yawn and checking her watch. "Almost closing time."

"We owe you an apology," Gianna said.

Darlene nodded. "Yeah, you do." She stuck out her hand and Gianna took it. "Accepted," Darlene said. "But just so you know, it hurts when your own people discriminate against you. Some gay people treat us worse than straight people. They won't even let us in that club cross town, that Louisiana place. And on top of that, we got the cops telling us it's our own fault what happens to us."

At that moment, the door opened and Linda Lopez emerged, followed by a trio of leering Latinas, all clad in baggies and backwards baseball caps. Her relief at the sight of Gianna and Cassie bordered on the comical, and Darlene did laugh. She also stood up and planted her feet.

"Why are you dudes hassling the lady?" she queried in her deceptively gentle way putting a protective arm around Linda's shoulders and edging her forward.

"We would never hassle nobody so pretty. We just tryin' to talk to her."

"Well, she's a little busy right now," Darlene said, using her body to create even more distance between Linda and her admirers.

"She don't look busy to me," one of them said, trying to step around Darlene, and making a grab for Linda, but there was too much of Darlene for success.

Linda hurried to the car, Gianna and Cassie following, slid behind the wheel, started the engine, threw the car into gear, and peeled off. Off-color jeers and taunts followed them.

"OK, help me out here," Linda said.

"We'll try," Cassie said, knowing what was coming.

"Those...women. They're scarier than men. I mean, the licking sounds and the wagging tongues and the pelvis thrusts and grabbing my ass. They're worse than men. What's that about?"

Gianna wished she could say, It's a gay thing, you wouldn't understand, but it was more than that and she didn't understand it, either. Not all of it. And Cassie seemed to be battling the same dilemma. She needed to give Linda an answer. Wanted to give her one because an answer was required, and not only because a cop had been rattled in the course of doing her duty. Linda was not one of the gay officers on the Hate Crimes squad, and that had never mattered, any more than it mattered that Cassie wasn't Latina or that Kenny Chang wasn't Black or that Bobby Gilliam wasn't Jewish or that Tim McCreedy wasn't straight or that the men weren't women. Their commitment was complete and total. Now, here was a situation that, as far as Gianna could tell, didn't have any easy answers.

"A sad fact, but a true one," Cassie said sadly, "women get more like men every day. What's a girl to do?"

"And what about how they're dressed?"

"You just blew it, kiddo," Cassie drawled. "How somebody dresses is how they dress, period. You can't judge somebody by how they look on the outside, you know that, Lopez. And not every woman who wears baggies and baseball caps calls women bitches and grabs their boobs."

"And whether they do or not, they can't be murdered for it," Gianna said, and punched a button on her cell phone. "Eric, where's my subway map?"

Gianna cursed under her breath and snapped her phone shut. Cassie leaned forward. "Maybe I can help, Boss. I ride the trains a lot."

"Our victim had a fare card in her pocket with one ride taken. She also had a single car key, but no wallet or driver's license. We're thinking that she parked somewhere and rode the train here but we don't know where."

"She probably parked at the Rhode Island Avenue station, just like we did. There's a big Park-and-Ride lot there. And this time of night, or morning, there won't be many cars left. We take her key, we might find a car it fits."

"But why not park in the club lot?" Linda asked. "Why bother with the train, then have to walk three or four blocks in this neighborhood?"

"I forgot about that lot!" Cassie said.

"Take a pass by it, Linda," Gianna said.

Linda made a U-turn and a hard right. The street that ran beside the club was dark as a tomb. Not a single street light still burned. Gianna didn't wonder that the club patrons came armed. What surprised her was that nobody had been killed before now. She sat forward in her seat as Linda slowed to a crawl, looking for the alley that ran behind the club. She found it and turned in. As soon as the car came even with the end of the building, motion detector lights flooded the alley with intense, bright light, and the parking lot was even brighter. It was enclosed by a fourteen-foot high steel fence with a remote control sliding gate. Despite her instant dislike of the woman, Gianna's respect for Dee Phillips as a savvy business woman continued to grow. She obviously was concerned about the welfare of her customers and her employees.

Cassie whistled when they reached the parking lot. "No wonder she keeps it locked! Will you look at that?"

They all looked. What they saw was a brand new Bentley, cream colored and shining like a polished diamond, parked right at the door. Next to it was an equally new Cadillac Escalade, all shiny black and chrome and damn near a block long. A dozen other cars were parked in the lot, none so new or so costly. Or so large. Cassie whipped out her notebook and started taking down license plate numbers.

"The Bentley, no doubt, belongs to Ms. Phillips. You think the monster SUV does, too?"

"I'd guess that belongs to Darlene," Gianna said, thinking the big woman would need a big car.

"And the regular cars belong to the dancers?" Linda asked?

Cassie nodded. "Probably. And the bartenders and Moms, who takes the money at the door."

"So how many's that? How many dancers are there, by the way?"

Cassie hesitated. "Don't make this sworn testimony, but I think there are twelve of them. I know there are two shows of an hour-and-a-half each, and there are different dancers each show, six of them. And four or five bartenders, I think."

Linda was counting personnel sheets. "I've got twenty-two," she said, "but I can't tell who works when or doing what."

"In any case, there's no red PT Cruiser back here and that's what Dee said Lili drove. And she did say she parked back here and left right after her set."

"And given how those women looked, I can't picture them walking up this street to catch the train. And given my reception in that place— and I don't look like Halle Berry— it's no wonder they need to be able to escape out the back door."

"Pull Lili's sheet out of that pile, Linda. We need to find her so we can ID our victim, since nobody seems to know who she is. Or they say they don't."

"They probably don't, Boss," Cassie said, and sounded so sad that it frightened Gianna, but that was a conversation for another time.

When they drove back around the corner the crime scene block still was lit up like a movie set and a sizeable crowd still hovered. As Linda parked, Gianna noticed that the ME and the body were gone. Crime Scene techs on hands and knees scrutinized the sidewalk and the vacant lot, though Gianna knew better than to hope for or expect anything significant or useful. She knew better, too, than to expect results from the neighborhood canvass. Still, it had to be done, all of it, by and according to the book. Gianna had never had a case in which, television-like, a piece of broken glass, a smudged fingerprint, a discarded cigarette butt, found and analyzed by the crime lab, had led investigators to the guilty party. She'd also never met a smart perp. She had, of course, encountered more than a few who'd thought themselves clever, but for whom arrogance or conceit was the predominant trait, with clever never making the top ten. This case, however, felt different, though Gianna could not articulate a specific reason for the feeling. It was more than just the extent and nature of the violence— the nature of the hatred. This one's clever, she thought, and the thought brought no comfort.

"Boss!"

She turned to see Tim McCreedy jogging toward her, loose-limbed, lithe and too good-looking by far. He was scowling, though, which was not a good sign. Tim was a genuinely light and happy being, even in the midst of a tortuous investigation. She'd seen him ruffled only once— he'd almost come unglued in the aftermath of the attack on Cassie. They were best friends, and not simply because they were the only gay members of the Hate Crimes Unit. They were kindred spirits, though Cassie was less light and happy these days.

"What is it, Tim?"

"There's a situation brewing over in the crowd."

"That's all we need," Gianna said, "is a brewing situation in an angry crowd in the middle of the night." She looked over Tim's shoulder toward the three dozen people still clustered behind the crime scene tape. Then she looked up at the sky, dark and dense with fast moving clouds heavy with moisture, and wished they'd release their bounty. "What exactly kind of situation is it, Tim?"

"Between some of the women from the club and some of the boys from the 'hood," Tim said.

He didn't need to say any more. Gianna, remembering Darlene's description of attacks on club patrons, nodded at him to lead the way. As she followed, she let her eyes roam the scenery. It was bleak, at best. The houses and businesses were ramshackle and run down, their best days in the past, and same no doubt could be said of the people who lived and worked in them. Except for Dee Phillips and her night club and the women who patronized it.

"Fuckin' ugly ass bull daggers!"

"Your mama is a bull dagger and she uglier than you!"

"Why don't you come over here and get some real dick?"

"How 'bout I shove your real dick up your ass? You know how you get it in the joint, just like you like it."

"Fuckin' bitch!"

"GUN!"

People screamed and scattered and Gianna was glad. Crowd disbursement, for whatever reason, was crowd control in a situation like this. Since she didn't hold out any hope for an eyewitness to the murder of young Tosh, the fewer people on the street right now, the better, especially given the nature of the hostilities that permeated the crowd. And the homogenous nature of it, Gianna thought, for she could barely distinguish between the armed, foul-mouthed man, now handcuffed and being hustled to the back seat of a squad car, and the women he'd taunted. All wore corn- rowed hair, oversized sports jerseys, butt-hugging baggy pants, and untied shoes, yet the man hated the women. Why? Because they looked like him? Because that threatened him? Because they took women he thought should belong to him? And what did the women feel? Did they hate the man? Gianna couldn't rationalize that: Why would a person emulate the person who hated her?

"Hey! Hey officer! I bet he shot her! Check his gun! I bet he's the one!"

A current of angry hostility re-ignited and coursed through the crowd along with the vocal speculation: Had the arrested man really killed the woman carried away in the Medical Examiner's van just a short time ago? That much coincidence was much too good to be true and Gianna didn't give it much credence. She also didn't waste any time wondering how anybody in the crowd knew that Tosh had been shot. The police hadn't and wouldn't reveal that information, but a good number of these spectators probably knew a bullet wound when they saw one.

"Lock him up anyway," somebody else in the crowd yelled out. "He's the one who shot at us in The Snatch line a couple of months ago!"

Good to know, Gianna thought, and worth a follow-up, though probably impossible to prove. Still, it would allow the cops to hold onto him for a couple of days while tests were run on the weapon. Gianna signaled for her team. "We need to get the rest of these people out of here. Start asking for names, addresses, and phone numbers, places of employment, parole status."

Less than a dozen people remained at the police barricade after the questioning began. Two of them, Gianna noticed, were older, and she thought them probably residents rather than by-standers. They would be good contacts to have, especially since they didn't balk at giving their personal information. Those who wouldn't do so evaporated, as Gianna knew they would. And her team would fan out, too, up and down the block, into the stores and alleys and side streets, checking license plates, whatever it took to convince the potential trouble-makers that this scene was shut down for the night. She stifled a yawn and looked at her watch, not understanding why anyone would need convincing to go home and go to bed.

Her cell phone chirped. Eric, calling from the Metro parking lot with the name and address of their murder victim: Natasha Hilliard, 29, of the 3000-block of Horatio Road in northwest D.C. Gianna knew exactly where that was— a quiet cul-de-sac of town houses and condominiums, jogging distance to Rock Creek Park. She knew because she and Mimi had looked at house there a couple of months ago, finding it a bit sterile for their tastes, but, she thought, it was a perfect fit for the owner of the expensive watch and the Ivy League class ring and the Mercedes Benz, and totally antithetical to the boy-clad Tosh now en route to the morgue a world away in Southeast Washington.

CHAPTER FOUR

Whoever said, "Be careful what you ask for because you just might get it," certainly knew and understood one of life's major truths. What Mimi Patterson didn't understand was why people— herself included— didn't heed the warning before the fact instead of afterward. Maybe because people— herself included— thought of it merely as an axiom, folk wisdom. Something to be repeated ominously while wearing a wry grin, but not to be obeyed, like the admonition not to speak ill of the dead or to look both ways before crossing.

Mimi had asked for— demanded— a respite from her investigative journalist duties. She was sick and tired of corrupt politicians and government bureaucrats. She was even sicker and tireder of spending her time exposing them, getting them fired or sent to jail. It didn't seem to matter. Every expose seemed to produce a new crop of the stupid, greedy bastards instead of serving as a warning to mend their evil, cheating, lying ways. So, when her editors finally realized that she really would quit if they didn't let her do something else for a change, she'd been thrilled. Actually, she'd been more relieved than thrilled. That would have been winning the battle and losing the war...or some other piece of folk wisdom. True, she really would have quit, but she had no idea what else she'd do. She'd been a newspaper reporter her entire life. Well, at least since finishing college, and in truth, she didn't want to do anything else. She just wanted to do it differently. So now, instead of being an investigative political reporter on the local desk, she was a profiles reporter on the national desk. That meant she got to travel around the country writing on a wide variety of topics. True, graft and corruption still reared their hydra-heads, but at least now she wasn't eating a steady diet of monster food.

She'd arrived back in D.C. from Los Angeles on a plane that was due in at 6:30 a.m. but which was almost three hours late. So, instead of going home to dump her bag and change clothes, she'd come directly to work. Big mistake. She couldn't stop yawning, she was hungry, she was tired, and the editor was hovering over her like a mother hen over a chic: If he could, he'd sit on her until her story hatched. Her story was a three-parter on the changing nature of the California population. Nobody had known or remembered or cared that Mimi was a California native when the story was assigned and she hadn't mentioned it. She'd been gone long enough to feel like an outsider. She couldn't have realized how much of one she'd feel by the time her three-week odyssey was over. The California population had indeed changed. The majority of the people who lived in the Golden State not only hadn't been born there, they hadn't even been born in America. So here she was writing a different kind of story, which was exactly what she'd wanted, yet feeling more depressed than if she'd been writing yet another story of graft and corruption in high places—and enjoying it a lot more. These would, she knew, be good stories.

"So, how're you coming?"

Mimi turned to find the editor standing behind her. Again. The third time in the last ninety minutes. "So, what do you think about the first two parts of the story, Bill?" She'd started writing while still on the road, so moved and motivated was she by what she was learning, and she'd written a good bit more during the four hours spent in the airport departure lounge waiting to board the plane. Depressed as it made her, what she'd learned during her sojourn was compelling and informative and she'd met some fascinating people. Immigrants still arrived in America seeking to grab hold of the brass ring, hope and awe alive in their eyes. That they were changing America as she knew it perhaps was to be expected; after all, didn't the immigrant wave of a hundred years ago change that America?

"It's just that I'd really like to have all three parts before I start to read. You know, for continuity's sake." Bill gave her the kind of half-smile that meant his patience was wearing thin.

"Ah, yes. Continuity," Mimi repeated, giving Bill the kind of smile that was mostly grimace and meant her already lousy mood was disintegrating rapidly. "I've heard of it. I think it's mostly overrated." She was saved from the rude follow-up that was forming in her brain by the ringing of her desk phone. She looked up at the editor, the message as clear as if the words had been spoken, and he strolled away. Mimi had to give Ol' Bill points for cool. Her former editor, the Weasel, would have stalked off, his anger an ugly aura sprouting from him like Medusa hair. Mimi picked up the receiver, hoping Gianna would be on the other end. What she got was security telling her she had a visitor in the lobby. On a Saturday?

She stood up and stretched. She hadn't asked who the visitor was and didn't care. It was an excuse to get out of the newsroom for a while, maybe even to go outside, walk to the corner for Chinese food. Her stomach rumbled at the thought. She stuffed some money and her cell phone into her pockets and strolled across the football-field sized newsroom. Even though it was Saturday morning, half the desks were occupied. It wouldn't get sparse until dinner time.

The elevator ride down was fast because it was Saturday— the other departments of the paper, unlike the news department, worked Monday through Friday— but the area of the lobby near the circulation and classified advertising desk was crowded, as usual. Mimi looked around for a familiar face and was headed to the security desk when she heard, instead, a familiar voice.

"Hey, Newslaper Lady!"

Not what she was expecting but not at all unwelcome. Mimi gave Baby Doll a warm smile of greeting and meant it. The ex-hooker and ex-junkie was using her given name these days— Marlene Jefferson— but she and Mimi still called each other by the names they'd each answered to when they'd met during a dark, ugly time when prostitutes were the targets of roaming serial killers. Two of Mimi's sources had been victims of the killers and Baby Doll had witnessed one of the murders. Gianna's Hate Crimes Unit had fought for the right to work the cases as crimes against women, and she'd won because Vice and Homicide didn't want them anyway since the victims were just some junkie hookers. Out of that dark, ugly time had grown a true friendship between the reporter and the young woman.

"Well, look what the cat dragged in," Mimi said, forcing a hug on Baby Doll who still recoiled from that kind of human contact and who, despite more than a year of clean living and healthy eating, still was little more than skin and bones.

"You callin' me a rat?"

"I'm calling you a sight for sore eyes. To what do I owe the honor of a visit from Miss Marlene Jefferson herself?"

Baby Doll grinned widely at the use of her proper name. "I'm glad you know you honored," she said with an affected air which made them both giggle.

"You look good, Baby," Mimi said. Free of the garish costume of the professional street walker, Baby Doll had grown her hair long and now wore the same kind of short, tight skirts and short, tight shirts that every other girl her age wore, and she looked like a pretty young girl and not like a hooker. "And don't take this the wrong way, but what are you doing here? How did you know I'd be here on Saturday?"

Baby Doll gave her the same kind of smile Bill had given her, this one tinged with pity. "'Cause you always at work. Saturday, Sunday, day time, night time, don't make no diff'rence."

"I must stop being so predictable."

"What's that mean, 'predictable'?" The question reminded Mimi of one of the things she liked most about Baby: She was inquisitive in the extreme, especially where language was concerned. It also was one of Baby's traits that most annoyed her: Once she got possession of a new word, she used it to exasperation.

"It means that people know what you're going to do before you do it because you do the same thing, the same way, all the time."

Baby nodded like some kind of wise sage. "That's you, all right: Predictable. And you need a haircut."

Mimi cut her a look that had no effect whatsoever. A waste of a good scowl, she thought, then said, "You have time to join me for lunch? I'm going across the street to the Chinese place."

"Sure," Baby Doll said, falling in beside Mimi as they exited the building. "I ain't had nothin' to eat since breakfast but you, bein' so predictable, you prob'ly didn't even have breakfast, I'll bet."

"For your information, I was on a plane this morning coming back from Los Angeles, and no, I didn't have breakfast because I never eat what's served on airplanes, which, these days, isn't much at all."

"What's in Los Angeles?"

"The story I was working on," Mimi said. "And my favorite aunt and uncle." They stopped at the corner to wait for the light. "That's my home town."

Baby Doll gave her a truly wondering look. "You from California? I didn't know that!"

Crossing the street and reaching the restaurant prevented Mimi from asking Baby Doll why the surprise. The lunch crunch was over which meant that even though the place was full, a table, way in the back of the dining room was available. Their waiter, a hip young guy with spiky hair, dragon tattoos up his arms, and rings in both ears, put water, chopsticks, a tea pot, and napkins on the table. His look was ultra-hip but his manners were old school. He smiled and bowed at Mimi. "Same as always, Miss Patterson?"

Mimi nodded. "But she'll probably want a menu."

"Maybe not," Baby said huffily. "What are you having?"

"Mu shu vegetable and you won't like it," Mimi said, remembering Baby Doll's revulsion at the mere notion of vegetarianism.

"What will I like then, since you're so smart?"

Mimi could have smacked herself. She'd forgotten that Baby couldn't read well enough yet to navigate a Chinese restaurant menu; that a year ago she couldn't read at all. "You like chicken, right? How about orange chicken. That's Gianna's favorite."

"Does it taste orange?"

Mimi shrugged and looked up at the waiter, who nodded.

"OK. Orange chicken," Baby Doll said to him. "And shrimp fried rice. And a fork. I can't eat with no sticks. And tea. "

Mimi pointed to the teapot. The waiter smiled again, this time directly at Baby, collected the menus, and walked away. Baby Doll picked up the pot and poured tea for both of them, and then dumped four packets of sugar into hers.

"It's a wonder you don't weight two hundred pounds, the way you eat."

"I got metabolism," Baby said smugly, enjoying possession of yet another new word. "That's what Adrienne said."

Adrienne Lightfoot ran the Washington Center for Spiritual Awareness, a non-sectarian organization that had made its mark working with street prostitutes to help them avoid AIDS. Adrienne and the Center had been helpful to Gianna and the Hate Crimes Unit during the prostitute murders, reaching out to women who normally would have had nothing to do with cops no matter what the danger. Adrienne had, of course, refused to give Mimi the reporter the time of day, but Mimi liked her anyway. "How is Adrienne?" Mimi asked.

Baby Doll turned up the tiny tea cup and drained it, licked her lips, and reached for the tea pot. "Chinese make the best tea," she said. "Did you know that? And they got green tea, too. That's my favorite. They serve it at the Center, and Adrienne's fine. She got me a job, you know."

"No, I didn't know that. Where? Doing what?" What job could she do that didn't require minimal reading skills?

Baby sugared her tea. "You know that adult education school over by the park? Well, I'm the new janitor. They pay me and they let me go to school for free! I thought I was too old but Adrienne says you're never too old to learn anything, and that's the truth 'cause you ought to see some of the people in that school! Old enough to be my grandparents, some of 'em." Baby got quiet and reflective. "That's admirable, don't you think? For somebody to try to learn to read and write at that age. That's what Adrienne called it: Admirable. It means doing something that people admire and respect."

"I think it's admirable that you're going back to school, Miss Jefferson."

Baby Doll, shocked speechless by the praise, was saved from formulating a reply by the arrival of the food, and she wasted no time digging in, after first saying of Mimi's Mu Shu vegetable dish, "I wouldn't eat anything that looked like that." And she got busy piling orange chicken and fried rice on to her plate.

The first time Mimi had seen her eat was at a diner on Connecticut Avenue. Baby Doll was still working the streets at the time and Mimi, trying to work her as a source, had assumed that Baby's appetite was either drug-induced or taking advantage of having somebody else pay for the meal. They'd dined together a few times since and it always was the same: Baby ate, as Mimi's father would say, like she had a hollow left leg. And a high-speed metabolism.

"So I guess you being on a plane from California is why your girlfriend was out in the street lookin' at dead bodies in the middle of the night," Baby said, and smirked as Mimi first choked, then shot her an evil look. "What's wrong, you think I don't know that cop is your girlfriend?"

"You're not making any sense."

"What don't make sense?" Baby stopped shoveling food in her face long enough to reach into her pocket and pull out a card, which she slapped on the table before reclaiming her fork. "That's her, right? Your girlfriend?"

Mimi pulled the card toward her. Sure as shit, Gianna's full name, rank and designation as head of the Hate Crimes Unit. "I take it you were on the scene of a murder that might be a hate crime?" Mimi asked, deflecting the question about her relationship with Gianna and striving to gain some control over the conversation.

"Not me, my girlfriend." Baby actually put down her fork and looked squarely at Mimi, totally oblivious to Mimi's surprise at the revelation that she had a girlfriend. "You remember that time when us girls were getting killed, right?"

Mimi put down her chopsticks and gave Baby Doll her full attention. "Of course I do."

Baby's face took on a strange, slack look that worried Mimi, until she began to talk. "That time feels like it was way back a long time ago, like it was somebody else's life, you know? I don't hardly ever think about it these days. I don't like to remember, you know what I'm saying? I like to think I always had a regular job and regular clothes and enough food to eat and a nice place to live, like I was a regular person. Then something happens like last night..."

Mimi reached across the table with both hands and took both of Baby Doll's hands and squeezed them tightly. "What happened last night?"

"This girl got killed."

"A friend of yours?"

Baby's eyes filled but she blinked away the tears, shook her head, and snatched her hands back from Mimi. "She was just some girl. She was at this club last night, where my girlfriend was, and she got killed. Terry— that's my girlfriend— she said they was gonna start killin' Ags, just like they killed the other girls." She inhaled deeply and her face and eyes hardened, transforming her into the Baby Doll of old. "Is that right, Miss Patterson? Can that happen? Can somebody do that?"

It was too much all at once. And Baby had called her Miss Patterson. "You're afraid somebody's going to kill your girlfriend?"

Baby nodded, picked up her fork and resumed eating but her eyes darted up and down, from her plate to Mimi's face, watching as the reporter picked her way through the labyrinth of pain, information, and challenge just laid out for her. It was so easy to forget that she was, clinically speaking, "a severely damaged personality." That was according to Beverly Connors, Mimi's best friend and ex-lover who also happened to be a psychologist who, along with Adrienne Lightfoot and Sylvia Richardson, Beverly's current lover, had helped several prostitutes kick the streets and their drug habits. "You don't wash away the effects of having lived that kind of life simply by taking a shower," Bev had said.

"Why does your girlfriend think she's in danger?" Mimi asked in what she hoped was a calm, non-challenging tone.

"I already told you why!" Baby snapped. "She's AG."

Mimi raised her hands, palms up, a supplicating, apologetic gesture. "I'm sorry, I don't know what that means, AG."

"And you supposed to be smart," Baby snarled, reaching into her purse again. This time she withdrew a wallet from which she then withdrew a photograph, which she passed across the table to Mimi. "That's Terry." Mimi looked at the photograph and saw a smiling, cocky, good-looking young man. Puzzled, she looked up at Baby, saw the warning flashing in her eyes, and looked back down at the photo. Then she got it. That was no boy, it was a girl. Baby didn't have the vocabulary to define what AG meant, but the photo spoke volumes. "So a girl who was AG got killed last night and it's being investigated as a hate crime," Mimi said, more to herself than to Baby Doll. Looking at the photo, she could understand why. "I haven't heard anything like that, Baby, but of course I'll ask around and I'll let you know." That was the best she could do.

"You think somebody would kill somebody just 'cause of how they look? How they dress? What kinda clothes they wear?"

Mimi looked down at the photo again, then remembered how Baby Doll used to look in a platinum blond, waist-length wig, thigh-high, six-inch red patent leather boots, and skin-tight spandex. Attire that identified her and all who looked like her as prostitutes— and got them killed? Yeah, somebody would kill somebody just 'cause of how they dress. "The girl who got killed last night, did Terry know her?"

Baby shrugged. "Just to see. They weren't tight or nothin' like that."

Mimi slid Terry's photograph back across the table to Baby Doll, who stashed it back in her wallet. "Right now, I don't think you and Terry have anything to worry about, but that's no guarantee of anything. There are a lot of sick people in this world, Baby, but you already know that. So if you all are worried, be careful, and tell your friends to be careful."

"But you'll ask your girlfriend, right?"

Not if I can help it, Mimi thought. Not and start an argument about her interfering in police business. "I'll ask her," she said to Baby Doll.

"When?"

"When I see her," Mimi snapped.

"You don't see her every day?"

"No, I don't see her every day. I haven't seen her for the last three weeks." And my get reacquainted conversation won't be about last night's murder, Mimi thought, becoming suddenly inspired to return to work and finish writing her story.

And while Mimi was doing that, Gianna was standing in the living room of Natasha Hilliard's townhouse, working to reconcile what she saw and what she'd learned with what she'd thought she knew of last night's victim. She knew better than to let stereotypes provide judgment and she should have been alerted by the watch, class ring, and Mercedes. Still, the house came as a surprise. No, more of a shock, in its elegance, Asian being the predominant aesthetic influence. The living room was sunken, the lighting recessed, the carpets Persian and thick, the artwork eclectic and much of it original. The kitchen was high tech and fully equipped and the equipment wasn't for show; this was the kitchen— utensils and food stuffs— of someone who enjoyed cooking and eating. The den-cum-library also was well equipped and comfortable— floor-to-ceiling bookshelves along two walls and a plasma television mounted on another. It was the office, however, which stopped Gianna in her tracks. The diplomas on the wall showed that Natasha Hilliard earned Bachelor's and Master's degrees at the University of Pennsylvania— which would explain the class ring now in an evidence bag— and a Ph.D. in History from George Washington University, and the papers in and on her desk revealed her to be a tenure-track professor of that subject, specializing in the Civil War, at American University.

"How old was this woman?" asked Linda in an almost whisper of awe.

"Twenty-nine," Cassie answered, "so there's still hope for me."

"The rest of us, however, are too far over the hill for hope," said Bobby.

"What've you got against a twenty-year pension from the D.C. police department?" Kenny asked. "You might even be able to buy a set of those pots and pans in the kitchen. Or maybe a couple of those wine glasses."

"College professors earn this kind of money?" Tim asked, his voice holding the awe they all felt, and since nobody knew the answer, they all looked toward the Boss for it.

Gianna, too busy internally reminding herself of the dangers of bias and prejudice, took a moment to answer. "Some do, especially the gifted ones who teach at prestigious universities, and this town is full of those." She sifted through a handful of papers, then put them back on the desk. "And our vic certainly seems to have been gifted. Bobby, are you and Tim finished in the kitchen?"

"Almost, Boss," they answered in unison.

"Then get finished. Linda, you get finished in here. Cassis, you get finished in the bedroom. We'll take the computer, answering machine, the bank and financial files, any address books." She surveyed the room again. "And look for receipts, and get an appraiser in here. I want to know how much this stuff is worth. And look for a will and a safety deposit box."

Tim shifted and they all felt it. "You thinking this was a crime for gain, Boss, and not a hate crime?"

"Somebody certainly stands to gain financially from her death. What do we know about the parents?" she asked. "Any siblings?"

Cassie whipped out her notebook. "Two sisters— one younger, one older, both parents living, mother an ordained minister, father a scientist for a chemical company, both parents and the oldest sister Ph.Ds, the youngest sister working on hers. They all live in the Philadelphia area."

"Sounds like they all live in the university library," Bobby muttered.

"Find out all you can about them, including where they spend their spare time. Start with the university library. And Lili Spenser. Have we caught up with her yet? She hasn't responded to any of our phone calls?"

Bobby shook his head. "She'd left the hospital when I got there, and she didn't go home. The ICU nurse said there were a bunch of brothers and sisters, so maybe she went home with one of them."

"We need to find her, and fast. Check the mother's address, and if that means going back to the club tonight, Cassie— ?"

Cassie nodded. "No problem, Boss."

Gianna was about to say something else when the phone rang. They all jumped, the sound making them feel what they always tried not to feel in such situations: That overwhelming sense of voyeurism, of violating the private and personal space of another human being, all the more uncomfortable because their very presence signaled that the rightful owner would never again claim his or her own space.

"Hi. Sorry I can't talk to you right now, but leave a message and I'll get back to you as soon as possible. Call 555-1234 to send a fax, otherwise, wait for the beep. Thanks for calling and have a good day." The beep sounded. "Tasha, darling," they heard, and felt more uncomfortably guilty than ever. "Where are you? Not out running with Fang in this disgusting heat, I hope. That's dangerous, you know, for you and the canine. Anyway, call me when you get in. There's been a slight change of plan for tonight, and really, I do mean slight, so don't stress, OK? Love you, Bye."

They stood there looking at each other, all immobile except Linda who was writing down the name and number from the caller ID strip on the answering machine. And they all were thinking the same thing: That the woman on the phone who had just called Natasha Hilliard 'darling,' who had just called Natasha Hilliard 'Tasha' and not 'Tosh,' was not Lili Spenser.

"Name's "Selena," Linda said. "D.C. area code, midtown exchange."

"Well, maybe it's not a crime for us after all," Tim said.

"Yeah," Bobby agreed, taking a closer look at the array of photographs on the desk and bookshelves. "Maybe our vic was a player who wound up getting herself played. Maybe we're looking at a revenge killing."

"Don't forget what was carved on her," Cassie said, and her words seemed to shift the mood in the room back to cop-like instead of guilt ridden, leaving Gianna to her own thoughts, which involved remembering what had been carved into Natasha Hilliard's torso: Die Dyke.

That spelled hatred, but there also were the incongruities to contend with. Natasha Hilliard, AG, also was Natasha Hilliard, Ph.D. And Darlene the Dangerous also was Darlene Phillips, big sister to Delores Phillips and co-owner of The Snatch, not just the muscle at the front door. Both Phillips sisters were college graduates, Dee with an MBA from Wharton, and in addition to the building that housed their night club, they owned a very successful family-style restaurant in midtown and three apartment buildings.

Dee, designer draped and coiffed, and Darlene homeboy-clad and easily able to mix it up with the best—or worst—of them. No, you sure as hell can't judge a book by its cover, and it's time we learned a lot more about Doms and Ags, Gianna thought. What she said was, "Somebody go find, feed and water Fang, then call Animal Control. And how do you tell a dog it's now an orphan?"

*****

"You're volunteering to tell me about a case?" Mimi raised herself up on one elbow and looked down into Gianna's sleepy face. "Will wonders never cease."

"There's a first time for everything and you'd do well to listen before I fall asleep. I've been up almost twenty-four hours," Gianna said, turning her face and yawning loudly into the pillow to prove her point. "And besides, I missed you. Couldn't you tell?"

Mimi sat up. "Yes, I could, and now I'm all ears."

"Not all, thank God," Gianna said, also sitting up. "I remember when I could work around the clock twice without yawning my tonsils out."

"That would have been a while ago."

"Don't mention it! I've had more than enough reminders in the past few hours how ancient and behind the times I am."

Mimi gave her skeptical look. "What fool risked your wrath, not to mention potential death, by reminding you...of what exactly? Certainly not how old you are. Nobody knows how old you are. I don't even know how old you are."

"Liar," Gianna said around another yawn. "And it wasn't as direct as a mention of how old I am as it was exposure to events and activities and names and places that I knew absolutely nothing about, that I would know something about if I weren't as old as I am."

"You're making absolutely no sense. Go to sleep and tell me whatever it is you want to tell me in the morning when you're lucid."

"No, no. I want to tell you now. Especially about a screw-up that I don't think means I'm old, but it may mean I'm a racist. But at least I'm not cruel to animals."

Mimi now was fully attentive. "What?"

"There's this club over on Lander Street. It's been open almost two years and the people who work and party there have never heard of the Hate Crimes Unit."

Mimi waited. Gianna didn't say anything else so Mimi did. "So that makes you a racist how, exactly?"

"Darlene was right: We've done outreach in Georgetown and DuPont Circle and on Capitol Hill, at the health clinics and in the health clubs, but nothing in her neighborhood. And if I ask myself why, I find that I don't like the answer."

"What's this club? Where's Lander Street? I've never heard of it and I know this town pretty well, and I'm Black. And who's Darlene?"

"I thought I knew the town pretty well, too. The street itself isn't much— one of those left over from the sixty-eight riots, still waiting for urban renewal or whatever was supposed to happen."

Mimi looked mean. "That should be a story: All the broken promises made by every city official since the sixty-eight riots. Or better still, what happened to all those hundreds of millions of dollars earmarked to help communities and neighborhoods that still look like war zones. Think how much crime you wouldn't have had to deal with over the years if the politicians had made good on just half the lies they told. Politicians, I hasten to add, who were as Black as the victims of the riots."

In the momentary quiet, Gianna reflected that this was a city they both loved but saw from completely different perspectives dictated by the completely different though often convergent nature of their jobs— and by the color of their skins. The one glaring similarity, Gianna thought, was that they both saw a lot of the ugly underside of the Nation's Capital— the people who lived in the city and the people who preyed on them.

"Anyway," Gianna said, "Darlene's the bouncer— Darlene the Dangerous they call her, and with good reason— and the club is called The Snatch—"

"Called the what!?"

"You heard right. And it's got dancing girls on the bar."

"Damn," Mimi said. "I guess you're not the only old biddy in the group. I never heard of this place. What kind of dancing girls?"

"Gorgeous ones, from what I could tell," Gianna said, "and pretty much unclothed. And they do much more than just dance."

"Uhuh. And what exactly was it that lured you into the jaws of The Snatch, Lieutenant? Certainly not an interest in gorgeous, unclothed dancing girls."

"Murder. The ugly, hateful kind," Gianna said.

"Oh, shit! The AG that was killed," Mimi exclaimed, smacking herself upside the head. "I forgot about that!" And before Gianna could put words to the look she was telegraphing, Mimi told her about Baby's visit and about Baby's girlfriend and about their fear that women who looked like Terry and the dead Tosh were or would be targets of a serial killer, like the prostitutes.

"You've heard of these Ags and Doms?" Gianna asked.

"Maybe," Mimi said through a yawn of her own. "I seem to remember reading something like that. It's mostly a Black and Latina thing, I think. I'd have asked Baby more about her girlfriend but you know how prickly she can be."

Gianna yawned again. "And Baby Doll has a girlfriend!"

*****

Baby Doll did indeed have a girlfriend, and though Terry Carson knew the truth of Marlene's past, Marlene is what she called her lady because Marlene was the only name she knew. And at that moment, Marlene and Terry were having a heated discussion—a term preferred by Marlene because argument portended hostilities—about Terry's desire to hang out at The Snatch, with her lady for company. "I told you I don't want to go there, and tonight I especially don't want you to go."

"But I thought you said that newspaper reporter said we didn't have anything to worry about."

"She doesn't think we do, Terry. Think. That's not the same as know for sure and she don't know for sure, but she said what we already know: There's a lot of crazy motherfuckers out there. So why you got to take chances?"

It was getting late and Terry was getting frustrated. "Look, Marlene, I just want to have a few beers, listen to some music, hang with my homies for a while. No biggie, all right? And after what happened last night, everybody's gonna be on the look-out for crazy motherfuckers. Ain't nobody gonna cap another one of us."

They were sitting on the couch in their living room. All of the furniture was new, purchased for cash at the big Ikea sale. No credit card debt for them— one of Adrienne's Life Lessons. Marlene loved this room—the clean-lined Scandinavian furniture, the colorful rug, the Art Deco prints on the walls. Terry had let her decorate the way she wanted, her only request being a big screen TV and DVR because she worked alternating shifts and would miss many of her favorite programs otherwise. Marlene hadn't minded because she had become a movie nut. She hadn't realized all she'd missed those years of walking the streets all night and sleeping all day. There really was a world that had passed her by and she didn't intend to miss any more of it. And Terry Carson was a big part of her new world and she wasn't about to let her get offed by some crazy dyke-hating son of a bitch. Terry, like she almost always did, knew what Marlene was thinking and feeling and grabbed her into a big, tight hug, the kind of hug Marlene had learned not only to accept but to welcome. But only from Terry.

"I just don't want nothin' bad to happen to you, that's all."

"You think I'm gonna let something happen to me, then some dude come along and snatch you up? Uhuh, no way Jose. It's you and me, Miss Marlene Jefferson. That's how it is, that's how it's gonna stay." Terry looked down at her, into her eyes, then smiled. One of the things Marlene loved most about Terry was her smile. Her whole face participated, especially her eyes, which seemed to twinkle like those little Christmas lights, and her teeth looked like an advertisement for that bleaching stuff, they were so white and straight and perfect. "Look, I got my phone, and I'll keep it on, and I promise I'll leave after the first set. How's that?"

Marlene sniffed and pushed Terry away. "That's what you really want to do is go look at naked women. You are so predictable."

The line outside The Snatch was predictable, too. At eleven o'clock the club was packed and the line snaked around the corner. Darlene had already called inside to Dee to have her activate the motion detector lights, but she still was worried. The crowd tonight was edgy. She could feel it. Instead of last night's murder being a deterrent, it had had the opposite effect. Saturday night usually was the biggest crowd but tonight's was unlike anything she'd ever seen. As she'd promised Cassie she would do, she waved her wand over everybody who entered the club, and had confiscated more knives and guns than she could keep track of; more than the lead bartender could safely store in the milk crate under the ice bin. She'd called Darlene a few minutes ago to say no more weapons.

"You gotta lock that piece in your car or something," Darlene growled to the tiny little dude glowering up at her. "You know you can't come in here with that."

"Then you keep it for me 'til I get ready to go." It came as an order and not a request, which annoyed Darlene even more.

"Not my job to keep it for you. Next in line."

The little dude was fast but Darlene the Dangerous was faster. She caught the gun half an inch from the side of her face in one hand. The other, in a fist, found her would-be assailant's mid-section in a tight, hard jab and the tiny little dude's knees buckled. "Damn, man" she said, as Darlene shoved her gently out on to the sidewalk so she could puke. Darlene kept the piece.

"Next in line," Darlene repeated in her quiet voice, but it sounded like a shout. Or a prayer. "And before you get to me, if you got a weapon, get outta line and take it somewhere else. I can't stash no more—"

The engine missed badly and loudly as the canary yellow Chevy SS roared down the street. The radio and the horn blared, and something was yelled out the window but Darlene couldn't make out what it was. The car was gone, however, and she was about to dismiss the event when a second car, a metallic blue Pontiac GTO, pulled up at the curb and slowed to a crawl. "Aw fuck," she said. That was enough. Everybody in line turned to look at the GTO, to look at the men inside it. Then the yellow Chevy roared back down the street. Darlene lifted her shirt and withdrew her SIG Sauer 9mm from the waistband of her pants. Half the ladies in her line scattered. The other half drew their own weapons. The Chevy and the Pontiac burned rubber peeling off, the Chevy's engine skipping like a school girl down the street.

Darlene watched them go, then called Dee and told her what happened. Then she took a card from her pocket, stared at it for a moment, and made another call.

Gianna had been asleep for exactly eighty-six minutes when the phone rang. She answered it in the middle of the second ring, wide awake and alert. She sat up, frowning, as the Dispatch Operator asked if she'd accept an emergency call from somebody named Darlene at something called Snatch.

"Put her through," Gianna said, getting out of bed, as if the bad feeling she was having would go away if she was standing up instead of laying down.

"Is that you, Lieutenant?" she heard Darlene's controlled voice on the verge of losing control.

"What's wrong, Darlene?"

"Did you mean what you said last night, about helping us out if there was any trouble?" Darlene was officially frantic at this point.

Gianna gave full reign to the bad feeling. "Yes, I meant it."

"Then you better get over before somebody gets killed," Darlene said.

Gianna switched off the phone and dropped it back into its cradle, then picked it up again and called Eric. She looked at the deeply sleeping Mimi, trying to decide whether to wake her. Unlike herself, Mimi did not awaken easily or gracefully in the middle of the night.

"Go 'way," Mimi mumbled when Gianna shook her. "Leave me alone."

"Don't you want to go to a rumble at the Snatch?"

On the drive down and across town from where she lived in Silver Spring to the lower part of Northwest D.C., Mimi slept and Gianna worked the phone. Her team would meet her on the scene and they'd assess the situation and decide whether to call in reinforcements. They'd operate low-key for as long as they could. Nothing like a phalanx of cops in riot gear to incite an already edgy crowd. Darlene was cryptic, acerbic, and borderline scared, and Darlene scared terrified Gianna. Shots had been fired, Darlene said, and unless somebody did something to stop it, more shots would be fired. Cars full of evil, nasty men cruising up and down, up and down the street. "They got to stop it," Darlene said ominously. The real danger, however, lay in the fact that men had penetrated her line and gotten into the club. One had been beaten senseless and tossed out the door and then kicked into the street, where his friends in one of the passing cars had picked him up, and the crowd inside was on the lookout for other imposters. Things were getting ugly in the line outside, too: Pants and shirts were being checked for the presence of dicks and the absence of breasts.

Gianna put the bubble on top of the car and gave the siren a quick twirl, startling Mimi awake, as well as the driver of the car in front of her. It was early enough that most of the drivers still were awake and alert enough that the flashing light behind them was sufficient to clear the street. From a block away, Gianna could see that the line to get into The Snatch still stretched around the corner.

"Let me off here," Mimi said, opening the door and scooting out while the unmarked sedan still rolled. Nothing to be gained by being identified as having arrived with the cops.

Gianna saw Linda Lopez talking to Darlene as she pulled up to the front door. The others would be nearby. She parked the car and got out, greeted by catcalls that were only half-heartedly hostile, probably because, Gianna thought, she was remembered from last night. At least she hoped so. "Where's Eric?" she asked Linda.

"He's inside with Miss Phillips. Bobby and Cassie are cruising around in Eric's SUV, and Tim and Kenny are parked in an unmarked two blocks away."

Gianna looked at her watch. The first show would begin in six minutes. If there were any men inside that club...She flipped open her phone and called Eric. "I'm outside. Stay in the office with Miss Phillips and watch the floor from the closed circuit cameras. Come out only to prevent a murder." She shut the phone then sidled up close to Darlene to whisper in her ear. "How much chance there's another man in there, Darlene?"

"I been over that in my mind a million times and as much as I hate to admit it, it's possible there's two more, real baby-faced looking fuckers. Short, thin, one of 'em's wearing glasses, gold rimmed, both have earrings."

"But not armed?"

Darlene shook her head. "No way. Everybody got wanded tonight. The only weapons inside there are the ones I confiscated."

Gianna's eye twitched with the effort not to betray her anger "There are contraband weapons in there? How many and what kind and where?"

"Behind the bar, in a crate under the ice bin. Eight or nine handguns and maybe a dozen switchblades," Darlene said. "Just a little while ago, though, I told everybody in line who was packing to get outta here."

"Where'd they go?" Gianna asked, scanning the eerily deserted street. Darlene shrugged. "Probably up to the subway station."

Gianna checked her watch again, then sent Linda inside. She walked to the curb and called Bobby. "Park at the north end of the street, Bobby, and keep alert," she said. Then she called Tim McCreedy and Kenny Chang with the message to bring their unmarked to the south end of the street. Then she positioned herself beside Darlene at the door to wait for whatever would happen next. The "whatever" appeared in the form of Mimi trotting purposefully toward The Snatch from the opposite direction from where she'd last seen her, notebook and camera in hand. Gianna stepped away from the building, over to the curb, to meet her.

"What?"

"Religious zealots," Mimi said, looking back down the street. "From that church down there. They're headed this way, waving signs and making dire predictions of doom and hellfire, or whatever it is they predict."

"Ah, shit. Like I don't have enough problems," Gianna said, and before she could say anything else, the sound of voices lifted in song wafted toward them on the heavy, humid air. "It's too hot for this kind of foolishness. Where's the rain?"

Mimi slid away from Gianna, angling across the street, and soon was invisible in the darkness. She kept on the look-out for cruising cars of men, but the real target of her interest was the contingent from the Ark of the

Covenant Tabernacle Church of the Holy Spirit. She counted as they approached: There were twenty-six of them, more women than men, led by a black-robed man with a big voice. What surprised her was their youth: No old fogeys, these, out to spoil young folks' fun. These people couldn't be much older than the people at The Snatch. They walked in the middle of the street, two abreast, in an orderly line behind the preacher, singing loudly and in perfect, majestic harmony.

"Come join us, sister!" the minister bellowed as he approached her. "Raise your voice against the forces of evil in our community!"

Mimi waved them along, then fell in behind them. She didn't know the song they were singing but it was spirited and vigorous and perfect for marching and waving placards. She whipped out her cell phone and called Gianna. "Here they come," she said, then hurried to the front of the church contingent. She didn't want to miss the initial encounter between them the collective object of their spiritual concern.

The church group ceased singing as soon as they reached the curb in front of The Snatch. The preacher raised the megaphone to his face. "It is never too late to come to the forgiving arms of the Master!" The preacher spread his arms as if to embrace the line in front of The Snatch.

"Jesus loves you!" one of the church people called out.

"Repent and come to Him," called out another.

"Cast not your lot with Satan, for surely you will burn for eternity in a hell of your own making." The preacher was preaching now, not talking, waving the arm that wasn't holding the speaker phone. The sweat began to   run down his face. "Renounce your evil ways and come home to Jesus!"

"Get the fuck outta here!" somebody roared from The Snatch line, and it was on. The two groups squared off, both side shouting and gesticulating, the church people with their bibles and placards, The Snatch people with the middle fingers of their hands.

Gianna inserted herself in the space between the two groups and snatched the speaker from the preacher, startling him into silence. "I am Lieutenant Maglione of the Metropolitan Police Department. Everybody be quiet, now." Everybody got quiet and Gianna returned the speaker to the preacher. "I don't want to arrest any of you, but I will if you make it necessary."

"You have no reason to arrest us, Officer," the preacher said in a more than slightly condescending tone. He was a round-faced man in his early thirties, of medium height and build, totally nondescript, except for his voice, which was raspy, deep and mellifluous. "We are exercising our Constitutional rights to assemble peacefully and to speak freely." He turned away from Gianna and faced his followers, his arms outstretched. "And we are doing God's will and His work."

"Preach, Brother!"

"Tell the truth!"

The preacher's crowd shifted around him, providing a wall of support.

"Do you have a permit, sir?" Gianna asked, taking a step closer to him.

"We don't need a permit, Officer, to exercise—"

"It's Lieutenant, sir, and this many people, with placards, and with a public address system, that's considered a demonstration and it requires a permit from the city. If you don't have one, you will have to disperse now. If you don't disperse, I will place all of you under arrest, and given the lateness of the hour, it is highly unlikely that you'll make church in the morning."

At that moment, Bobby and Cassie appeared from one direction, Kenny and Tim from the other. No doubting that they were cops. The minister's round face, which had been openly expectant, caved in on itself and he resembled a child denied permission to watch a favorite television program. "But what about them?" he asked, pointing to the line.

"Mind your own fuckin' business, asshole!" And the line surged toward the preacher and his flock.

Gianna faced the line and raised her hands, palms forward. Darlene walked the line, making eye contact with everybody she passed. Quiet returned, if not the peace. She turned to face the church group. "What's it going to be, folks?"

The preacher had regained some of his starch. He squared his shoulders and took a step toward Gianna. "Do you have a card, Officer?"

"What part of 'lieutenant' don't you understand?" Gianna had spoken so quietly that only the preacher could hear her but he backed up several steps as her hazel gaze fixed on him.

"I...uh...I meant to say...Lieutenant. Do you have a card?"

Gianna reached into her pocket, withdrew a card, gave it to him, and watched him read it. "Anything else? Any more questions?"

"I've got one." Mimi stepped toward the minister. "Are you aware that a young woman was murdered a block from here last night?"

The preacher nodded vigorously. "Yes, sister, and while we pray for the salvation of her eternal soul, we warn all who walk an ungodly path that surely death and destruction are to be expected—"

The Snatch line surged forward as if one body and one mind, the roar that emanated coming as if from one mouth. Acting with comparable unanimity, the cops wedged themselves in a line between the two groups and, with help from Darlene, they managed to keep some distance between them. Gianna grabbed the speaker again.

"You all will disperse now or be placed under arrest."

"They'll disperse now or I'll kill the motherfuckers!"

Darlene employed force, pushing her line back, away from the church people. She got help from Cassie, while Bobby, Tim and Kenny helped Gianna move the church group back and down the street.

"This is uncalled for, Lieutenant, and I will be lodging a formal complaint," the minister said, resisting Gianna's attempts to move him back until Tim added his weight. "This is police brutality!" the minister cried out as Tim propelled him into a serious backpedal.

"Just move back, sir," Tim said, literally adding weight to his words.

One of the church women began to sing, another picked up the song, and in an instant they all were singing in perfect *a capella* harmony. They turned as a unit and marched back down the dingy street to their church, followed closely by Tim, Kenny and Bobby. The crowd in the line broke into loud cheers and an impromptu rendition of "Hit the Road, Jack." Not as harmoniously as the church group but just as spirited. Darlene, not needing much force at all, got her line back in order, singing along with them, until order was restored. She raised her hand for silence, and got it. Then she reached down beside her chair and retrieved a roll of tickets. "Everybody gets a free one on me tonight. Get a ticket going in the door."

A cheer went up, then changed tone and shape as Tim, Bobby and Kenny returned. The Snatch line gave them an ovation. Kenny and Bobby gave sedate bows and waves, but Tim went into his High Queen routine, contorting his six foot-four inch weight lifter's body into something fluttery and preening. He broke both wrists, added a mincing, tight thigh walk, and left the women in line screaming for more. For the moment, the ugliness was forgotten.

"Thanks, Lieutenant," Darlene said. "It makes me queasy to think what would have happened if you hadn't been here."

Gianna didn't want to think about that, either. "Have they done that before?" she asked, not as relieved of tension as the crowd. She knew that despite their antics, Bobby, Kenny and Tim were back on patrol, ever on alert.

"Yeah," Darlene said, "almost every week, but we mostly ignore 'em. Some of the homies would shout stuff at 'em, dirty stuff, especially at the good church brothers. Did you happen to notice how many of them were sissies? Especially the preacher. Big ol' queen, and he's got the nerve to be talking about somebody burning in hell. He better hope God's got a sense of humor—" Her phone rang, cutting off her rant and, at the same moment, so did Gianna's. Both answered. "Oh, fuck!" Darlene said.

Gianna raced for the door. Darlene unlocked it and started to follow. "You need to keep the peace out here but don't let anybody else in." She looked toward the street and signaled to Cassie. "You come with me." She raised her hand in a stand-by gesture to Kenny and Bobby and knew they saw it.

It was wild inside. The music thumping and pulsing, the women dancing on the bar, and five hundred people in motion. Gianna pushed her way through the crowd, toward the back door. The movement back there was decidedly different from that in the front. Nobody back here was watching the bodies gyrating on the bar. They were watching the bodies writhing on the floor. Four of them. Eric and somebody, Linda and somebody else. Eric was holding his own. Gianna waded in to help Linda, who was straddling what

Gianna assumed was a man, struggling to get both of his arms behind him.
He was flailing and kicking for all he was worth. Linda had him pinned but
she couldn't get both arms together to get the cuffs on. Gianna stood over
him, one leg on either side, and grabbed both his arms. Linda handcuffed him
and yanked on the cuffs. Hard.

"Goddamn bitch!"

Linda yanked again, harder, and he howled even louder.

Gianna walked around him and bent down. "You're going to stand up now,
and you're going to keep your mouth shut, or I'm going to let the women in
here have their way with you. Understood?"

He nodded and struggled to his feet, with Linda's help. Eric and Cassie had
the other collar on his feet as well. Both men, Gianna realized, were bloodied
and battered, as were several of the by-standers, and Dee Phillips was ready
to chew nails.

"Get them out of here," she snarled, and pointed toward the back door. "I'll
unlock the gate so you can get out."

Eric and Linda led the handcuffed men out and Dee slammed the heavy
steel door shut so hard Gianna swore the brick wall surrounding it vibrated.
The woman was rattled. Gianna turned toward the bar and watched the show
to give her time to recover herself, using the moment to tell Cassie to mingle
with the crowd, making sure there would be no aftershocks.

"I owe you an apology, Lieutenant, and my gratitude," Dee finally said, her
voice vibrating a little.

"I'll accept the apology but no gratitude is necessary. This is what we get
paid to do. Just think of it as your tax dollars at work, and I'm certain you
pay enough taxes to keep a couple of us employed full time."

Dee relaxed and almost smiled. "More than a couple of you," she said, and
headed for her office. Gianna followed. Two chairs sat side by side in front
of the security monitors and Gianna guessed that Dee and Eric had spotted
the two imposters before they had time to cause any real trouble. "Your
Detective Ashby is a real eagle eye," Dee said, confirming Gianna's
speculation. "He watched those monitors the whole time, never moving a
muscle. Then he calls me over, still not taking his eyes from the screen.
'Watch these two,' he says, pointing to the screen. 'Tell me what you think.'
So I watch for about a minute. 'Those are men,' I say. 'That's what I think,'
he says, and calls Officer Lopez. I watched them, Lieutenant. They moved
into that crowd without causing hardly a ripple, grabbed those two, and were
hustling them to the back door before anybody noticed. If I had gone out
there sooner I could have prevented the melee that occurred, but I was in here
fuming. I just want you to know that your people didn't cause that free-for-
all. They are true professionals, both of them"

And Gianna knew that if anything mattered to Dee Phillips, it was true
professionalism. "I'm glad to hear it, Miss Phillips. And the only people to

blame for what happened in here are those guys. They came in here looking for trouble."

"Well, they found it," she said. "Now what? Will you arrest them?" Gianna hesitated, then shook her head. "I don't think so, not unless they have outstanding wants and warrants. We'll make sure we know who they are and where to find them, and we'll make sure they understand that if there's any more trouble here, we'll blame them."

Dee Phillips paced up and down her office. She wore what Gianna knew was an expensive designer pant suit, though she couldn't have named the designer, and expensive designer shoes that Gianna did recognize because she hadn't been able to afford them. Dee's jewelry— watch, rings, ear studs— were solid gold and obviously costly though not flashy. Her haircut was as flawless as it had been last night and Gianna wondered if anybody, even a rich anybody, got a haircut and a manicure every day, because both looked that fresh. She glanced at her watch, then at the monitors. "I need to go out on the floor," she said, and while it wasn't quite asking permission, the tone was more conciliatory than before.

"Of course," Gianna said, moving toward the door.

"Do you think we're going to have any more trouble tonight?"

Gianna had been wondering the same thing, and wondering what to do about it. What she didn't want to do right now was alert the district commander of her presence here tonight. She had plans for dealing with him. But she also didn't want to leave her people here— they were up all night last night; and granted they were younger than she was, they still needed a night of uninterrupted sleep. They were scheduled to meet at the office at ten the next morning. She'd push the meeting time back to noon. "I don't think so, Miss Phillips but I don't have a crystal ball. I'll give you my home number, and if you need to, you can call me." She wrote her home and cell phone numbers on the back of a card and gave it to the still tense night club owner.

"I don't imagine these numbers are scribbled on the bathroom wall," Dee said, locking the card in her desk drawer. Then she headed for the door. She offered Gianna her hand, opened the door, waited for Gianna to exit, then closed and locked the door. It, like every door in the place, was reinforced steel surrounded by brick.

"You've got some of the best security I've ever seen, inside and out," Gianna commented.

"Imagine how it would be if we didn't," Dee said, and the two women separated, moving off in different directions, Gianna acutely and intensely aware of the noise. It had been absolutely silent inside Dee's office. Silent and cool to the point of being almost chilly. It was anything but chilly out here, though air circulated— Gianna could feel it. She looked for its source and found the huge fans. As she slithered through the swaying, gyrating bodies, she wondered why Dee didn't install central air conditioning.

Outside, she called Eric, told him to drive the beat-up and bloodied home boys out of the neighborhood and drop them off, relayed Dee Phillips's' praise, and told him to send everybody home, with the new start time for the following day. Then she called Mimi. She didn't wonder where she was, she knew: At the church with her zealots, looking for the story that the eternal reporter within her knew was there somewhere. Mimi confirmed her location and promised to meet Gianna at the front of the club in fifteen minutes.

"Lieutenant?"

Gianna turned to find herself eye to eye with a young woman she recognized from the night before, part of the crowd standing behind the crime scene tape. The one who had said 'It wasn't no love crime, that's for sure.' "Yes?"

The young woman approached Gianna and extended her hand. "I'm Terry Carson, Marlene Jefferson's friend." Gianna shook the hand while searching her memory for a clue to who Marlene Jefferson was. "She said you were on the up and up, and I guess she was right. You all really treated us like were citizens tonight."

This was Baby Doll's girlfriend. "You are citizens, Terry. Just don't forget to vote, and keep paying your taxes."

"Like I got a choice about the taxes. Fuckin' government takes what it wants before I even get mine, and I'm the one doing the work."

Gianna commiserated properly and waited to see if Terry wanted anything else. "Tell Ba...Marlene I said hello."

"I'll do that," Terry said.

As she walked away, Gianna couldn't stop herself from thinking how much like a young man the young woman looked. She called up the memory of herself at that age, remembered the butch and femme looks, thought about the butches who were more than a little masculine in appearance. This was not a new phenomenon, she told herself. But it felt new. It felt different. Was it?

CHAPTER FIVE

Sunday morning was as leisurely as Mimi and Gianna could make it under the circumstances. They were at Mimi's house—they'd come back here after the excitement at The Snatch to unwind in the hot tub that was the centerpiece of the former toolshed in her back yard. Mimi also had food because, after a three-week absence, she'd had to shop, and the fridge was overflowing with culinary goodies. Breakfast was herb and cheese omelets and raisin toast and fresh squeezed juice and some Trader Joe's coffee Mimi brought back from California. She had just about convinced Gianna that it was better than what she called "that overpriced and overrated pseudo-gourmet crap" sold by the chain coffee bars.

So, after her second cup of coffee, and despite the events of the previous night, Gianna felt relatively rested. She'd gotten more sleep than Friday night's three hours and she was starting the day with real food, which was a rare treat for her. For Mimi, it was a necessity. Both the sleep and the food. Mimi didn't function well unrested and unfed; in fact, she was, Gianna told her more than once, surly and snarly when deprived of those basic necessities. Mimi had not gotten sufficient sleep and she planned to make up for it sometime this afternoon, but the food revived her. So did Gianna's busy hands beneath her bathrobe before she pushed her away with the admonition not to start anything she couldn't finish. And that Gianna couldn't finish—at least not to Mimi's satisfaction; she had to rush off for her noon meeting with her team.

After Gianna left, Mimi cleaned the kitchen, showered and dressed, and headed for her own office, but at a more leisurely pace. She didn't mind going into the paper on Sunday, especially since she wasn't on the clock. She'd turned in the third part of her California series the day before. Today, she would clean her desk, organize her files, and prepare for the coming week, and do it all without some editor's warm breath on the back of her neck. She contemplated riding the subway because even on Sunday, parking downtown was a pain, what with all the restricted parking zones and parking meter rates in effect even on weekends. She didn't really need the car today. Then she thought maybe, after she finished at work, she'd drive over to Georgetown or perhaps to DuPont Circle and get a haircut.

She paused before the fireplace mirror and took a good look at herself. She was surprised Gianna had offered only one "you need a haircut" comment. In truth, she'd needed one before she left town, and she'd planned to get one in California. What she hadn't expected was the dearth of Black people in her home state. Why hadn't she been more aware, she wondered, that Blacks had become the third-place minority in California, so scarce in some places as to be non-existent? Why hadn't she known that she couldn't just pop into any salon anywhere in Los Angeles or San Francisco or Sacramento or San Diego and find somebody able to do something with her hair? She really had been away from home for too long. There was a reason it was said you couldn't go home again.

Mimi parked three blocks from the paper and was locking the car and setting the alarm when a fat raindrop smacked her in the face. "Oh, yes, please!" she implored, peering up at the darkening sky. What a relief rain would be. The globe might be merely warming in other parts of the world, but in D.C., it was sizzling. There hadn't been much rain over the summer and despite the fact that it was a few days past the middle of September, fall hadn't even peeked around the corner. There probably was something untoward about wishing for a hurricane but a rainy Sunday afternoon or evening—no matter that it would mean that the storm tracking up the eastern seaboard likely had gotten close enough to do damage somewhere in North or South Carolina—truly would be something to look forward to.

The newsroom was busy but not hectic. People lounged at their desks, reading fat Sunday papers from around the country, or talking on the telephone, instead of hunched over keyboards, one eye on the clock, struggling to make deadline. Mimi exchanged pleasantries with several colleagues and real conversation with a couple of others. She was halfway through the three-week accumulation on her desk when the weekend editor of the local section, Carolyn Warshawski, stepped into her sight line.

"Hey, Mimi," Carolyn said. She was one of the few people at the paper who called her Mimi; everybody else called her Patterson, which was her preference. The name served to separate her personal life from her professional life but Mimi liked Carolyn; liked her enough not to mind that her appearance at Mimi's desk meant she wanted something.

"How's life, Carolyn?" Mimi asked, really wanting to know. Carolyn Warshawski was reminiscent of Sissy Spacek in that she was tiny and blond and fragile looking; but at the ripe old age of whatever she was—thirty-two or thirty-three—Carolyn had endured a big enough chunk of bad luck to last most people a lifetime. She'd fallen in love with a musician, against all advice, her first year at the paper. She'd met him on assignment—she the rookie reporter doing a story on a no-name but promising band for the entertainment section. Both their stars rose quickly: Carolyn was as good a reporter as Monty Murphy was a musician, and she quickly moved from low reporter on the totem pole at the entertainment desk to major player on the national desk, seeing the world at its ugliest and winning a drawer full of reporting prizes in the process. Monty also was seeing the world— and doing half the women in it. Then Carolyn got pregnant and asked to be assigned back home. She didn't want to have the baby in a foreign country, alone. And by that time she was alone more often than not. Then the trouble really started. Something happened to the amniotic fluid and both mother and baby almost died. Then mother and baby survived, but baby was little more than an amoeba. After a valiant year-long struggle, Carolyn's baby girl threw in the towel and Carolyn began the process of rebuilding her life, sans Monty Murphy.

"Life's not half bad, Mimi, thanks for asking. And as good as it is to see you, I'm standing over you because I need a favor."

That was another thing Mimi liked about Carolyn: There was no bullshit about her. Most other editors would hem and haw and beat around the bush if they were about to ask a reporter for the kind of favor that involved working on a day off. Not Carolyn. She was as up front as they came, which was why Mimi didn't balk at the intrusion. "I'm happy to help you out if I can, Carolyn."

The movement behind her deep-set, pale-colored eyes spoke her appreciation. What she said was, "I wouldn't bother you if I had anybody else to put on this."

Mimi's eyes did a quick roam and spied at least four other reporters who were on the clock and who didn't look like they were engrossed in writing the next Pulitzer Prize winner. "What's the story?"

"A woman was raped last night over on Harley Street. It seems she'd just left a night club called The Pink Panther. I'm interested because it's a gay club, because it may not be the first incident involving patrons there, and because the cops don't seem to have much interest in the thing. I mean, wouldn't you think the district commander would be a little worried about three felony assaults in the vicinity of the same gay nightclub in less than a month?"

"If the district commander isn't worried, I'd like to know why," Mimi said, and meant it.

"I thought you might," Carolyn said, pushing a strand of reddish-blond hair out of her face, only to have it flop right back.

"Are you looking for something by deadline?"

Carolyn shrugged. "Only if there's something there. But call and let me know as soon as you can, OK? I'll hold space just in the event. And thanks, Mimi."

The editor walked back to her own desk, leaving Mimi to sort out her thoughts, and it was no small job. Another gay club she'd never heard of, located on another street she'd never heard of. Carolyn had said the victim was raped. Because she was a lesbian? Was she, in fact, a lesbian? Had she, in fact, been at the Pink Panther or merely in the vicinity? And what were the other "incidents?" The answers certainly could spell hate crimes. She grabbed up the phone and started calling sources— cops, paramedics, crime scene technicians, assistant medical examiners, gay community activists, gay bar owners— looking for somebody on a Sunday afternoon with the Redskins playing the Cowboys on television who would give her the deep and skinny about a rape last night in the vicinity of the Pink Panther. She got lucky on the fifth call. Jose Cruz, the supervisor of the crisis hot line at the Metropolitan Washington Gay and Lesbian Community Organization, was at work because the Sunday hot line coordinator was raped last night after leaving the Pink Panther night club. He was still so mad he'd be happy to talk to her about it.

Mimi got her tiny digital camera, tape recorder and cell phone from her desk, put them in her bag, and headed for the door. She detoured mid-stride and aimed for Carolyn's desk, noticing the on-duty reporters the editor had by-passed to throw Mimi into the mix on her day off. And no wonder: Two jerks, an idiot and a drunk, all of them white males. The next snide Jayson Blair remark that came her way she was going to unload. "I have no idea where Harley Street is."

"I didn't, either," Carolyn said, digging around in the pile on her desk, coming up with a computer-generated map with a yellow-highlighted area clearly marked. "Who'd think to put a night club in there?"

The same people who'd think to put a night club on Lander Street, Mimi thought, gazing at the map. Lander Street appeared to be perhaps two miles from Harley Street and, if she recalled, in the same police command district. Then it occurred to her that she probably didn't want to park her car on Harley Street, even on Sunday afternoon. Her brand new Audi convertible, purchased mere months ago in the wake of the theft and destruction of her prized, classic 1966 Karman Ghia. She'd go to Metro GALCO first and talk to Jose Cruz, and if she got lucky, he'd arrange for her to talk to the victim. And if she got even luckier, the victim would know the name of somebody she could talk to at the Pink Panther. It was all about luck. Well, maybe not all, otherwise, Carolyn would have sent the idiot, the drunk or one of the jerks.

"We're not even forty-eight hours into this case and it's already got more twists and turns than a two-lane West Virginia road," Detective Eric Ashby groused. He was standing at the wall chart in the Think Tank, the Hate Crimes Unit's basement lair in police headquarters, trying to create a time, event and character line. Across the room, his boss, Lieutenant Gianna Maglione, was hanging up an array of crime scene photographs on the board. Kenny Chang and Linda Lopez were busy at the computers. Tim McCreedy and Cassie Ali were poring over a foot-high stack of files, while Bobby Gilliam took notes as they dictated them, maintaining a separate notebook for each principal. So far there were eight of them: The victim, Natasha "Tosh" Hilliard; Delores Phillips; Darlene Phillips; Robert, Christine, Felicia and Jill Hilliard, Tosh's parents and sisters; Lili Spenser, The Snatch dancer identified as Tosh's girlfriend; Selena Smith, a Literature professor at George Washington University and also a girlfriend of the victim; Starletta "Tree" Davis, scholarship basketball player at the University of Maryland; Aimee Johnson, Snatch bartender. There would be more but these people would provide the police with their early information about the victim— and already it was clear that information would be contradictory at best.

"Who's got the vic's personal papers?" Gianna asked.

"I do...we do," Tim said, "and we're not even half through 'em."

"That's the bad news," Cassie said. "The good news is that Professor Hilliard was extremely well-organized. The other bad news is that she seems never to have thrown away a single piece of paper in her entire life. Were you looking for anything in particular, Boss?"

"The will," Gianna snapped. "Or a key to a safety deposit box. If this is a crime for gain, I want to know it sooner rather than later."

"Well, there's no file that says, 'WILL' with the stuff from her desk and file cabinet. Maybe it's in her computer," Tim offered.

"Who's her lawyer?" Gianna asked.

"Don't know yet, Boss. Sorry."

"Yeah, me too." Gianna crossed the room to stand between Kenny and Linda at their computers.

"The Phillips sisters are sterling citizens times ten, Boss." Kenny Chang was their resident computer geek and he looked the part: Spiky black hair topped a youthful, round face upon which sat wire-rimmed eyeglasses. But Kenny wasn't just a nerd, he was a detective first grade, outranking everybody in the room except Gianna. He'd spent half a decade working major crimes and as one of a handful of Chinese-speaking officers in the Department, worked a few cases with international aspects. But when the Hate Crimes Unit was formed, he, like every member of the team, quickly volunteered.

"Yeah," Linda said, not raising her eyes from the screen, "I wish I was that sterling. They're worth well over a million. Each. They've been buying real estate since they first started working."

"Please tell me they're older than twenty-nine," Bobby said.

"They are, but not by much," Kenny offered. "Big Sister Darlene is all of thirty-four and Dee is two years younger."

"And get this," Linda injected. "The head bartender, Aimee Whatever? She's their first cousin. She's got a business, degree, too, and she's only twenty-six. Dee co-signed her loan when she bought a three-unit house last year. She lives in one, rents out the other two. The rents pay the mortgage and she banks her paycheck. Already she's headed toward Darlene and Dee's kind of security."

"And by the way," Kenny added, "the only lawyer to turn up in any of Natasha Hilliard's computer records is somebody named Allison Jenkins. She's a divorce lawyer."

Eric started to pace. "I'd like this thing a whole lot better if we had just a whiff of slime and low lifes and underworld characters and nere-do-wells. All these upstanding, righteous citizens— this is making me nervous."

"Not me." Gianna dropped down chair and put her cowboy-booted feet up on the desk, legs crossed at the ankles. She folded her hands behind her head and leaned back in the chair, the very picture of not nervous. "In fact, Eric, you just clarified my thinking for me. This is a hate crime for the very reason that you're unnerved. There is absolutely no reason to target these women other than—"

"How they look?" Cassie was riled up and ready for a fight. "Mainstream society finally decides that maybe it's OK to be queer as long as the girls look like they belong on The L Word and the boys are interior design and fashion queens, but heaven help anybody who doesn't fit inside their straight little lines! It sucks!"

The room and the people in it went still and silent. Everybody needed a moment and Gianna gave it to them. "Let's talk about that, about Doms and

Ags. It's something I need help with, too, because until Friday night I didn't know there were designations other than 'Butch' and 'Femme.' And maybe that's because I'm just a behind-the-times old biddy—and I'll cop to that—and don't you dare laugh, Ashby, you're not that much younger."

With his bright red hair and wide blue eyes and looking more like a choir boy than a detective, Eric did exactly that and the others joined in, glad to have the tension released, especially at the Boss's expense and instigation. They could laugh because with the possible exception of Cassandra Ali, they all were in the same out-of-touch boat as their boss. "So the question is," she continued as calm returned, "are we just out of date, are we just...what's the terminology? Not still 'square' or 'lame,' I'm guessing."

"Even I know better than that," Eric said. "I think the term you're looking for is, 'old school.'"

Gianna bowed in his direction as several heads nodded that he was correct. "So, as I was saying, the question we have to answer is are we just too old school, or does there exist a subculture, a counterculture within the homosexual community that we don't know anything about? And if that's the case, how effective can we be in our jobs— or rather, how ineffective have we been in our jobs— ignorant of this fact?"

All the humor evaporated. Every one of them was somber and serious as they pondered the question, including Cassie. Then she felt eyes on her and realized that she was expected to take a stab at an answer. She raised her hands, palms upward, in a helpless gesture. "That's a really good question, Boss, and I wish I could give it the answer it deserves. Yeah, I knew about Doms and Ags before Friday night, but a counterculture? A subculture? Either that's way over my head or, and don't take this wrong, it's just an excuse for not wanting to deal with people as they are. I mean, like you just said, there's nothing new about butch women."

"So why aren't we calling them 'butches' like before?" Tim asked. "What's with this 'Ag' and 'Dom' stuff if we're talking about the same thing?"

"That's a question we need to answer," Gianna said, looking at Cassie. "Can you give us any insight?"

Cassie shook her head. "I don't think so. I mean, I know some people think the wardrobe and the language and the behavior are kind of extreme and, I guess in a way, it's meant to be. It's kind of an in-your-face-don't-mess-with-me attitude that sends a definite message, you know? But it also could be more than that..." Cassie shook her head again. "I'm sorry I can't be more help."

"Let me ask you one more thing," Gianna said. "Is it your belief that it's a Black and Latina thing?"

Cassie was thoughtful, then began slowly nodding her head. "Yeah, I think that's fair to say. Up to a point. I mean, does everything have to have a label? Does everything always have to come down to race?"

"You're right," Gianna said. "Let's not get bogged down in that. We've got a homicide that's a hate crime to deal with. We follow the same procedures as always. We still work the files and information and the details, and when the forensic evidence starts to come in, we work that, too. And we strip Natasha Hilliard down to her very essence. We know from her closet that whatever else she called herself—Dom, Ag or butch, Dr. Hilliard didn't go teach history at AU dressed the way she was dressed at The Snatch on Friday night, and I'd bet my paycheck that she wasn't going anywhere with Professor Selena Smith on Saturday night dressed the way she was dressed at The Snatch. But did she go places with Lili dressed like that, or did Lili and The Snatch and Tosh exist only one night a week?" Gianna stood up and took Eric's place pacing. She knew her paycheck was safe. What she didn't know was why a paycheck much larger than her own hadn't kept Natasha Hilliard safe. "What time are the Lili and Selena interviews?"

"Simultaneous," Eric answered, "at two-thirty. Cassie and Kenny have Lili and Linda and Tim have Selena. Bobby has the Maryland basketball player who Aimee the bartender says was talking to Hilliard at the bar, and I've got Aimee herself, both interviews at three."

"Make sure you find out the full extent of Lili's relationship with Tosh. I'll see everybody back here in the morning at eight-thirty. Thanks for your weekend, folks. I'll make it up to you as soon as I can." She didn't know when that would be— days off in a case like this weren't an option— but she wouldn't assign any all-nighters if she could avoid it, and she'd alternate half days off among them as often as possible, as long as the all the bases were covered. They were good cops who worked their asses off, as much for her personally as for the cause they all believed in, and she knew it and was grateful. Eric had passed the sergeant's exam, then passed up two chances at promotion to remain her second-in-command, and Kenny and Bobby could have their detective shields any time they chose. In fact, she had just about decided it was time to push them in that direction—Eric, Kenny and Bobby. All that talk about getting older, the laughter notwithstanding, was no joking matter. A police department was the kind of organization you either moved up or stagnated. All her people were too good to let them stagnate.

"I'll get it," she said when the phone rang, wondering if one of their interviews was calling to cancel. "Hate Crimes, Lieutenant Maglione," she answered, and listened for a full minute to the caller. Then she said, "Your information is correct and I'll meet with you whenever you say but the sooner the better." She grabbed a pen and notepad. "May I have your full name, phone number and address, please?" She wrote, listened and wrote some more. "Thank you for calling, Miss Harper. I'll see you tomorrow morning at nine o'clock."

Every eye in the room was on her. "What was that?" Eric asked in a tone of voice that suggested he really didn't want to know.

"Joyce Harper. She was raped last night— early this morning— after leaving a night club called the Pink Panther. It's on Harley Street. There were three of them who took turns. They called her 'dyke' while they raped her, saying she ought to die."

The silence was ice cold. "Oh, fuck," Bobby said, shattering it. He started to crack his knuckles, then quickly stopped; he knew it drove everybody crazy.

Linda wrapped her arms around herself as if she were, in fact, cold. "Where's Harley Street?" Tim asked.

"About a mile and half from Lander Street," Cassie answered, and Gianna snapped out of her reverie.

"In what direction?"

"East," Cassie answered, and they knew immediately what Gianna knew: That Harley Street was in the same command district as Lander Street. The Snatch and the Pink Panther were in the same police command district and the Hate Crimes Unit had never been advised of the possibility of hate crimes being committed there, either.

"I'm meeting Miss Brown at her home tomorrow morning at nine. Linda, you switch off The Snatch and onto this," she said, handing over the notebook with Joyce Harper's information. "She was at GWU ER until eight o'clock this morning, and they did a rape kit. Bobby—"

Bobby jumped to his feet. "On my way, Boss," and he was out the door.

"Was there any kind of crime scene investigation?" Eric asked, the wishful thinking so heavy in his voice it sounded like begging God.

Gianna shook her head. "She lives in the neighborhood and walked home after the attack. The woman walked four blocks after that."

"Maybe it's not too late if we know the exact location," Cassie said, standing, her own wishful thinking dashed on the rocks as Bobby rushed back into the room.

"Rain's finally here," he announced, grabbing an umbrella from the makeshift closet at the rear of the room and rushing back out.

Possible trace evidence sloshing down the gutter with the rest of the city's accumulated grit and grime, Gianna thought, though without deep regret because she was planning in her mind the exact words she'd say to the chief of police when she showed up at his office at seven tomorrow morning. She'd begin his Monday the way she was ending her Sunday: with a pile of shit nestled in her lap. As for the remainder of Sunday? Well, at least they had Joyce Harper's rape kit. That was something, which was better than nothing.

*****

Jose Cruz was a little gnome: Wizened and witty, full of life and energy, walking proof of those old axioms, "age ain't nothin' but a number" and "you're only as old as you feel." Jose must regularly have felt twelve or thirteen because he bounced around the offices of the Metropolitan Washington Gay and Lesbian Community Organization as if on a pogo stick, usually trailed by a swarm of teens who'd normally rather die than give props to an adult. Jose was seventy if he was a day, a recent arrival in D.C. from New York, which he left, he said, "before the damn place killed me."

Harsh words coming from a native New Yorican but for him, necessary and true. So true that he'd brought his 'baby' sister with him: Emelia, sixty-five and a dead ringer for the late, great Salsa singer Celia Cruz, to whom Jose and Emelia bore absolutely no relation, they told everybody before the question was asked. Celia, they'd tell you, was Cubana. Jose and Emelia were Puerto Ricans from Spanish Harlem.

Mimi still wasn't sure how somebody who hadn't even seen Metro GALCO six months earlier now seemed to own the place, but such was the nature of Jose Cruz. One day he came in "looking for something to join," the next he was in charge of organizing for senior lesbians and gays, and shortly thereafter, he was tapped to supervise the hot line because he'd managed a crisis line in New York City. Like everybody else who met him, Mimi was captivated immediately, a feeling enhanced by the fact that Jose didn't begrudge her the nature of her work. "Everybody's gotta do something," was a favorite motto of his. "Even you," he'd say, giving a sly glance to whomever he was chatting up.

"Mimi, mi hermana," he sang out, giving her a rib bruising hug and smacks to both cheeks. "How are you, darling?"

Mimi kissed the top of his shiny bald head. "Always better after I see you, you handsome devil."

"Flattery will get you everywhere. And you're looking quite fetching yourself, *cara mia*." He ogled her up and down, totally unaware that nobody called anybody fetching except in British novels. "I've heard of casual Fridays, but casual Sundays must be something new."

Mimi had forgotten that she left home wearing jeans— the skintight variety— and a tee shirt. That she had the benefit of a jacket was owing only to the threat of rain and cooler temperatures. Technically, she wasn't working, and this she explained to Jose. "And I know you don't normally work on Sunday either, so thanks for agreeing to see me, Jose."

His face fell and sadness was such an unusual emotion to see in him that it was a bit unnerving. "That whole situation with Joyce makes me want to do violence to somebody," he said, looking much less gonme-like.

The Metro GALCO building had been an elementary school in its former life, one of the old ones, built with character and meant to last, built way before accessibility became the norm. Consequently, all programs and services for seniors and the physically challenged were on the ground floor except the crisis intervention hot line, which was in the basement. Fortunately, there was an old fashioned lift that descended the one level, since several of the hot line monitors were elderly and or disabled. Jose did not consider himself elderly; nevertheless the hot line operation was in the basement, behind a heavy iron door, because in New York the crisis line office once had been attacked and several workers wounded by an angry ex-lover of a client who hadn't appreciated the advice dispensed.

Mimi followed Jose into the creaky old cage and watched him pull the accordion gate shut and manipulate the lever, dropping them slow as molasses to the basement. Jose probably remembered when elevators like this were the height of cool. She said as much and he gave her a happy, wistful grin. "They all had operators, too, and it was a skill to run the car smoothly, without jolting and jerking, and to bring it to a slow, smooth stop. Like this." And the lift came to a slow, smooth stop.

"Not many people working today," Jose said over his shoulder as he sped down the hallway. "Not usually too busy this time of the month. But from next month straight on through until the first of the year, we'll be busy, busy, busy, especially on weekends."

He opened an unmarked door at the end of the hall and entered a classroom sized interior square. The windowless room was brightly and warmly lit. There were half a dozen long tables placed at various angles, each with three partitions and a phone headset in each. People sat at three of the partitions, one talking on a headset, two others reading novels. All three waved at Jose and he waved back. His office, a smaller room off the main room, held a desk, chair, three tall filing cabinets, and a phone console from which he could monitor any call out front. He waved Mimi toward a chair and went to one of the file cabinets and pulled open a drawer. A moment later he had a folder in his hand.

"I wish I were that well organized."

"When you're my age, you will be," Jose promised. "You won't be able to afford not to be if you want to get anything accomplished. And why, you wonder? I'll tell you: Because your memory runs and hides." He plopped down behind his desk and opened the folder, read through the pages quickly, and closed it. "How did you know what happened to Joyce?"

"My editor. All I knew before I talked to you was that a woman was raped in the vicinity of the Pink Panther and it's not the first time patrons of that club have been assaulted, though I don't know if they were all women."

"But Joyce is the story you care about right now?" Jose asked.

Mimi answered carefully. "I need to let my editor know whether or not her information was correct. Then I need to find out if there is in, in fact, a pattern of harassment, and if so, where the cops are. After that...well..." Mimi shrugged.

Jose's lips lifted at the corners. He knew enough to know the shrug meant if Mimi found any hint that the cops had ignored what looked like a pattern of harassment against any particular group there'd be hell to pay. And, no matter who her girlfriend was, it would be the cops doing the paying. "Joyce called me at home at two-thirty this morning as asked me to meet her at the

George Washington University Hospital Emergency Room. What I heard in her voice, I didn't ask why, I just got up, woke Emelia up, and to the hospital we went. As her parents. She said to tell them we were her parents because she doesn't have family here." Jose sighed, shook his head, and muttered something in Spanish that Mimi didn't catch.

"What, Jose?"

"Ruby should have been with her."

"Who's Ruby?"

"Her lover supposedly, though you can't prove it by me," Jose said. "Care to guess where she was last night while Joyce was being brutalized in a dark alley?"

Mimi settled herself more comfortably into the hard wooden chair and crossed her legs. Getting this story out of Jose was going to take time. Good thing she had a reliable source at George Washington University Hospital who didn't mind being disturbed by a reporter on Sunday. Good thing Carolyn Warshawski wasn't the kind of editor who'd break all her knuckles for not having a story this Sunday evening, because there would be no story today. But next weekend? She'd make Carolyn one happy editor next weekend. She already was planning what she'd say to her boss tomorrow morning to clear the way for that to happen.

CHAPTER SIX

"I don't want you in my house, now get away from my goddamn door!"

Gianna didn't blink or budge but Linda Lopez flipped the safety off her Glock. "Joyce Harper asked me to come here. When she asks me to leave, I will," Gianna said calmly, hoping it would rub off on the woman blocking the door.

"You'll leave when I tell you to or I'll kick your ass down those steps." The woman glowering at her in the doorway took a menacing step in her direction and Gianna was trying to decide on a course of action when she heard somebody speak from within the house.

"I asked her to come, Ruby. I want her here."

"Well I don't."

"Then leave, like you always do. Go back wherever you were Saturday night." Joyce Harper somehow managed to move Ruby aside and took her place in the door way. She wore a beautiful silk dressing gown and matching slippers and she looked like hell. "Come in, Lieutenant," she said, her bruised, swollen lips barely able to form the words. She saw Linda behind Gianna, Glock in hand, and nodded her in, too, unfazed by the weapon. Ruby closed the door and followed them.

"Shouldn't you be in the hospital, Miss Harper?" Gianna asked.

"Probably," Joyce answered, leading the way slowly and painfully down a narrow hallway with a polished, hardwood floor and white walls covered with framed photographs. The hall led, like the typical row house, through the center of the structure. Joyce turned right, into the living room, narrow but bright because of the floor-to-ceiling bay window. The sofa bed was open and Joyce lay back down on it, groaning with the effort. "But if all I'm gonna do is hurt and cry, I'd just as soon hurt and cry at home, in my own bed. At least I don't have to worry who hears me."

"Can I do anything to help?" Gianna asked, seriously concerned about the woman's well-being, emotional as well as physical.

"Catch the bastards who did this to me."

"You had no business out there! If you'd been home, nothin' like this would 'a happened." Ruby's face was scrunched up in equal parts anger and sorrow and her mouth quivered. She was a thin woman, and older than Gianna had first thought—closer to forty than thirty. She wore a pale blue, long sleeved oxford shirt and jeans and leather slippers. She had a beer in one hand and a cigarette in the other, neither of which she'd had a moment ago at the door. Gianna looked from her to Joyce, then sat down in the armchair at the foot of the sofa bed. Linda assertively took a chair opposite.

"What did happen out there, Miss Harper?"

"Can't you see what happened?" Ruby unleashed her anger again. "Why you got to make her say it all over again? Why she got to talk about it? Why you can't just leave it alone?" Ruby demanded.

"Because I don't know what happened and Miss Harper is the only person, other than her attackers, who can tell me, and the sooner I know, the sooner I—we—can do something about it." Gianna, her arms resting on her knees, leaned toward Joyce Harper. Her clear, hazel eyes, direct and unwavering, met and held the other woman's. The Maglione gaze was well known among victims and witnesses; it was comforting and reassuring. It spoke to them: Talk to me. It's all right. To perps, the message was different but it was just as clear: You'd better start talking right now. And they usually did.

Joyce sighed deeply and the tears swimming around in her eyes spilled out. Her pretty, round face was puffy and discolored by the beating she'd suffered, and the tears tracked into the welts and bruises. She wiped her face and winced. "Ruby's right about one thing: I shouldn't have gone there. To the Panther. It's nothin' but a dive. But I had to get outta here. I wasn't thinkin' what could happen, you know? And I know better! That's what's hurting me as much as the rest of it: That I know better. I can't believe I was so stupid."

Gianna moved herself from the chair to the bed and grabbed the box of tissues, pulling out a few. She gave them to Joyce then looked at Ruby. "Would you get a bowl with some ice cubes and water and a cloth, please, Ruby?"

Ruby hesitated briefly, then left the room. Linda exhaled and took out her notebook and tape recorder, which she turned on and put on the bed beside Joyce, who started talking. She was upset, she said, because Ruby had promised to come straight home after her shift at the UPS loading dock and take her to dinner and a movie. A rare Saturday night out since Joyce herself usually worked Saturday nights at the hotline at Metro GALCO. "She should've been here by quarter to nine at the latest. I must have called her cell phone six or seven times but it was turned off. She still wasn't here by eleven so I left." And went to the Pink Panther and sat at the bar alone and drank Canadian Club on the rocks until she calmed down.

Then, Gianna thought, a woman wounded in spirit and dulled by too much alcohol after a couple of hours in a bar decides to walk the four blocks home to clear her head instead of calling for a taxi. Four of some of D.C.'s roughest blocks. Yes, it was a stupid thing to do, but then Joyce Harper already knew that, better than Gianna ever could or would.

Ruby returned with a heavy ceramic bowl of cold water and a brand new linen dish towel. She put the bowl on the floor, dipped the towel in it, then wrung it out and placed it gently on Joyce's face. She repeated the action three times while Gianna and Linda watched. The puffiness around the wounded woman's eyes and cheeks seemed diminished. Joyce said it felt better and she thanked her partner. "It's time for me to take those pills. Can you get 'em, please? I left 'em in the kitchen when I should 'a brought 'em in here."

Ruby gave a grudging nod and left the room again and Joyce quickly related the details of the rape. Quickly and clinically and unemotionally. Until she had to repeat what the men said as they raped her. "They called me a dyke and a lesbo and unnatural and they said I ought to be dead. I look like every other woman out there. I had on a skirt and a blouse and some sandals. How they know what I am unless they were in there with me?" She broke then, and began to cry. Gianna dipped the towel in the icy water, told Joyce to lie down, and put the towel to her face.

Ruby returned with the pills and glass of water. "Is she asleep?" Gianna shook her head. "Emotional. Frightened. Guilty."

"She ain't got nothin' to be guilty about. I'm the one should be guilty. It's my fault. I said it was hers but that's a lie. It's my fault and if I could do last night all over again, I swear to God I would."

Then Ruby was crying but Gianna was finding it difficult to conjure up any sympathy for her. She looked at Joyce, deathly still, the towel still covering her face, and felt nothing but anger toward Ruby. Gianna stood and picked up the tape recorder and put it in her bag.

"I'm sorry, Lieutenant. I don't mean to run y'all off. I know you just tryin' to help, just tryin' to do your job."

Gianna turned to look at Ruby, to study her, and what she saw drained away some of the anger she felt. "Can I give you my card, Ruby, and will you call me when she's better able to talk?"

Ruby sniffled and wiped her face on her sleeve. "Yes you can, and yes I will." She took the card and read it, then looked at Gianna through her tears. "Hate Crimes. What—" The answer presented itself before she finished asking the question. "They did this to her 'cause she's gay. Oh my Lord. Oh my dear Lord."

Gianna and Linda made their way back down the hallway to the front door, Ruby following. Gianna stopped in the doorway. "If either one of you needs anything, please call. And Ruby? Lay off the booze, OK? It's too early in the day to be drinking, and Joyce needs you. She can't get through this alone."

"She might be better off alone," Linda said when they were in the car. "What a jerk! She's smoking and drinking like she's the one in pain."

A scared, helpless, powerless, guilt-ridden cheat is what Ruby was, Gianna thought, not simply a jerk, but she definitely was in pain. "Let's drive by the Pink Panther, then from there to The Snatch. I want to see these neighborhoods in the light of day and on a weekday instead of a weekend night."

What they looked like in the daylight was what they looked like at night: Rough, ugly, dangerous terrain, no place for a woman to be walking. Any kind of woman. Not Tosh and not Joyce, not even a woman with a gun who knew how to use it. Though the Pink Panther's geography was, Gianna noted, a bit more stable than that of The Snatch. There were more residential structures here, and no vacant lots, and more different kinds of business— a dry cleaners and tailor, a little grocery store, a cafe, a storefront church, and two liquor stores. A night club and two liquor stores within two blocks. What the hell were they thinking in the Business Permits office to approve such a thing? Just four blocks away, where Joyce and Ruby lived, was all residential. Pretty, well-kept though small houses, home to decent working people. Why should there be two liquor stores and a night club in their neighborhood?

*****

"There was a time when the police department and citizen groups worked together on things like that. I don't know what happened and we don't have time to talk about it, Maglione. O'Connell should be here any moment now. If he's smart." The Chief of Police was up on the balls of his feet and pacing, his shiny black shoes reflecting the royal blue of the plush carpet in his office. The stars and bars on his jacket and shirt glittered, and the creases in his pants were razor-sharp. He wore his uniform every day, proud of it and the job he did. His hands were stuffed deep into his pockets, jiggling the change. Gianna knew him long enough and well enough to know the action meant that he was barely containing his fury. She also knew not to say anything else, so she crossed her legs, folded her hands in her lap, and waited. She too, was in uniform this Monday, a rare enough occurrence these days that he'd known when she appeared at his office door eleven hours earlier that something was up, and when she told him what it was, he'd sat looking at her for a full minute before speaking. Now they were waiting for Inspector Frank O'Connell to arrive for the six o'clock meeting the Chief had ordered him to attend. Gianna looked at her watch. It was one minute after.

The phone on the Chief's desk buzzed but instead of answering it, he charged across the room to the door and swung it open. Frank O'Connell removed his hat and stepped in. "Come in, Frank. You know Lieutenant Maglione."

"I don't believe I've had the pleasure," O'Connell said, barely covering his surprise at finding her seated in one of the two arm chairs adjacent to the big desk in the center of the room as the lie rolled easily out of his mouth.

"We've met several times," Gianna said, deliberately flouting protocol by keeping her seat in the presence of a superior officer. She kept her eyes on the Chief.

He stood behind his desk. He opened a folder, looked down at it, closed it, and looked up at O'Connell. "Tell me about The Snatch and the Pink Panther, Frank. About your problems with those places in the last few months."

The color drained from O'Connell's face, leaving a red patch high on each cheek. "What's this all about, Ben?"

The Chief came from behind his desk like a cannonball. "What did you call me?"

O'Connell, in the process of lowering himself into the other armchair, stumbled backward, away from his boss. He raised his palms protectively. "What is this? What's going on here?" He kept back-pedaling as the Chief kept coming at him. "I don't know what you want, Chief."

"I want you to tell me about problems having to do with places called the Pink Panther and The Snatch. They're nightclubs. Gay nightclubs. One of 'em's on Harley and the other's on Lander. Both in your command last time I checked. How many incidents at that Snatch place, Frank?"

"None...nothing...no incidents..."

"So explain that meeting you had with the owners on May the eleventh with Miss Delores Phillips and Miss Darlene Phillips. You remember that meeting. You kept 'em standing in the hallway."

If he paled any more O'Connell would either faint or disappear. He glared hostility at Gianna. "What's this all about, Maglione?"

Gianna, legs still crossed, hands still folded, kept her eyes on the Chief, which is what O'Connell should have been doing. He didn't see the folder aimed at his head until it hit him.

"What the fuck!" he yelled.

"You know what the fuck, you sorry bastard. Or maybe you don't, and that's worse. Tell me you don't know about the woman murdered half a block from The Snatch on Friday night or the one gang-raped half a block from the Panther on Saturday night." The Chief was up on his toes in O'Connell's face, his fists granite balls at his sides. He'd been a Golden Globe boxer in his youth and still worked out with the bag several times a month. If he hit Frank O'Connell he'd damn near kill him.

O'Connell backed up some more. "I haven't had a chance to look at the weekend stats but I will as soon as I get back to Command, Chief, and I'll call you right away with that information."

"You're not going back to Command. As of this moment you're officially on administrative leave with pay and I'm looking for a way to take your money, O'Connell. You're a disgrace."

"On her word? You're doing this to me on her word?"

"I'm doing this to you on your record. You've violated at least half a dozen Departmental rules and three of my own directives. Lieutenant Maglione should have been notified at the first hint of trouble at both those night clubs, but because she wasn't, we got a rape and a murder on our hands and I'm putting that right on your head. Do not go back to Mid-Town. Eddie Davis has already taken over. You are to go directly to Administration and sign the paperwork, then you go to Operations where you report to Deputy Chief House until further notice."

O'Connell's face went from white to purple. "Mildred House! That bitch! She's a dyke just like this one!"

The gut punch was so sharp and so fast that O'Connell was down on his hands and knees before he fully understood what had happened to him. The Chief stood over him as he struggled, first to catch his breath, then to stand. Neither man spoke. O'Connell stood, swaying, waiting. When he realized that the Chief had nothing else to say, he moved toward the door in daze, not all the fuzziness in his head due to blow to his solar plexus. He stopped, stooped, and picked up his hat, his progress slow and halting. "I deserve a chance to talk about this, to tell my side."

"That's what Administrative Hearings are for. Get outta here."

"You hit me! You can't get away with that."

The Chief visibly relaxed. He took his hands out of his pockets and perched his butt on the edge of his desk and actually grinned at O'Connell. "You gonna ask Maglione here to be your witness to that? Besides, Frank, everybody in the whole damn Department knows that if I'd really hit you,

you'd still be laid out in the middle of the floor with a broken jaw, spitting teeth. Now get outta my office."

O'Connell had enough sense left not to slam the door on his way out though Gianna almost wished he had. Something was needed to dissipate the charged air in the room. "Inspector Davis will be good for that Command," Gianna offered.

"I know that, Maglione. That's why I put him there."

"Yes, sir."

He got to his feet and walked around a bit, coming to stop beside her chair. "You did the right thing, coming to me with this."

"Yes, sir," she said again.

"But that's not how it's going to smell when it hits the fan."

"I know, Chief, but like you said, it was the right thing to do."

"You anywhere on those crimes?"

She shook her head. "Too early."

He was furious again. "Too damn late you mean! Shit's been brewing for months around those places and if you'd known about it you could've put some people in there and maybe kept a woman from being brutalized like that, kept that kid from getting killed." He opened and closed his fists, the fists that wanted to hit O'Connell again. "Twenty-nine years old and dead forever and for nothin'! I could break O'Connell's neck."

"I could help you."

He gave her a look as sharp as her comment. "What else you got on your mind, Maglione?"

She was grateful that she had Frank O'Connell to rail at, to share the blame, but sharing the blame didn't lessen her burden. She said, "I'm wondering whether we shouldn't hand off the rape to Sex Crimes and concentrate our efforts on the Hilliard murder. We can't work them both effectively."

He shook his head. "Nobody can work those cases better than your people, Maglione, and you know that. That woman, the rape victim, she called you on a Sunday afternoon, she didn't call nine-one-one and ask for a Sex Crimes investigator. And didn't she tell the ER doc that she didn't trust cops? No, you've already got her in hand and I won't risk that."

Any other time she'd have welcomed the praise. Now it just felt like too big a weight to carry. "Then I need some help."

"Sure you do. I'll send you Alice Long. I don't know why I don't let you just keep her, as much time as she spends in your outfit. And I'm sure you and Eddie Davis can work something out for getting somebody assigned to you from over there, somebody who knows the terrain. Give him a couple of days to get settled. I'll tell him to expect to hear from." He looked at his watch, then went back to his desk. "I gotta go. Tonight's my anniversary. I've been married twenty-five years and I've been warned that this is one night I'd better not be late getting home."

Gianna stood up. "Congratulations, Chief, to you and Beth."

He nodded, then came from behind the desk and stood beside her. "Do me favor, Maglione. You go home, too. Directly home. Don't argue with me and don't disobey me. I know what time you left Lander Street on Friday night and I know what time you left Harley Street on Saturday night and I know what time you left here on Sunday night and I know what time you got here this morning. Go home, Maglione. I need you at full speed when the feces hit the rotating mechanism, and that's going to be sooner rather than later."

"You think that's going to happen?"

"I know it is. Now go home."

"Yes, Sir." She threw him a salute and got as far as the door before his attention-getting throat clearing stopped her.

"How's Mimi these days?" he asked, and laughed at the expression on her face, waving her on and out. He was still chuckling to himself when he picked up his private line phone and dialed.

"How's my favorite reporter?" he asked.

Mimi got her tape recorder out of her desk drawer and attached the telephone recording device to it. The chief of police didn't just call to chat with her, or with anybody for that matter. He wasn't a chatty kind of guy. "I've been out of town for three weeks, so whatever it is, I didn't do it."

"You might want to ask Maglione how it is that Eddie Davis replaced Frank O'Connell as Mid-Town District Commander effective immediately."

"Shouldn't I ask you that?" she asked, switching on the tape recorder.

"You certainly should, but not until after you've asked Maglione," he said, and hung up on her. The only thing on her recorder was buzz and hiss.

Mimi switched the thing off and sat back in her chair, feet up on the desk, hands behind her head, and pondered how to play this one. She'd already put in a call to O'Connell requesting an interview about the murder on Lander Street and the rape on Harley Street but she hadn't known that Gianna knew about Joyce Harper's rape. Of course, they hadn't done much talking the previous night...but at least now she knew why she hadn't gotten a call back from O'Connell. And she'd much rather talk to Inspector Eddie Davis any way, though he wouldn't tell her anything unless ordered to. She sat up straight. Would the chief be in that generous a mood?

The phone rang. Mimi snatched it up and switched on the tape recorder. "Patterson," she said, waiting for the chief to add some more details.

"I want to soak in the hot tub for an hour listening to Miles Davis and Carmen McRae, then eat sushi and tempura and drink Chinese beer, and be asleep by nine o'clock," Gianna said.

The Chief had called this one just right, Mimi thought. She said to Gianna, "You go put yourself in the hot tub and I'll go pick up the sushi and beer. Just don't fall asleep in the thing and drown before I get there."

Mimi disconnected the recording device from the phone and cleaned off her desk. Then she called Carolyn Warshawski and told her to expect front page stories for both Saturday and Sunday. She was packing her rucksack when the phone rang again. This time it was Jose Cruz. Joyce Harper would see her tonight, after Ruby left for work, but he, Jose, would have to be present—at Joyce's request. Mimi hesitated, then accepted the offer and the terms. She needed to talk to Joyce Harper but she wished it didn't have to tonight because she didn't want to talk to Gianna about all this tonight. Not after she just owned up to being completely exhausted.

"Too bad you won't get to meet Ruby," Gianna said, and added, "I'll be dead to the world when you get in. Just letting you know ahead of time." She dipped another salmon skin make into the wasabi and soy sauce mixture and popped it into her mouth, then squeezed her eyes shut when the fiery condiment hit the roof of her mouth and penetrated her nasal cavities. "That is so good. Sure you won't have one?" Her eyes were watering and she was breathing through her mouth.

Mimi, drinking seltzer water instead of beer because of her meeting with Jose Cruz and Joyce Harper, shook her head. "Thanks, but I've got to go." She looked at her watch. "The way Jose described Miss Harper, I'm surprised she's still alive. I don't want her to die before I get there." Gianna stopped chewing. "I thought she should've been in the hospital. The poor woman was—" She shook her head, unable to produce the words. "No matter how many times I see it, I'm still rendered speechless by that kind of brutality, and by the bravery of some people to withstand it."

"Gianna, are these two cases connected in any way?"

She shook her head. "We don't have any reason to think so at this point."

"Thank you," Mimi said, her gratitude palpable. This was new territory for them, such open discussion of their work in that place where it had collided in the past, with disastrous results. "That helps, but it doesn't totally explain why, or exactly how, Frank O'Connell is out on his ass and buried so deep inside the bureaucracy the sun won't shine on him for a light year—though it couldn't happen to a more deserving asshole."

Gianna laughed out loud. "I love that analogy," she said, lifting another piece of sushi with her chopsticks. "Be sure to share that one with His Excellency. He'll appreciate it." She wanted so much to tell Mimi how he'd put O'Connell on his knees with the chop to the gut but knew that she could not. Could never.

Mimi kissed her quickly and hurried out the door, equal parts amazed at how relaxed Gianna was with their open discussion, and grateful for it. Since neither of them was a candidate for a career change, this definitely was the least stressful approach. Of course, it probably wouldn't stay that way for long. Similarities notwithstanding, they did different jobs, and the point of divergence often was the point of contention and conflict. Gianna's job was to apprehend a killer and a rapist. Mimi's job was to find out why a police captain had allowed a murder and a rape— because that's in effect what he had done by not reporting potential hate crimes to the Hate Crimes Unit.

While the owners of The Snatch had come to appreciate if not exactly welcome the presence and attention of the Hate Crimes Unit, the owner of the Pink Panther harbored no such warm feelings. In fact, Raymond Washington said, the only people he hated worse than D.C. cops were FBI and IRS agents, and he suggested that if Officers Linda Lopez and Bobby Gilliam knew what was good for them they'd get their asses out of his bar double time. He had, he said, too much work to do before opening to waste time talking to them. Bobby, an intense, sometimes nervous, but usually mild-mannered man, tried reasoning with Washington, appealing to his sense of decency, and when that didn't work, to his common sense: It couldn't help his business if it became known that patrons were subject to assault on a fairly regular basis, for Hate Crimes had learned, from the newly installed and very cooperative Mid-Town commander Eddie Davis, that Joyce Harper was just the latest Pink Panther patron to be assaulted within a block of the place. The first and so far only woman— the bar catered primarily to gay men— but the attack on her was much more violent than on the four men before her. Two of them had been robbed, one chased three blocks to his car in a hail of verbal abuse, the fourth beaten and kicked and saved from a worse fate by passers-by who heard his screams and either were brave enough or foolhardy enough to intervene.

"You won't have to worry about being ready for your customers if you don't have any customers," Bobby said to the bar owner in what he thought was a very reasonable tone, "and you won't have any customers if they come to think that having a drink in your bar means getting their asses kicked."

"If I want your advice, asshole, I'll ask for it," was Washington's response. "I don't care what happens outside. It's none of my business what happens outside."

Bobby remembered that Dee Phillips had had that same attitude— until they showed her the error of ways— but what he wanted to show this Washington character was a close-up of his fist. The two men were about the same height but Bobby clearly was stronger of the two. He could knock Washington down with a single shot. That's what he wanted to do.

Linda Lopez, quiet and bookish, tried a different approach. After all, Dee Phillips had come to have a change of heart and mind. Ray Washington would, too. One way or another. "I need to see your business license, your occupancy permit, your ABC permit, your food service permit—"

"Who the fuck do you think you are?" If they were in were a cartoon instead of a mid-town D.C. dive, steam would be puffing from Ray Washington's ears. "You can't come in here ordering me around, intimidating me. No crime has occurred here and nobody here has been accused of a crime—"

"Yet." The way Linda said the word, it was a threat, and that's how Ray Washington took it. Linda was in the man's space, crowding him. Bobby circled around behind, still wanting to hit him, waiting for a reason to take a shot.

The man was caught between those two places—between those two cops— and it was not comfortable for him, but he was no limp-wristed sissy, liable to come apart at the seams at the slightest hint of discomfort. Besides which he could serve up attitude with the best of them. "I don't know what you think you mean by that and I don't really care. I haven't done anything illegal."

"What do you call setting a woman up to be raped?" Linda demanded.

"What the fuck are you talking about, setting up a woman to be raped? Are you fuckin' crazy? I didn't...you mean that woman from Saturday night? I never even knew anything happened to her until you people called and said you were coming here to talk to me."

"Miss Harper thinks maybe she remembers you talking to the men who followed her out of here and raped her. Do you remember something like that, Mr. Washington? Talking to three men at this end of the bar while Miss Harper sat down there drinking her CC on the rocks?"

Ray Washington looked from one end of the bar to the other as if it were foreign territory. Unlike the long, curving, polished, shimmering bar at The Snatch, this one was short and ugly, scarred and stained. In fact, the whole place was ugly, scarred and stained, and it stank like old beer and whiskey and cigarette smoke and bodies. The mirror behind the bar was smudged, the neon beer lights out of date. "You know this is a gay bar, right? So what kind of sissies—drunk ones at that— you think followed a woman into an alley and raped her? Y'all ain't makin' no sense at all." Washington was adamant but he also was out of steam. "Why y'all hassling me like this?" He almost whined the question.

"Because we don't like your attitude, Mr. Washington," Bobby said. "We came here asking for your help and what we got was an earful of how much you hate D.C. cops. How 'bout I tell you how I feel about you? Better still, how 'bout I show you?" Bobby took a step toward Washington and he backed up.

"No cause for you to be treating me like this, Man."

"I've got plenty of cause, but I'm a reasonable guy. So, how about we take it from the top?"

Washington looked at his watch, looked around his establishment, gave a heavy, resigned sigh, then pulled out a chair at the nearest table and sat down. Bobby and Linda looked around, too, both of them comparing it to the inside of The Snatch. This room was about one-fourth of size. There were three booths along the back wall with a tiny square of a dance floor fronting them, and a dank hallway leading to bathrooms at the rear. Tables and chairs filled the rest of the room—square tables with four chairs, round tables with two chairs, all on top of a sticky, grimy carpet the color of which was not discernable. Washington sat at one of the round tables. The two cops checked out the chairs at the adjacent table, took in the ripped, sticky-looking faux leather seat bottoms, and opted to stand.

"We're listening," Linda said as Bobby took out his notebook.

"You don't want to be bothering the people who come in here, the regulars," Washington said.

"You don't get to tell us what to do, sir," Linda said.

"I'd appreciate it if you wouldn't. Lot of those guys, they're on the DL, but that don't make them rapists, you understand what I'm telling you?"

"They're on the what?" Linda snapped. She was out of patience with Ray Washington and didn't mind letting him know it.

"DL means Down Low," Bobby said. "It's when dudes won't own up to being gay. Kinda like being in the closet, but different. They're not really gay, they just like to have sex with other men."

Linda looked from one man to the other. "You're telling me that gay guys pretending to be straight guys...or is it straight guys pretending to be gay guys—anyway, whatever they are, they hang out here in your gay bar and what, Mr. Washington, they couldn't possibly be rapists because, why? There's obviously something I'm not understanding here." Linda was in no mood to give Washington any wiggle room. "I want the names of the men who were in here Saturday night."

"I don't know their names." Washington spat the words at her.

"You said they were regulars. Every bartender in the world knows the names of his regulars."

"First names is all I know, and I don't know nothing else about 'em."

"Fine," Linda said, heading for the door. "Come on, Bobby, let's go."

Bobby, commanding his face not to register the surprise he felt, slapped his notebook shut and followed her to the door, where she stopped and turned back to the bar owner. "By the way, there'll be a cruiser parked outside your door by the time you open and we'll have some trainees from the Academy roaming around, taking down license plate numbers. Let's see what that does for your low down business."

The very idea had a miraculous effect on Ray Washington's knowledge bank. He discovered that not only did he know the full names of the three men who drank at the other end of the bar from Joyce Harper on Saturday night, he knew where they lived and where they worked. "But I'm asking you again not to tell 'em I gave 'em up. My customers need to believe they can trust me."

"Too bad Joyce Harper couldn't trust you," Linda said, slamming the rickety door behind her and understanding and appreciating Dee Phillips's preference for steel doors anchored in brick walls. Ray Washington also made her appreciate Dee Phillips, and the DL men who hung out at the Pink Panther made her appreciate the Ags and the Doms who hung out at The Snatch. At least they were, fully and proudly, who they were. And at least being who they were didn't put anybody else's health and life at risk, unknown to them.

CHAPTER SEVEN

MID-TOWN COMMANDER RE-ASSIGNED;
INACTION MAY HAVE LED TO HATE CRIMES
By M. Montgomery Patterson
Staff Writer
Inspector Francis X. O'Connell, a 22-year veteran of the Metropolitan Police Department, abruptly was relieved of his command duties at the Mid-Town Police District and reassigned to administrative duties following the murder of one woman last Friday night and the rape of another last Saturday night. Both crimes occurred in the vicinity of nightclubs known to cater to a gay and lesbian clientele, and both were reported to be only the latest in a series of what now are being investigated as hate crimes.
Police Chief Benjamin Jefferson confirmed

O'Connell's re-assignment but refused to give a reason for it. However, Lt. Giovanna Maglione, head of the Hate Crimes Unit, has confirmed that both the rape and the murder are being investigated by her Unit. All District commanders are under orders to turn over suspected crimes against persons based on race, religion, gender, or gender preference to the Hate Crimes Unit. Not only did O'Connell fail that directive, but there is no indication that Mid-Town Command investigated half a dozen incidents in the four hundred block of Harley Street where The Snatch Club is located, and the six hundred block of Lander Street where the Pink Panther Club is located.

"We have not had any success bringing our concerns to Inspector O'Connell in the past," said Jose Cruz, director of the Victim Assistance unit at the Metropolitan Washington Gay and Lesbian Community Organization. "But even though Inspector O'Connell has not been at all sympathetic to our concerns, I hate to think that his inaction has resulted in something so horrible as rape and murder."

At the same moment that O'Connell was learning his fate, Inspector Eddie Davis was taking over at Mid-Town. Chief Jefferson emphasized that moving Davis, who was head of the Criminal Investigations Division, was not a demotion but rather "an expression of confidence in his abilities."

Davis, a 20-year veteran, formerly commanded both the Downtown and the East River Districts, and is well-regarded as a fair and able administrator. His job at CID is being filled on an interim basis by Deputy Chief Archie Johnson, head of the Police Training Academy, the Chief said, adding that Davis will be returned to CID "as soon as is practical and possible."

Davis called the murder of 29-year old Natasha Hilliard, an American University History professor, and the rape of a 39-year Mid-Town resident "horrible, inexcusable tragedies," and already has increased patrols in the areas around the bars. He refused to comment on what his predecessor may or may not have done. "My focus is on what I do," he said. He also declined to speculate on whether the two crimes might be related. Hate Crimes' Lt. Maglione said, "We have no reason to think so at this point."

HATRED TAKES ONE LIFE,
SHATTERS ANOTHER
By M. Montgomery Patterson
Staff Writer.

By all accounts, 29-year old Natasha Hilliard was on a track so fast she had few fellow travelers, but all who knew her liked and respected her, and none of them can comprehend the horror that befell her last Friday night as she walked from a local night club to the Metro station three blocks away. Police are calling Hilliard's murder a hate crime. Family, friends and colleagues say there must be some mistake.

"Tasha is one of the most likeable people I've ever met, and I've met a lot of people," said Dr. C.L. Jerzey, head of the History Department where Hilliard was a professor specializing in the Civil War. "Yes, she was young, but she was brilliant without the brashness that can come with that. And before you ask, yes, we knew she was a lesbian. She'd never tried to conceal the fact, so I can't believe that someone would kill her for that."

Hilliard, a Philadelphia native, graduated with honors from the University of Pennsylvania and did her graduate work at American University, where she taught, and where she was popular with both faculty and students. On the Monday after her murder, students sat numbed and quiet in her classes, whispering among themselves, staring at the empty podium at the front of the room, as if waiting to learn that the bad news was a bad joke.

"This sucks!" said one student who wouldn't give his name. "Hilliard is cool, you know? She really makes history come alive. I'm thinking about changing my major because of her."

Jane Doe (not her real name) changed lives, too. The 39-year has been the voice of hope and reason at the Metro GALCO Hot Line on Saturday nights for years. She had the night off last Saturday, had a few drinks at a bar in her neighborhood, and was brutally beaten and raped as she walked the four blocks to her home.

"She is loving, compassionate, giving, and a tireless worker," said Jose Cruz of Jane Doe. "I wish everybody could know her as I do."

Everybody can't because this paper does not publish the names of rape victims, but perhaps it is enough to know that a woman who, after working a 40-hour week, spent every Saturday night in a windowless room talking to strangers on the telephone, listening to their pain, finding words of comfort for them, often the words that kept them wanting to live for another day.

Cruz oversees the Victim Assistance Program at Metro GALCO, which runs the Hot Line. "That she should be a victim—it makes me think their is no justice in the world," he said. "Why did this happen to her?"

Here's a possible answer: Both crimes— Natasha Hilliard's murder and Jane Doe's rape— occurred outside bars known to cater to a gay and lesbian clientele, and both victims are lesbians. Are these hate crimes? The Hate Crimes Unit is investigating, so the Police Department thinks so. Lt. Giovanna Maglione, who heads the Unit, said, "There's no reason to think so at this time," when asked if the two crimes are connected in any way. Aside, that is, from the hatred that apparently gave rise to them.

Gianna poured another cup of coffee, returned to the living room sofa, and re-read the stories. It never ceased to amaze her how much information Mimi could amass— how much accurate information— from her various sources. The only facts she herself had shared was the apparent lack of a connection between the two crimes, and that Inspector Frank O'Connell had failed to inform the Hate Crimes Unit of potential problems related to two gay nightclubs in his district. And, of course, Gianna had taken her to The Snatch the night of the church demonstration against the club and its patrons. But where did she get the other stuff? From the Chief? Gianna knew that Mimi had as close and personal a relationship with him as she herself did, and that Mimi credited him with bringing the two of them together, though that was a real stretch of the imagination for Gianna. Her boss, the Chief of Police, playing matchmaker for one of his lieutenants and one of the city's premiere investigative newspaper reporters? Still, he was a crafty son of a bitch, no denying that. M. Montgomery Patterson was pretty crafty herself, Gianna thought, wanting to call her but knowing that she'd get nothing but grunts and growls at this hour of the morning. Mimi had worked until well after midnight on the stories for Sunday's paper, which she promised would be as interesting as today's.

Gianna drained her coffee cup, got up, and switched on the television, and found the Weather Channel. Hurricane Isadore, now losing steam as it tracked north toward Maryland, had managed to make a pretty good mess of parts of the South and North Carolina coastal areas. It finally reached the D.C. area overnight, dropping a couple of inches of much needed rain and, she and everybody else in the area hoped, cooler weather. It was almost October and as hot as it had been two months earlier. She would welcome cool but she'd settle for wet.

While she listened to the international weather report, she fixed a bowl of yogurt and granola, and a turkey and cheese sandwich for later, after the gym. She'd been diligent about keeping her promise to eat with some regularity. Perhaps not as often as a nutritionist would recommend, but some food during the course of a day was better than none, and this day probably wouldn't allow time for a regular meal.

She listened to the local forecast— rain all day, occasionally heavy— followed by cooler temperatures by mid-week, then changed to a local news channel. As she expected, Mimi's stories were Topic A. She switched from channel to channel while she ate her breakfast, switched back to the weather channel while she loaded the dishwasher, then watched the storm clouds and rain move across the sky from the vantage point of her seventh floor condo. She loved apartment living when she was here, and she loved the simple pleasure of walking barefoot in the grass when she was at Mimi's house. Their talk of living together had taken them no further than visits to various condominiums and townhouses and houses with gardens and patios and discussions about whether they both preferred to live on the ground or above it. They'd not seen anything that either of them liked well enough to force a decision, and unless their work schedules changed dramatically, Gianna didn't know when they'd find the time to make one. She took a last look at the newspaper, at the headlines of the two stories, and knew this would be a long, tough day. For them both.

Minister Charles William Bailey checked the four buckets in the sanctuary of the Ark of the Covenant Tabernacle Church of the Holy Spirit, one in each corner of the room. "The roof leaks," he said to Mimi in an explanatory tone that bordered on the condescending, eroding whatever positive feeling she'd convinced herself to try to have for him. Then he looked over his shoulder at her expectantly, as if he expected a response. The rain was coming down in torrents outside, and only slightly less forcefully in the four corners of the little church. The tin buckets were filling rapidly and required constant emptying. Is this how the minister would spend his Saturday, Mimi wondered. Since he seemed to need a response from her, that's what she asked him and he explained that one of his deacons was en route to the church with four thirty-gallon plastic garbage bins. Mimi refrained from asking how he planned to move a thirty-gallon barrel of water without sloshing it all over the floor. Instead, she wished him luck.

"No such thing as luck, sister," he said, lifting his eyes to the ceiling. "It's all in God's hands, the good and the bad. Whatever happens is the will of God."

Mimi looked at steady stream of water flowing from the corner eave as if from a faucet and, against her better judgement, opened her mouth. "You think God wants your church destroyed by rainwater?"

The minister's round face wrinkled, then relaxed. "God isn't responsible for this, an incompetent contractor is." Then his eyes widened, as if the light switch had been flipped to the on position. "Maybe you could put in a good word for us with the Problem Solver."

Mimi's look was as blank as Bailey's was expectant. "The what?"

"You know, that lady on television who solves people's problems for them, especially those dealing with crooked contractors and mechanics. It's a special segment in the news program called The Problem Solver."

"I'm a newspaper reporter. We don't have a problem solving segment."

"But you people are all connected, you're in the same business—"

Mimi stopped him before he could say anything else stupid, and before she could tell him how stupid he was. "You told my editor you wanted to tell me why you think Frank O'Connell should have his job back as district commander?"

The minister looked at his watch, then unrolled the sleeves of his black robe so that they covered his arms. Finished being the maintenance man, back to being the man in charge. "Brother Joseph should be here any minute with those big cans. I hope you don't mind if we talk in here?" He cast a worried glance back at the tin buckets, then gathered the folds of his robe around him and sat down on the front row pew. He gave Mimi a beatific smile. "Closer to God in here anyway."

Mimi sat down next to him and took out her tape recorder, notebook and pen. "Why shouldn't Inspector O'Connell be punished for all the rules he violated?"

"It's only God's rules that matter, sister, and brother O'Connell is a God-fearing man who abides by the rules of the Almighty."

"So he doesn't have to obey the chief of police or the laws of the city?"

"Not if their laws go against God's laws."

"What about the oath he swore, to uphold the laws of the city?"

Bailey shook his head. "Only the laws of God matter."

"And if one woman is murdered and another woman is raped while O'Connell is ignoring the laws of the government he works for, that's OK with you?"

"If people— whether they be men or women— violate the laws of God and the laws of nature, punishment follows. We pray for those souls and hope that others like them see the error of their ways, but we stand up for Christian soldiers like Inspector O'Connell. The Christian army he serves is more powerful than the secular one. If God had wanted those women saved, they would have been saved."

Mimi was saved from a response by the sodden and noisy arrival of two men and four huge, green plastic garbage bins. Bailey jumped up from the pew, clasping his hands together, and hurried toward the two men with cries of welcome and delight. She kept her seat and watched the exchange of tin bucket for plastic tub and thought what she'd thought when she saw them for the first time the previous Saturday as they marched on The Snatch: These men were gay. Or perhaps merely effeminate? She tried balancing their appearance, which her best friend Freddy Schuyler would call "queen to the extreme," against their behavior, which was homophobic in the extreme, and came up stymied every time. Was this an example of the Clarence Thomas Syndrome— a manifestation of rampant self-hatred? She shook off the thought. She didn't have to understand them to do her job; her job wasn't to explain them, it was to report their words and their actions and the effect of their words and actions on the community. Same thing for Frank O'Connell. Same thing for the chief. Same thing, for that matter, for the head of the Hate Crimes Unit.

"I'm sorry," Mimi said, as she realized that Bailey had spoken to her.

"I asked whether you had any more questions for me," he said, looking as if he was trying to decide whether to resume his seat.

"You said you planned to do something to support Inspector O'Connell. What did you mean by that?"

Bailey rubbed his hands together and his eyes sparkled. "A demonstration! I'll announce it from the pulpit tomorrow. So will God's messengers in churches all over the city, including Inspector O'Connell's pastor. God's soldiers will line up together to bring the words of truth and salvation to—"

"You know Frank O'Connell's pastor?" Mimi picked up her notebook and tape recorder and stood up to face him. "You've talked to him, and to other ministers, about organizing a demonstration?"

"Indeed I have," Bailey boomed, his big voice taking on the resonance of the pulpit. He must rattle the rickety walls of this tiny space on Sunday mornings. "Reverend Doctor Elwood Burgess, a true man of God. He'll lead our prayer march."

"This thing just changed shape for me," Carolyn said when Mimi told her what Bailey said about Burgess and local ministerial involvement in the O'Connell matter. "But you knew what it was all along, didn't you? You knew it last Saturday," she said, sounding certain she was right.

Mimi shrugged. "I didn't know, no, but I've heard enough stuff about O'Connell over the years that I was concerned when I found out he was involved."

"What kind of stuff about O'Connell? Has any of it ever been reported?"

"No," Mimi said, shaking her head. "None of it ever was reportable, it was just talk, the kind of stuff you hear when people are complaining about this or that boss, and cops whine and complain more than reporters, if you can imagine that. You consider the source, then ignore most of it. But sometimes—"

"Sometimes what, Mimi? Is there something off about O'Connell?"

"I think maybe it's worth asking about, and maybe connecting some dots," she said, already making some connections in her memory.

"I have to take this to the bosses. You know that."

Mimi nodded. She knew. "If they want to give it to somebody else, I don't care." And she didn't, not really, for this was about to turn into yet another story about a high government official doing wrong and Mimi had had her fill of those.

"Well, I care," Carolyn said. "You developed it, it's yours."

"You had a bad feeling about this from the jump, too," Mimi said. "At least about the Joyce Harper rape angle. That's why you passed it on to me, because you knew something smelled funny. Don't sell yourself short."

"Yeah," Carolyn said hesitantly, "but my bad feeling was more about the Hate Crimes outfit. I was thinking maybe they'd dropped the ball. I didn't know anything about O'Connell."

Mimi hoped she didn't sound as defensive as she felt when she told the editor that so far as she knew, Hate Crimes had yet to drop the ball. Then she remembered Gianna's worry about being a racist because the same outreach hadn't been done in the Mid-Town District as had occurred in the wealthier, trendier, hipper areas, and thought OK, maybe a ball had been dropped in the Hate Crimes court...

*****

Gianna hated everything about the post mortem process, including the name. The very words sounded dead and decaying, conjured up nauseating odors and descriptions of body parts and organs. Her presence at the forensic dissection of Natasha Hilliard was necessitated by her urgent need to find something, anything, that would give a clue not only to the identity of the murderer, but to the reason for it, because Gianna simply didn't believe that it was a crime of opportunity: Natasha Hilliard was not dead because she was in the wrong place at the wrong time. Dozens of women passed up and down Lander Street on Thursday, Friday and Saturday nights, entering and leaving The Snatch. Why that woman at that time on that night? Because she was there? And yet, if she had been deliberately targeted, how could the killer know what time Natasha would be on the street alone unless he or she had followed her into and out of the nightclub? Darlene was adamant that Tosh had arrived alone and had left alone, and Gianna trusted that. Her team had had no success locating a witness to anything relating to the murder itself, which left her relying on forensics for a solution. It was not a position she liked.

"Didn't expect to see you here," Wanda Oland said, backing into the frigid cut room ahead of the morgue attendant who was trailing behind her, trying to tie her gown in the back. "Where's Ashby? You usually send him."

"Don't want to be here," Gianna said, reaching for goggles and a mask, "but you're my last best hope for something resembling a lead."

"Your boss is a real son of a bitch," Wanda said, sliding the tray containing Natasha Hilliard's body out of the refrigerated cabinet. "He's been calling over here since Wednesday ordering us to get this PM done or else. My boss asked him, 'or else what?' I left the room. Even I didn't want to hear the tail end of that."

Gianna didn't blame her. Wanda's boss, Chief Forensic Pathologist Dr. Asa Landing, was a legendary son of a bitch himself. "How is the old bear?"

"Old bastard, you mean, and he's the same old bastard he always was," she replied, helping her assistant roll the body onto the dissection table. She checked the tool and equipment tray, swung the microphone around and switched it on, said the day, date, time and name of the autopsy subject, and began to work. Gianna closed her eyes, anticipating the first cut, only to hear a description of the cut marks on the torso. "You sure you don't want to see this?" Wanda asked.

Gianna sighed. No, she didn't want to see it, but she got up and went to look. The mutilation was as horrible a week later as it had been upon first glance the previous Saturday night. "What am I looking at?" she asked, willing the nausea back down as she leaned over the mangled torso. She didn't know why she'd originally thought these were mere hacking marks when they definitely and distinctively were words carved into a young woman's body.

"These cuts are deep and deliberate. Angry. Intentional. No hesitation marks, like the person was afraid or remorseful or even worried about being seen. Definitely a hate crime, I'd say."

"So, wrong place at the wrong time?"

Wanda Oland hesitated and Gianna jumped right on it. "Is this a hate crime or isn't it, Wanda? I can't use a 'maybe.'"

"It is, and in my opinion, the hatred is directed specifically at this person—at Natasha Hilliard— and not just at some random dyke the killer happened upon while walking down the street. But the thing is— the head SOB and I talked about this and we don't fully agree —it tracks like a revenge killing to me. I'm thinking this is just your average, garden variety revenge murder and the victim happens to be gay."

"Then why call her a dyke? Why carve that into her?"

Wanda shrugged. "Because she was a dyke."

"She also was a Gemini and an Episcopalian and a history professor. Why not carve that into her if whoever did it just hated Natasha, the person?"

"Why carve anything at all," the doctor said, and it wasn't a question. She sighed. "And here's another thing to keep in mind: I don't think there was any sexual assault, and I'd expect to see that if this was a random attack against a random lesbian victim. The absence of the sexual element is another thing that points me toward revenge of a personal nature."

Gianna looked at Natasha Hilliard's mutilated body. "So do I have a revenge murder or a hate crime?" She walked away from the dissection table, as much to calm herself as to get the hideous image out of her sight.

"You waiting for an answer?"

Gianna turned back to face the surgeon. "Do you have an answer, Wanda? One that tells me why this kid is dead? Because if the killer hated Natasha the dyke because she was a dyke, and killed her because she was, then that makes it a hate crime, not a revenge murder or a crime of passion."

"You're the cop, Maglione, I'm just the cutter."

"But you've never cut one like this, have you?"

Wanda looked down at the ugliness laid out before her and shook her head.

Garden variety murder my ass, Gianna thought as she slogged through the heavy, steady rain to her car. Despite the slicker and the umbrella, she was soaked through, compliments of the gale force winds that had blown the rain around like an egg beater in a mixing bowl until about half an hour ago. Now the storm seemed to have settled itself into the kind of soaking downpour the region so desperately needed, and it even seemed a few degrees cooler, so she didn't mind being sopping wet. She had changes of clothes in the trunk of her car, in her office, and in a locker in the Think Tank, so she wasn't worried about being wet. What worried her was the challenge of looking for a murderer within Natasha Hilliard's circle of family, friends, and professional colleagues. Whether Wanda Oland was correct in her assessment, or whether Gianna herself was, the crime still was specific to that specific victim. Either way, it was Gianna's problem because even if it was a 'garden variety revenge murder', no way the chief would consider re-assigning it now. Not after the response to Mimi's stories in that morning's paper.

The phones had started ringing before daybreak— in the chief's office, in Hate Crimes, at Mid-Town Command, in Community Relations, and in the mayor's office— and they were still ringing. Gianna didn't need the chief yelling at her about how the mayor was yelling at him about how the community was yelling at her to "do something." The only something that would be satisfactory would be the immediate arrest of Natasha Hilliard's killer and Joyce Harper's rapists. She felt pretty good about the latter possibility and positively glum about the former. True, they were in the early stages of turning over the stones of her life, but Natasha Hilliard's feet seemed never to have strayed from the good path.

According to the reports coming in from the Hate Crimes team investigation, Natasha's entire family knew she was a lesbian— had known since she was in high school— and had found no fault with her for it. The Hilliard parents, Robert and Christine, were equally proud of their three daughters—Jill, Natasha and Felicia— all of whom were upstanding citizens and successful professionals. Natasha had adored and been adored by both her sisters and a close knit family of aunts, uncles and cousins, all of whom appeared devastated by her murder. She was admired and respected by her colleagues and peers in academia, and very much liked by those she'd allowed close enough to form friendships. There were five of those in the D.C. area and a dozen others scattered across the country and into Canada. Professor Hilliard had traveled widely, attending meetings and conferences and lecturing. A rising star in her chosen profession, she also was being recruited by universities in Chicago, Boston and New York. And though it would take some time to run checks on the out-of-town connections, if the in-town connections were any indication, there'd be nothing to find. While both Lili Spenser and Selena Smith were dismayed to learn of Tosh/Tasha's involvement with the other, neither seemed surprised or angry.

"It's funny," Lili said through tears shed for both her lover and her mother, "I always felt she was faking the AG thing, pushing it too hard. I told her that once and she got mad, so I dropped it."

Pushing it how, Gianna had asked.

"Always talking the talk, walking the walk. Sometimes the words sounded really strange coming out of her mouth. 'Bitch' this and 'dog' that, constantly, and it sounded fake. Now I guess I know why."

And you never knew how she was employed, Gianna asked.

"She just said she worked in the straight world, but so do I. Dancing at The Snatch isn't my profession. I teach dance at Performing Arts High School but

I earn more on the bar three nights a week at The Snatch than I do in a month at school."

And what did you know of Selena Smith, Gianna asked.

"Nothing," Lili said with a sad smile. "But I'm not surprised. Tosh really loved women, all women. No reason for me think I was the only one."

"You're kidding!" was Selena's response to learning about Lili. "I went there once with some friends. We'd heard about this place and couldn't believe that women actually...well, we couldn't believe what we'd heard, so we went to see. And sure enough, there they were! But what freaked me out was all those male-looking women! Some of them were scarier than men— and you're telling me Tasha was one of them? I don't believe you! She was much too refined for that kind of behavior. I never saw a hint of that in her. Never."

For the last year, according to Selena, she'd seen Tasha at least twice a week for dinner and until recently they'd spent weekends together. They often traveled together to conferences and meetings. "We shared our lives. I just don't believe that there was such an enormous part of hers that I knew nothing about. I can't believe she would dump me for a stripper. You can call them dancers all you like. Strippers is what they are. I know a stripper when I see one, and those women are strippers."

Gianna hadn't seriously considered that a woman had carved Natasha Hilliard's body so grotesquely but she was interested in the revenge angle. It made sense given the nature of the crime. But revenge for what, if being a lesbian was at least partially the reason for the murder? She didn't see a way to connect either Lili or Selena to a revenge killing. Both were as unequivocally and openly lesbian as Natasha, and she was certain that they hadn't known about each other until told of the fact by Hate Crimes investigators. So, somebody else hated her enough to kill her; and not just to kill her but first to stalk her, to wait until she was alone on a deserted side street in a shitty neighborhood, and then, finally, to maim her, to destroy her body. That much hatred usually took a while to fester to the point of eruption, which meant it would take time to find its source, time they didn't have. What they needed was a lead, a direction to follow or a reason to follow a certain direction, and they didn't have that, either.

Gianna looked at her watch and picked up the phone. Directionless was not a comfortable feeling, and she needed to change it quickly.

"Dyke."

Gianna stopped mid-stride, turned and caught up with two patrol officers she'd just passed in the hall, caught up with them, fronted them, and stopped so fast they almost slammed into her trying to halt their stride. "What did you say?"

They were young, one blond, the other dark. The blond one smirked, the dark one looked nervous. "Come on, let's go," the dark one said, grabbing the blond by the arm. They started to walk around her.

"You're not going anywhere," Gianna said, the cold finality of the order in her tone of voice nailing them to the spot. She took her notebook and a pen from her pocket and wrote down their names: Blondie was Ferrell and Atkins was his nervous buddy. "Which one of you made the remark?"

"What remark was that?" Ferrell asked, opening his eyes wide in mocking, feigned innocence, the smirk turning surly.

"Look, Lieutenant, we gotta go. We got roll call right now," Atkins said.

"You know me?"

"N..n..no, Ma'am. Not personally. That is, I've never met you, but we all know who you are," Atkins said.

"I know you." Ferrell literally snarled, his thin lips curling with the effort. "You're the dyke who got the boss shit-canned."

"What did you say?" Inspector Eddie Davis had appeared so quietly and so quickly behind the two cops that Gianna hadn't had time to react to his presence and she was looking right at him. The young cops whirled around coming face to face with their new commanding officer. "What did you say?" Davis asked again, and at the quiet authority in his voice the rookie cops literally trembled.

"N..n...nothing, sir," Atkins said.

"Then I'm not talking to you. Get your ass to roll call and I'd better not hear of you even breathing too many times in a minute or you'll be looking for a new job. Do you understand me, Officer Atkins?"

Atkins stuttered so hard he couldn't get any words out, so he fled down the hall, leaving Ferrell to face the music alone.

For his part, Ferrell tried for bravado through his terror. "I didn't mean anything, Inspector. It's just a word, that's all," he said, shrugging and exchanging bravado for nonchalance.

"Until further notice, Ferrell, you're assigned to foot patrol in the four block area around The Snatch, starting now. I'll inform the WC."

Ferrell's nonchalance evaporated. He went white. His eyes bulged. "That's not... you can't...they'll..." He was stuttering worse than Atkins.

"Not fair? This is the police department, not the playground, and yes I can. I just did. As for what they'll call you out there? Don't worry about it, Ferrell. It's just words. Now get your ass out there and protect the citizens who pay your salary. All of the citizens."

They watched Ferrell stomp away. Then Gianna looked into the darkly handsome— now darkly angry— face of the man who had been her boss before the chief put her Hate Crimes Unit under his own direct command. "It's good to see you, Inspector," she said. She'd always liked and respected Eddie Davis and he'd always returned the sentiment.

"It's good to see you, Anna. You've done a hell of a good job with Hate Crimes. My only regret is that I wasn't able to take credit for it." Clearly he still smarted from having her unit taken from his command when he headed CID.

Gianna didn't say anything and they both knew why: They both served at the pleasure of the chief and just as it had pleased him on Monday night to move O'Connell and replace him with Eddie Davis, it had pleased him the year before to move Gianna's Hate Crimes Unit from Davis's command. "I'm glad you're here to straighten out this mess," she told him.

"And I thought you liked me," he said, feigning hurt feelings, and if Gianna hadn't been too old to swoon, she might have. Davis looked exactly like a young Sidney Poitier, and women— those who'd known him for as long as Gianna had and those just meeting him— often experienced difficulty breathing normally in his presence. Except for those who thought, as Gianna did, that they were too old for such behavior. Davis never seemed to notice one way or the other.

"His Excellency told me to give you time to get the lay of the land before I came over here to beg for favors," Gianna said. "Is five days long enough?"

"Long enough being a relative term," he said, heading down the hallway. Gianna followed, studying her surroundings. She'd been inside the Mid-Town command only once, years ago. It had been renovated and spruced up since then but it still was ugly, in that uniquely governmental, functional kind of way: Fluorescent lighting bounced off the highly polished tile floor, cheap-looking beige paint covering the walls in between. Wooden benches were placed at intervals between the front door and the shoulder-high barricade that separated the public area from the official police area. When Gianna was last here, the barricade had been waist high and had a swinging, cafe style door. Entry now required a code. Davis punched in his, a buzzer sounded, he pushed through, and Gianna followed, immediately recognizing three familiar faces—two sergeants and a civilian. Davis had brought his top staff with him. Smart move if he wanted to get anything accomplished in a hurry, and he did. Was, in fact, under orders to do just that.

Hello, Mrs. Williams." Gianna surprised herself and pleased the woman by remembering her name. She was Davis's administrative assistant and ran his office the way all offices should be run— effectively and efficiently and with a deep commitment to service.

"It's good to see you, Lieutenant. I've been following your exploits. Way to go, girl!" She shook Gianna's hand and gave her a quick embrace. "I just made a fresh pot of coffee. The good stuff. I'll bring you some."

Gianna thanked her, threw a greeting salute at the two sergeants whose names she didn't know because the Inspector always referred to them as Frick and Frack, and followed Davis into his inner sanctum.

Controlled disorder ruled. O'Connell's out-going belongings were boxed and piled on one side of the room, Davis's stuff on the other. The walls were barren, the outlines of former hangings clearly visible. The desk top was clear except for two telephones, a stack of folders, and the morning newspaper. The computer on a small table behind him was on, the screen saver flashing circus animals. Two chairs faced the desk. Davis waved her into one of them as he dropped down into the one behind the desk. "This is a real mess."

"How bad?" she asked.

"I'm not ready to be quoted yet but there seems to be a pattern of ignoring certain kinds of complaints and jiggling with the crime stats. Because of the way this thing went down, I think we have a pretty good chance not only to find out how bad things really are, but to make some things right."

"We can't make right what happened to Natasha Hilliard and Joyce Harper, or even to Delores Phillips."

"No, we can't, and I didn't mean that. But to citizens who thought they didn't matter, we can show them that they do. We've already started. Foot patrols on every shift, squads making regular runs in known hot spots, hard, take-down busts in open street corner drug dealing. And I personally paid a visit to Miss Phillips and Miss Harper, and if I personally have to go undercover to do it, I intend to nail the bastards who brutalized that woman like that." His jaw muscles worked as he controlled his emotions.

Mrs. Williams provided an assist as she arrived with two mugs of coffee. "Ethiopian," she said to Gianna, placing a mug on a napkin before each of them. "Inspector likes it even better than the Kenyan."

Gianna thanked her— for the coffee and for remembering how she took hers— and the woman left, closing the door firmly behind her. "What would you do without her?" she said to Davis.

"Retire," Davis said, and his tone of voice said he wasn't kidding. "Half a dozen of O'Connell's crew put in transfer papers on Tuesday morning after Miz W showed up with Frick and Frack in tow. I signed off on every one of 'em. But what they don't know is that they're all going to be assigned to the Chief's office until the dust settles from this thing." He took a sip of coffee. "So, what can I do for you, Lieutenant?"

"I don't really know." She told him everything she did know about the Hilliard and Harper cases, and about the victims themselves and the circumstances that put them in harm's way. "We might get enough for a sketch from Joyce Harper. Once the shock wore off she realized that she remembered quite a bit. I've got a female I can put undercover in the Pink Panther, and I'll need a couple of males from you to provide back-up for her. But I'm absolutely nowhere on Hilliard."

He walked her again through what she knew, starting from the night of the murder, the crime scene results, the autopsy results, the street canvas, the family and friends interviews, all the time asking the kinds of questions that required the kinds of answers that served to sift and evaluate information and evidence. She knew that she'd missed working under his direction and supervision; she just hadn't realized how much she'd missed it. "So you're not exactly nowhere on this thing, Maglione. You are somewhere, you just don't like where you are."

Gianna acknowledged the truth of that. "If we accept that Natasha Hilliard's murder was specific to her and not a general attack against certain kinds of lesbians, Doms and Ags, then we have to accept that we may never know who killed her. Her best friend lives in Montreal and two ex-lovers that we know of live in San Francisco and Chicago. Lack of resources alone narrow the scope of our investigation."

"And suppose you don't accept that hypothesis?"

"Then we wait for the next murder to happen," Gianna said, "and I like that scenario even less than the first one."

"Tell me what Doms and Ags are," Davis asked, and at the look on her face, he gave her wry grin. "Good! You didn't know, either. Now I don't feel so...so..."

"Old school would be the term you're looking for." And at the look on his face, Gianna began explaining, as best she could, what she'd learned of Doms and Ags, not as much as she wanted to know, but a little bit more than she had, the latest information coming earlier that day from Beverly Connors, a clinical psychologist and good friend who also happened to be Mimi's former lover. And while Bev had insisted that her understanding of things might be flawed, it made sense to Gianna that young Black and Latina women, struggling to find a place in a society that marginalized them in the best of times, would adopt the some of the mannerisms of people, of men, especially those who seemed to garner some measure of respect.

"And these days," said Davis, "that would be the gangstas and gang-bangers."

"Unfortunately, yes," Gianna responded.

"Are these women as violent as the men?"

Gianna shook her head. "Not as a rule. But, of course, there are always exceptions. Some Doms and Ags mistreat their women, but that is the exception rather than the rule."

Davis steepled his fingers and almost looked as if he, in fact, was seeking some guidance from elsewhere. "What do you want from me?"

"Back-up for my female undercover at the Panther as soon as possible, and continued foot patrols and drive-bys outside The Snatch. And speaking of which, is Ferrell a good idea for that?"

Davis's answer was an evil chuckle. He picked up the newspaper off his desk and pointed to Mimi's front page stories. "You have anything to do with this?"

"Just my several 'no comments' strategically placed throughout."

Davis tapped the folded paper against the desk top. "That Patterson is a damn good reporter. And a tough one. I wouldn't be Frank O'Connell right now for all the Bushmill's in Dublin."

"Jesus Christ, Patterson, when are you gonna stop going after cops?" Mimi stared out at the rain water sloshing against the windows of the snug little U Street cafe. It was early afternoon and as dark as if it were dusk. The storm center had settled in over the mid-Atlantic coast and was, it seemed, making itself at home. Which is where Mimi wished she was instead of sitting across a table from Vice Squad Detective Ernie Binion. He shot her nasty look and tossed a wadded up napkin in her direction, though not exactly at her. It skidded across the table and she caught it before it landed on the floor.

"When cops stop behaving like jerks and assholes and doing things that make me go after them," Mimi said calmly and reasonably, not wanting to incite further ire. She needed him, needed the information only he could provide. Ernie was a source, a good one, and had been for many years. He also was a good cop, and he didn't like it when cops went bad. He liked it even less when police department dirty linen was aired in the newspaper.

"Well, I'm not gonna help you this time, so go away and leave me alone." Ernie swallowed the last bite of his third lemon-filled Krispy Kreme, drained his coffee cup, pushed his chair back, and heaved his heavy bulk up to a standing position from which he glowered down at her, strands of his stringy blond hair escaping its ratty pony tail. He leaned toward her and anybody but Ernie she would have considered menacing. "You ever think that maybe some times you go too far?"

"I think sometimes people like O'Connell go too far and they take people like you with them, people who don't deserve to get nailed to the same cross."

Ernie, Mimi was glad to see, was genuinely confused. "Me? What do you mean people like me? What have I got to do with any of this shit, Patterson?"

"You're connected to O'Connell, Ernie, connected long and deep and tight and everybody knows it. You know it, too."

"We trained together, we rode together for a while, and we drank together, whored around together, but that was a long time ago. Then I got married and Frank found success." Ernie slapped his hands together in an up and down motion. "That was it as far as him and me bein' tight. I made detective and that's as high as I wanted to go up the ladder, which was a good thing, 'cause that's as high as I was going up the ladder. I'm not smooth and polished like Frank, I don't kiss ass and I don't play politics. So here I am— on the top rung of the detective ladder, hoping and praying I don't take a bullet or have a heart attack before I get my twenty-five years and my pension. And what you're doing to Frank just proves I made the right choice."

"You mean what Frank's doing to himself, and to you and McGillicuddy by extension." Ernie's face changed and Mimi's internal self heaved a sigh of relief. She was beginning to think that either her information was faulty or she had badly misplayed this guy, which would mean she'd learned nothing in the years she'd known him and worked him as a source. He looked around the crowded cafe, as if noticing for the first time that it was crowded, that every table and booth was occupied, that vintage Janis Ian was playing from the sound system, that the noise from the rain driving against the plate glass windows was louder than Janis.

The waitress made a pass with the coffee pot and Ernie sat back down when she filled his cup. "I got nothin' to do with McGillicuddy."

"That's not how I hear it, Ernie."

"You hear it any way other than how I'm tellin' it to you, you're hearin' it wrong. Listen close: I got nothin' to do with McGillicuddy and nothin' but memories of the past to do with Frank. Like I told you, we went separate paths some years back when he found success."

"The way I hear it, what he found was religion. A new kind."

Ernie swallowed too hard and almost choked. "Is that what this is about?"

Mimi didn't say anything. She'd played almost all her cards, used almost all her bait. To say any more now could be dangerous. Ernie often was a jerk and occasionally was an asshole, but he was smart and he was a good cop, whatever that meant any more. Best thing for her now was to play it cool. She stole a glance over her shoulder, as if worried that they'd be seen together. That got him. "I am no part of that. Never was. You hear me, Patterson? And you better not connect me to those weirdos, I mean that."

Mimi put some money on the table and stood up. "I think we should go for a walk." She grabbed her raincoat, umbrella and bag from the chair beside her and turned toward the door.

"It's fuckin' rainin' cats and dogs out there! Go for a walk?" Almost out of breath from the combined effort of standing up too fast and being angry, he grabbed her arm to stop her. "Go for a walk why? Is there somethin' I need to know, somethin' you haven't told me? Play it straight, Patterson."

She took a step toward him. "People do strange things in the name of God these days, no matter what they call their god, and think they have not only the right but the obligation to do them. The law that you and I know about means nothing to them. But you already know all that."

"I don't, I tell you!"

"I've always trusted you, Ernie, and you've always known you could trust me. We've never liked each other but you've used me and I've used you and we've done all right. But I'm telling you I know how close you were to O'Connell, McGillicuddy and Burgess." That was her last card. She played it and waited and he folded.

Now it was Ernie's turn to look over his shoulder. "Does the chief know?"

"You know about the Chief's Monday morning strategy meeting that all the division chiefs and district commanders attend, right? Well, at that meeting, he ordered O'Connell to come back to his office at six o'clock that evening. While Frank was at headquarters with the chief— he probably thought he was going to get promoted or something—Eddie Davis shows up at Mid-Town command with a department locksmith and a department computer programmer and his personal staff. In half an hour, the janitor had O'Connell's name off the office door and all his belongings in a box. What do you think, Ernie: Does the chief know?"

"I guess we better go for that walk."

It was still raining, steady and hard, but the wind wasn't howling and turning umbrellas inside out and blowing buckets of water down the backs of coat collars, so foot traffic on U Street was moderate, though light for a Saturday afternoon in what was becoming a trendy neighborhood. They walked side-by-side, slowly, heads down, hands stuffed in their pockets, both hoping not to be recognized. City Hall was a couple of blocks away in one direction, the city's gay and lesbian newspaper office a couple of blocks several more in the other direction, with a subway stop that could discharge almost anybody from almost anywhere in the middle. Mimi rationalized that few people could distinguish both of them for what they really were. They were just a guy and girl walking in the rain on a Saturday afternoon, not a newspaper reporter and an undercover cop talking about cops at the highest level in the police department committing crimes in the name of a god created especially for them.

CHAPTER EIGHT

THE STREETS THAT TIME FORGOT
By M. Montgomery Patterson
Staff Writer

Harley Street. Lander Street. Nobody who doesn't live or work in the area would know where they are. The general area is Mid-Town. Both streets are in what the bureaucrats like to call working class neighborhoods, though there are more working people on and near Lander Street than there are on or near Harley Street. And for a very good reason: Most of Harley Street burned to the ground in the 1968 riots following the assassination of Dr. Martin Luther King Jr. Despite more than 30 years worth of promises and hundreds of millions of dollars spent and misspent since, vacant, weed-and trash-filled lots proliferate on Harley Street. An encampment of the homeless recently spawned on one of the empty lots, the one adjacent to the gas station that doubles as a betting parlor, two blocks from where 29-year old Natasha Hilliard was murdered a week ago.

The people who live on Harley Street rent from people who live in the suburbs and who haven't stepped foot on their property since those riots way back when.

The people who own businesses on Harley Street eek
out a meager living by charging too much money for
sub-par goods and services to people who have too little
money but who are willing to pay for the convenience
of shopping close to home. There are no chain restaurants
or stores within two square miles of Harley Street.

Lander Street is posh in comparison. It's closer to
the Mid-Town commercial district, there are no vacant
lots, and the people who live in the area are, for the most
part, homeowners. Low and mid-level government and
office workers who cut their grass and paint their houses
and pay their taxes. People who don't complain about
the presence of two liquor stores, three carry-outs and a
nightclub in one three-block area. People who appreciate
the dry cleaners, grocery store, cafe, churches, day care
centers, barber and beauty salons that make this a
vibrant neighborhood. People who either didn't hear
or didn't care to hear the cries of a 39-year old woman
who was raped and beaten in an alley not 50 feet from
somebody's living room window.

The best thing on Harley Street is The Snatch night
club, a renovated warehouse whose owners last year
paid more than $100,000 in various taxes to the city.
The worst thing on Lander Street is the Pink Pussycat,
a dilapidated structure whose owner hasn't paid taxes
to the city in three years. Both streets and both
night clubs are located in the Mid-Town Command
District of the police department. Both night
clubs cater to homosexuals. Women were attacked
within two blocks of both clubs two weeks ago, chosen
as victims apparently because of their sexual orientation.

The police department's Hate Crimes Unit is
investigating the murder of Natasha Hilliard and
the rape of Jane Doe (this newspaper does not
print the names of rape victims.) Lt. Giovanna
Maglione, who heads the Unit, won't say whether
there are suspects or motives, but it is believed that
HCU is finally getting the necessary cooperation
from the Mid-Town police precinct, now under the
leadership of Insp. Eddie Davis, who recently replaced
Insp. Frank O'Connell in the wake of allegations that
he ignored incidents in the area that could have been
considered hate crimes. No charges have been brought
against O'Connell and he's made no comment.

"How does she know the stuff she knows?"

Eric asked what everybody was wondering and all of them, except Eric, looked toward Gianna for an answer. She knew they knew about her relationship with Mimi although Eric was the only one of them with whom she ever discussed her personal life, and that's because they'd been discussing their personal lives with each other since their training academy days. They also knew that Gianna maintained a strict separation between her professional obligations and her personal relationship with the newspaper, though not even Eric would ever know how precarious that balance sometimes was.

It was noon on another Sunday in the Think Tank. They all had cups of coffee and muffins or Danish or doughnuts, and they all had a newspaper with M. Montgomery Patterson's story on the front page. Gianna had read it the night before, when Mimi brought the early edition home with her, and she, too, was impressed, both with the amount of information Mimi was able to collect, and with the way she arranged it into the kind of stories that always demanded action or reaction.

"Reporters have sources just like cops have sources," Gianna said, repeating what Mimi had told her on more than one occasion.

"I wish she had one who'd tell us where to look for Natasha Hilliard's killer," Tim McCreedy said. "I don't think we've ever worked a case where we had absolutely no leads, have we, Boss?"

"We got leads, McCreedy," Cassie said in her deadpan tone of voice. "We just don't know where they are yet."

"Too bad Fang can't talk," Tim said.

Gianna looked momentarily puzzled, then she got it, and displeasure replaced puzzlement. "You are not supposed to still have that dog." Cassie and Tim had fallen in love with Natasha Hilliard's dog, a shaggy-haired mutt of indeterminate mixed heritage with a sterling personality.

"We don't, Boss," Cassie quickly interjected. "The sister came and got him. Jill, the older sister."

Gianna looked from Tim to Cassie.

"Honest, Boss," Tim said, and raised his right hand. "Though I wouldn't have minded being able to keep him."

"Me, too," Cassie said, then added, "I don't know why some stupid humans think animals are dumb. That dog knew something was wrong."

"Like I said, too bad he can't talk."

Eric gave Tim a look. "We're not that desperate, McCreedy."

"No, we're not," Gianna said. "So, let's get to it. Eric?"

"So far, everybody that we know about who knew Hilliard is accounted for at the relevant times, and we haven't found any connection between her and any of the people at The Snatch except for casual contact, Lili Spenser being the exception. She's been very cooperative, under the circumstances. What are the chances, her mother and her lover die the same night? Talk about a bummer."

There was a moment of silence, as if somebody in charge had asked for it, then Eric resumed. "There's no hint of discord at the University. The important people in her department knew she was a lesbian, by the way, and considered that no big deal, but they didn't know about the Dom/Ag thing. The dean and the department chairman both allowed as how that could have presented a problem, but since it never came up, it was only speculation as to how they might have responded if presented with a Dr. Hilliard dressed like a dude, and blah, blah, blah. The only loose end in this whole thing is a—" He struggled to recall a name, then flipped a folder and pulled out a sheet of paper with a photograph attached. "Here it is...Stephanie Blackstone. Lot of calls from Hilliard's home and cell phone to her. She, too, is a professor of history, but she's been on sabbatical since the spring, somewhere in Europe. Everybody who knows this woman also knows we're trying to reach her. We'll hear something soon, tie a knot in that loose end, and then we're officially and completely screwed."

Eric stood and took a bow in the midst of the cheers, jeers, whistles and cat-calls that greeted his presentation and final pronouncement. In the middle of all that, the door opened and Detective Alice Long walked in. "I'm glad to see y'all, too," she said in her distinctive South Carolina Gullah drawl, and it was several minutes before something like order was restored. They all were genuinely glad to see Alice, who had been assigned to help the Hate Crimes unit on two previous big investigations. She was older than most of them, and more experienced, seasoned by both undercover and special ops experience. She fit in easily and worked well within the Hate Crimes structure. Alice wanted full time assignment to HCU but there was no money in the budget for that. Only if someone left could Alice come in and she wasn't crass or cold enough to wish Cassie Ali's injury had sidelined her permanently.

"All right, you guys," Gianna said, and the room got quiet and down to business. "Did Natasha Hilliard become 'Tosh' only on the Friday or Saturday nights that she went to The Snatch? Is The Snatch the only hang out for Doms and Ags? How long had she lived that dual life? Who else knew about it? I think somebody had to know. Nobody can keep a secret like for very long. Somewhere, there's somebody who knew both Tosh and Tasha and we've got to find that somebody. I'm thinking the Phillips sisters might be inclined to help steer us toward the Dom/Ag community, and we need check out Baltimore, too. If D.C. was too risky for Tosh, maybe Baltimore was safer, or New York, even. Cassie? You and Tim."

Tim assumed his queenly posture so quickly that he actually surprised his colleagues though they were by now used to the performance. And a performance it was: McCreedy compressed and contorted his six-foot-four-inch weightlifter's body into a prancing, mincing, limp-wristed caricature, which included a locked-thigh walk that was as gravity-defying as it was hilarious. "You can't send me back there, Lieutenant! You just can't! They don't like me. They won't talk to me. And I simply can't imagine why! I mean, I'm a white male! Why wouldn't they want me around?"

They all went silly and giddy again and this time it took longer to reign them in. Gianna got the message: Unless there was a compelling reason not to, she needed to send them home. They'd been ten straight days on the clock. Their silliness was merely a reflection of their fatigue. "On to Joyce Harper. We may have a sketch tomorrow and Bobby's going to pester the lab for DNA test results. Alice was at the Pink Panther last night, and there should have been some back-up provided by Inspector Davis from Mid-Town. Alice?"

"There were all kinds of people in the Pink Panther last night, including quite a few women. I think they were trying to make some kind of statement, like, we're not afraid to come here, we won't be intimidated. But I gotta tell you, Lieutenant, if that's supposed to be a gay bar, then most of the men in there were lost."

Then Bobby and Linda related their conversation with Ray Washington, earning Linda a whole chorus of atta girls for her handling of the situation and a new designation of DL as Low Down. "It is low down," Linda said. "All those so-called straight men going home to their wives and girlfriends after a night in Pink Panther bathroom, and they wonder why so many straight women have AIDS."

"I appreciate the explanation," Alice drawled, "'cause I was having trouble trying to figure out why all these so-called gay guys were giving me sideways looks."

"Miss Long, honey, I give you sideways looks and I haven't been straight a day in my life!" Tim said, giving full, buffed butch, and Gianna sent them all home.

Alice Long was, without question, one of the most stunning women Gianna had ever seen and she knew that Mimi thought so, too. She also knew that something had happened between Mimi and Alice, though she wasn't sure what, and she wasn't especially worried about it as long as it didn't get in the way of Alice's work, and there was nothing to indicate that it would. Still, she wondered. Then she pushed the thought away and pulled the stack of reports toward her. She opened the top folder, Stephanie Blackwell's. She looked at photograph— standard studio portrait— then at the info sheet. Older than Natasha Hilliard by almost fifteen years, a tenured professor, a former chair of the department, twice a visiting professor at other universities. And married. To a man. Gianna paged quickly through the file looking for the husband's information: Allen Cureton, a professor of art history, currently on Sabbatical. Gianna felt a flash of something familiar.

She pulled Natasha Hilliard's telephone records. All of her phone calls to Blackwell were to her office or to her cell phone, none to her home.

She stood up and began to pace, then sat back down and began to check the dates. Then she checked the dates of Hilliard's involvement with Lili Spenser and Selena Smith, then with the other intimate relationships the Unit had discovered— and there were quite a few of them. As Lili Spenser had said, Tosh/Tasha loved women. Gianna returned her attention to the record of phone calls to Stephanie Blackwell. Then she got up and paced some more. Natasha Hilliard had had an affair with Stephanie Blackwell. She'd check their travel records but she knew what she'd find. And then she knew what she'd felt, knew what the flash of familiarity was: The peculiar logistics of an affair with a married woman. Gianna able to call Dorothea only at work and never at home, able to see her or to be with her only when the husband was working late or out of town. Dorothea had dumped her, opting to remain with the husband who earned more money and offered a more comfortable lifestyle than a cop ever could. Especially a woman cop. Had Natasha dumped Stephanie? How had that been received? Had Stephanie's husband been aware of the affair? She made a note to expedite locating Blackwell and Cureton, clipped it to the outside of the file, closed it, and reached for another file. She realized that she'd thought about Dorothea without pain or sorrow for the first time since their break-up three years ago.

*****

Elwood Burgess had one of those huge, monster churches across the D.C. line into Prince Georges County, Maryland, in an area that now was so chic and trendy that probably nobody but Burgess remembered its redneck origins. But Burgess certainly remembered; that's where he was from, and so was a notorious cadre of D.C. cops and an even more notorious cadre of PG County cops who had been so violent that Black residents equated them to the cops of Mississippi and Alabama and the Carolinas and Georgia.

The members of Elwood Burgess's church probably didn't know that the man they called Reverend Doctor ever had been called Officer. Or Pig. Mimi knew, the same way she knew most of the history and lore of D.C. and its origins— from a couple of retired reporters and cops who were has-beens when she was a cub reporter but who, for whatever their reasons, took a liking to her and whom she still respected and from whom she often sought advice and counsel. The Burgess story was one told by both cops and reporters and as old as the story was— more than thirty years old now— it still was worth telling, how Burgess had kicked and stomped a sixty-year-old man to death following a routine traffic stop: One of the tail lights on the man's car was out. Months of protests by outraged citizens finally resulted in a review board which cleared Burgess of any wrongdoing, based on the testimony of his partner. Like a Boston priest, he was transferred to another Division and two years later, while responding to a burglary-in-progress call, he shot a fifteen-year-old boy in the back. Again, a review board found no fault with his actions based on the testimony of his partner, and again he was transferred. The third time was the final strike. Burgess put a forty-year old housewife in a wheelchair for life when his shot at a fleeing suspect whom nobody else but his partner had seen, severed her spine. Another person shot in the back. Another Black person a Burgess victim. Another police review board finding in his favor, based solely on supporting testimony by his partner. Then a citizen stalker with a high powered rifle began to follow Burgess and take pot shots at him, scoring a series of dramatically—and intentionally—narrow misses. Even followed him home one night and put a bullet in the wall so close to Burgess's sleeping son that he put in his retirement papers the following day. He found Jesus shortly thereafter, got a couple of mail order divinity degrees, bought a couple of acres of still cheap PG County farmland, built a little clapboard church, and went into the soul saving business. His current church, a brand new eight-million-dollar edifice, boasted a membership of more than five thousand. Burgess had his own TV ministry, a stretch limousine, a mansion, and he was a chaplain to the D.C. police department.

*****

Mimi's eyes burned from three hours of reading old newspaper clips on microfiche and her head ached at the thought of the rampant and unchecked racism and injustice, and at the knowledge that this man still was welcome inside the D.C. police department. Did people ever change? Could they change? Maybe, maybe not. That was a question for philosophers and theologians and ethicists to ponder. Mimi's concern was Burgess's former partners: Frank O'Connell, Darren McGillicuddy, and Ernie Binion. O'Connell and McGillicuddy were deacons in Burgess's church. Binion still was the Catholic he'd been raised to be: Went to confession on Friday night, Mass on Sunday morning, and spent the time between Sunday afternoon and Friday afternoon trying to dodge hell. For a cop, no easy task; hell was everywhere. For people who either thought they were God or thought they had a direct line to Him— people like Elwood Burgess and Frank O'Connell and Charles Bailey— sitting in judgment was what they did when they weren't interpreting Divine pronouncements for the masses.

Mimi had returned to Bailey's little church for Sunday morning service and Carolyn Warshawski had sent another reporter to Burgess's big church. The message, though delivered in different cadences, was the same: Homosexuality was a sin against God and nature. Homosexuals deserved to be punished. Homosexuals would be punished, either by God or by nature. It was not the job of the police to protect homosexuals and sinners. The D.C. Police Department had erred grievously in its sanction of Inspector Frank O'Connell, who had refused to provide comfort and protection to homosexuals. The true sin was that a God-fearing Christian soldier like Frank O'Connell was expected to entertain homosexuals in his office! And prostitutes and drug dealers and others like them. Mimi didn't know how many other congregants throughout Metropolitan Washington heard the same message from other preachers. The message was shocking: Frank O'Connell, the preachers said, had "refused to provide protection" to homosexuals on his watch. Both Bailey and Burgess had said it. Both Mimi and the other reporter had it on tape.

"What next?" Carolyn pulled up the chair from the adjacent desk close to Mimi so they could talk without being overheard.

"Find a cop from Mid-Town who'll say that O'Connell issued a specific directive: Don't patrol at the gay bars, don't protect citizens at the gay bars, don't investigate crimes against homosexuals."

"You think he was stupid enough to put anything like that to paper?" Carolyn's face was as hopeful as kid's on Christmas.

"If he was, Eddie Davis'll find it, but he won't give it to me." As far as Mimi knew, Davis had never leaked anything to a reporter in his entire career. Of course, there was a first time for everything...

"You want to know about O'Connell, and you want me to ask Davis to answer your questions, but you don't want to know anything about the Hilliard or Harper investigations. Am I getting this correctly?" They were finishing a Sunday dinner at Gianna's—soup, salad and lasagna, with apple pie for desert—and talk had been about everything but work until mention of their friend, Marianne, owner of a Louisiana-themed lesbian nightclub led to mention of The Snatch and recent events.

Mimi nodded. "Right."

"So, you wouldn't be interested in an artist's sketch of one of the rapists."

Mimi shook her head. "Nope, not unless it looks like Frank O'Connell."

"And the fact that we may never know who killed Natasha Hilliard, that doesn't make your pulse race and sweat pop out on your brow?"

Mimi started to laugh. "You make my pulse race, Lieutenant."

"By the way, Alice Long's working with us again."

Mimi stopped laughing. "Where'd that come from?"

Now it was Gianna's turn. She worked to control a sly grin. "Must've been talk of racing pulses. Alice seems to have that effect on people, including half the low down men in the Pink Panther, as well as our very own Tim McCreedy."

"How about on a certain lieutenant?"

"I have only protective and proprietary feelings where my team is concerned."

"And what about when Detective Long isn't on your Team?"

"That may be a moot point. The chief may let me keep her."

"Wow," Mimi said, duly impressed. "What brought that on?"

"Amazing, isn't it?" Gianna mused. "Six months ago the City Council was about to remove us from the budget with an eraser the size of Alaska, now we're getting an extra body. Unfortunately, the hate business is booming."

"Which reminds me," Mimi said, "O'Connell. We were talking about what you know about Frank O'Connell."

Gianna got up and began clearing the table. "You were talking about him, I wasn't. Do you want more pie?"

"Are you kidding? I need an hour in the gym and work off that second helping of lasagna so no, no more apple pie. Unless you've got a better idea for an intense caloric burn."

"I just might have a thought or two on the matter...oh, hell." She scurried into the kitchen to answer the phone. The instant change in her facial expression brought Mimi to her feet. Gianna said, "Yes, sir," twice, then, "I think I should be there, if you don't object."

"What?" Mimi demanded as Gianna ended the call.

"The Snatch clientele are having a memorial service for Natasha Hilliard followed by a demonstration outside the Ark of the Covenant. Retaliation, I suppose, for the church group's rally the other night, only theirs is larger. About three hundred people, which is about three times the number in attendance at the Sunday evening church service."

"I wonder if that's because they had somebody at this morning's service and heard what the good reverend had to say."

That stopped Gianna in her tracks. "I'm assuming you know what the good reverend had to say at this morning's service?"

"He said, among other asinine, ignorant and stupid things, that Inspector O'Connell was right not to offer protection to homosexuals, no matter what police department regulations say."

"He said O'Connell intentionally ignored the assaults on the patrons of those nightclubs? How would he know that?"

Before Mimi could answer, her cell phone rang. She grabbed it from her pocket and it was Gianna's turn to watch Mimi's face, which converted from frown to grin. "I appreciate the call, Miss Jefferson, and I'll see you there." She shut the phone. "That was Baby Doll, I mean, Marlene, calling to tell me about the demonstration. She didn't call earlier because she didn't want to bullshit me, in case nobody showed up—her words, not mine. She also called your office and left a message for you."

Gianna headed for the bedroom and a change of change of clothes. Davis was right— she didn't need to be there, his call was purely courtesy. But she didn't want to risk any cracks in the shaky foundation of her relationship with the Phillips sisters and their patrons, especially in light of what Mimi just told her. Eddie Davis hadn't been at Mid-Town long enough to impact and affect behavior, and if the cops in O'Connell's command thought it was acceptable to withhold protection from lesbians, things could get out of hand and very ugly in no time.

Mimi came up behind her to kiss the back of her neck. "Not exactly how I'd planned to spend Sunday night," she said.

Gianna turned to face her, claiming the kiss. "Maybe there's still hope," she said hopefully.

"Yet another of the many reasons I love you: Your cockeyed optimism." Mimi was out the door.

Optimistic, perhaps, Gianna thought, but cockeyed? Was it really so outrageous to think that they still could salvage some of their Sunday evening? And as she strapped on and fastened her shoulder holster, she knew the answer. Even if the demonstration was short-lived and peaceful, Mimi would have to go to the paper to write up the story, and she herself would go back to Mid-Town command with Inspector Davis to talk over with him what Mimi had told her about Frank O'Connell and to try and learn what he already knew about the man he'd replaced.

She used the quiet time on the drive to The Snatch to mull over the facts of the two cases. With an artist's sketch and DNA evidence they had a better than even chance of getting their hands on Joyce Harper's rapists, but in the Natasha Hilliard case there still were no witnesses, no forensic evidence, and no apparent motive— no way to catch a killer. Unless young Miss Hilliard's apparent predilection for loving them and leaving them led to a motive for murder, and certainly jealousy constituted as good a motive as any. There still were backgrounds to be checked and the second round of interviews with those closest to the victim. Let the shock wear off and often other emotions surfaced— anger, resentment, revenge, jealousy. Combine those four emotions and there surely was a motive for murder. But for mutilating a body?

Then there was greed. Natasha hadn't left a will but she did have insurance policies that paid off the mortgage on her house and the loan on her car. Throw in the art work, the Persian carpets, the first edition books, and there was an estate worth close to a million dollars that her parents would inherit, but Gianna didn't really believe that Robert and/or Christine Hilliard had murdered their second-born daughter for her assets; they had plenty of their own. Tosh Hilliard wasn't killed for her earthly possessions. She was dead because she was a dyke and somebody didn't like that fact. Somebody had been angry enough that Natasha Hilliard was a lesbian to kill her. But who? Gianna didn't have time to ponder the question further. The Snatch demonstration, she saw when she turned the corner, was in full swing. Television equipment and personnel were as plentiful as mushrooms in the forest after a rain, which made Gianna nervous. TV cameras seemed to impact people and events in bizarre ways, especially in a situation already rife with unusual twists and turns.

Gianna drove her unmarked sedan up on the sidewalk across the street from Charles Bailey's Ark of the Covenant Tabernacle Church and to the rear of the crowd and studied the gathering as she worked her way to the front. It was a multi-ethnic, mixed gender conglomeration as amazing for the spontaneity of its organization as for the sense of purpose it conveyed: The camaraderie was palpable. Cross-dressers in full bloom sang and danced beside Doms and Ags, butches and femmes joined arms with gay men and lesbians— all of them their own rainbow of Black, white, Latino, Asian. Many of them looked young enough for Gianna to wonder if their parents knew where they were and more than a few were old enough to be grandparents. Impressive as the gathering was, however, it still was illegal, and Gianna wondered how long Eddie Davis would allow it to continue, wondered how long its sanguine nature would continue in the presence of television cameras, especially once the church contingent put in an appearance..

Police presence was heavy but non-threatening: An unobtrusive phalanx of uniformed officers had the group boxed in on three sides and a line of blue separated the church itself from the demonstrators, which counted, Gianna saw, quite a few undercover cops among its number. They blended in well, under the circumstances, but any cop, or anybody looking for differences, would easily identify them. It wasn't their purpose, however, to spy; they were there for control purposes should violence occur. And given the number of them, Gianna wondered how much notice Davis had received in advance of this thing, for he certainly seemed to have things well in hand. Squad cars blocked both ends of the street and though she couldn't see them, that's where the riot control personnel and gear would be, ready and available if needed, and if not, unprovocatively out of sight.

She spied Inspector Eddie Davis coming from the direction of The Snatch and headed toward the cluster of television cameras and personnel at the front of the crowd and she wondered whether the Phillips sisters had a hand in organizing the event, whether they controlled its tenor and tone, and if so, whether they could call it off as quickly and as easily as they seemed to have called for its existence. She scanned the crowd and saw familiar faces, among them Baby Doll (Marlene!) and her girlfriend, Terry; Jose Cruz from Metro GALCO and his sister, Emilia, who had helped take care of Joyce Harper; Ruby Dawson, Joyce's lover; Aimee Johnson, one of The Snatch bartenders and cousin to Dee and Darlene; Darlene herself, though not Dee; Alice Long, and Cassie Ali. As much as she wanted to question Cassie about her presence here, she wanted more to talk to Inspector Davis. Cassie would have to wait until later.

"Quite a little confab you've got here," Gianna said when she got close enough to Davis for him to hear her over the singing and chanting.

"It is kinda nice, isn't it?" His benign gaze meandered over the crowd. He was, she knew, taking the pulse of the people as well as pinpointing the strategic positioning of his cops.

"How long have they been out here?"

"Little over an hour." He looked at his watch. "If they keep their promise, they'll disperse in about five minutes."

She looked at him in surprise. "You didn't want to break it up right away? I don't understand."

"That would've taken force, or at least a show of force and I didn't want that. Can't go from ignoring people to locking them up."

"Then I may have created a problem for you..."

He already was shaking his head and waving his hand at her. "No problem and no conflict and I already told that to Reverend Bailey."

"Told him what?"

"Told him that you had every legal right to break up his demonstration the other night, and that I have every legal right to break this one up when I think it's time to break it up because this began not as a demonstration but as a memorial service for Miss Hilliard."

"And was there really was a memorial service?"

He nodded. "At the crime scene, where her body was found. They laid a wreath and lit some candles and said some prayers and sang a song, then they walked down here. They said they had a message for Reverend Bailey—"

Who appeared in the doorway of his church as if on cue, his pastoral robes flowing about him, his congregation surrounding him. The crowd saw him, too, and let out a roar, then began to cheer and sing. They sang, For he's a jolly good fellow. Bailey was so shocked that he turned and fled back inside his church, closing the door behind him. Then the crowd, as if a single entity, turned away from the church and headed back toward The Snatch, chanting, "We're here, we're queer, deal with it!"

"You want to explain to me what just happened here?" Gianna's relief was tempered by annoyance, which increased as she saw Mimi dodging in and out of the crowd across the street, heading for The Snatch. That she could have stayed home was her first thought, followed closely by wondering what exactly had she wanted to happen here, expected would happen, for she realized that she had prepared herself for wide scale violence and, in its absence, felt more let down than relieved.

"I told you I met with Miss Phillips?" Davis asked. "Well, she came to see me yesterday. Seems that everything that's happened since the Hilliard girl was killed has created the need for people to do something."

"To do something." Gianna repeated the words, looking for more meaning than existed on their surface, looking to Davis for that meaning.

"Your response to them was the first positive thing they'd experienced since they opened for business almost two years ago. Then there were the newspaper stories that dealt with them honestly and respectfully. Then O'Connell got the axe because of his treatment of them. Then I showed up offering more of the same support that you'd already given. To paraphrase Miss Darlene Phillips, they felt like it was time for them to stand up for themselves, and in front of Reverend Bailey's church is where they wanted to make their stand."

"You gave them permission?"

He shook his head. "They didn't ask my permission, they told me what they were going to do, without placards, banners and a bull horn, which they learned from you constituted a demonstration and therefore was illegal."

She sighed. "I'm sorry. I didn't mean to create a monster for you."

He waved her off again. "No need to apologize. Once I understood that a couple hundred people already had planned to show up here for the memorial for Hilliard, my only options were control and containment. So, I made a deal with Darlene to keeps the cops at bay if she'd keep the crowd under control and disperse in an hour. We both bargained in good faith, and we both got what we wanted."

"And what did they want? To tell Reverend Bailey what a swell guy he is? Did you see the look on his face?"

Davis turned on his Poitier smile. "Priceless. He'll be mad at God for that one for weeks! Imagine, a couple hundred homosexuals serenading him!" He laughed out loud. "Miss Phillips— Delores— said they felt they actually owed Bailey and O'Connell their gratitude."

"Speaking of which, I need a few minutes, Inspector."

He checked up and down the street. "OK, but first I want to make sure all those people get out of here without incident and that the Phillips sisters get that place emptied out and locked up. Technically, they're not even supposed to be in there on a Sunday night. Meet me at the Command in thirty." He charged away.

"All right, everybody! Listen up!" Darlene stood at the end of the bar, a crowd of about a hundred people still energized by the events of the evening milling about. Despite their presence, the place seemed strangely quiet without the pounding music and the roaring fans, and empty with only a hundred people standing around instead of five hundred people bumping and grinding. "What we did out there tonight was very special and very wonderful."

A cheer went up, followed by a chorus of 'for she's a jolly good fellow' when Dee came and stood beside her. Darlene raised her hands to quiet them. "We showed tonight that we can put aside our differences and come together to face a common enemy. We need to remember that and stop getting so hung up on giving ourselves names and labels, 'cause people out there— they don't care if you call yourself Dom or Ag or femme or fag or Miss Thing or Stud Muffin. They hate us all the same, which means we got to love ourselves all the same."

This time the cheer was deafening, the applause lengthy, and Darlene's pleas for quiet ignored. Finally, it was Dee who managed to restore order. "I know that we all feel more comfortable with those like ourselves and nobody's asking you to stop gathering with your friends," she said. "We certainly don't intend to stop serving our clientele—"

A cheer went up for that announcement. "—but I also promise to keep in better touch with the entire homosexual community in D.C. so no cop or no preacher can ever again cause any one of us to feel any less than any other citizen in this city. Now: Go home, all of you. I'm not allowed to be open on Sunday night. Loving you doesn't mean letting you cost me my license."

After a long minute of cheering and foot stomping, the crowd began to trickle out of the door, all except Mimi and Cassie, both of whom were parked in the lot behind the club, the result of Dee's appreciation for what she called their courtesy, but which both of them insisted was merely the performance of their respective jobs. Still, they both appreciated the convenience and safety of the lot.

"We were talking about you this morning," Cassie said while they waited for the room to clear.

"Who's we?" Mimi asked.

"The team. We were wondering how you find out so much, how you know so much. The Boss said she didn't know any more than we did, except she said reporters have sources like cops do."

Mimi controlled the urge to smile. "If we're lucky we do," she said.

"They were good stories. I especially like that you wrote about the women as people, as human beings, and about the neighborhoods where human beings live."

Mimi nodded her thanks and changed the subject. "How're things with you these days, Officer Ali?"

Cassie's cell phone rang saving her from having to find an answer, but the respite was short-lived. "Yes, Ma'am," she said, and Mimi knew who she was talking to, so she stepped away, but not too far. She heard two more "Yes, Ma'ams" before the call ended. "Guess you know who that was," Cassie said, returning the phone to her pocket.

"I should go," Mimi said. "I still want to do a few more interviews."

"You doing a story on this?"

Mimi nodded. "It's good to see you again, Officer Ali, and I'm glad you're doing OK." She turned back to Cassie and pointed to the bar. "I hear the show is something to see."

A slow grin lifted Cassie's lips. "At least once before you die," she said, "you should experience The Snatch Dancers."

The Snatch Dancers. Mimi couldn't get the phrase out of her mind— the rhythm of the words or the image they conjured up. Snatch Dancers. So alluring that they came and left via a steel gate. As Mimi drove through that same gate, she noticed the speed with which it slid shut. She had taken a good, close look at the steel-reinforced doors inside the club, and the security system inside Dee Phillips's office. These women were terrified and the people charged with protecting them not only didn't understand the nature of or reason for their fear, they contributed to it. In a long talk with Dee Phillips following the stories in Saturday's paper, Mimi had learned that Frank O'Connell had actively attempted to block the Phillips sisters' application for permission to own and carry a weapon following several attacks on them and their customers. Only the forceful intervention of their City Council representative— bought and paid for with a generous campaign contribution— overrode O'Connell's interference.

Mimi drove slowly toward the Metro stop, looking for more people to interview. She already had a dozen interviews but the more she learned, the more she wanted to know. She found herself feeling as guilty as Gianna had felt upon learning of both the existence of The Snatch and of their lack of awareness of the existence of an entity— the Hate Crimes Unit— specifically to aid and benefit them. Gianna thought her ignorance could be due to some heretofore unknown racist tendency or attitude on her part. Mimi, from the vantage point of being Black, thought it something else entirely. She blamed a form of cultural elitism that separated and divided members of the same group, the same way that educated, economically secure Blacks allowed the separation from those not so well-heeled. The cultural arbiters grudgingly had decided on a level of homosexual acceptance: They had to look and sound good on TV. That meant they had to be white, preferably male, and certainly funny. Women who looked and dressed like the feared and loathed boys in the 'hood most certainly did not fit the bill.

She slowed her car as she approached a crowd half a block from the Metro station and let down her car window. As she was about to call out a greeting, one was called out to her. "Hey Newspaper Lady!"

Mimi pulled to the curb and got out as Baby Doll sashayed across the street toward her. "Hey, Marlene. I was looking for you," she said, giving the girl a quick hug, feeling her surprise and pleasure the open gesture of friendship.

"You got a new car! 'Bout time."

Mimi was about to defend her former vehicle, a classic Volkswagen Karman Ghia which Baby had mercilessly maligned, when they were joined by three other women, one of whom draped a proprietary arm across Baby's shoulders. This would be, Mimi thought, the girlfriend. She extended her hand and introduced herself.

"Thank you for coming," Terry said.

"I told you she would," Marlene said smugly.

"So how do you know Marlene?" asked one of the other women, who were standing slightly behind Terry.

Mimi saw Baby stiffen, saw the haunted look return to her eyes, a look that had gradually eroded as the girl shook off her past. Eroded but not gone. "She helped me out on a story a couple of years ago," Mimi said, "and we kept in touch, became friends."

"What kinda story?" the woman demanded to know.

Mimi shook her head. "I can't discuss that." She extended her hand to the woman and introduced herself, then waited for their names: Tyra and Kelly. "What did you think of the demonstration?"

"We've been reading your stories in the newspaper," Tyra said instead of answering the question, which was fine with Mimi, as long as it achieved the objective of moving the discussion away from the nature of her relationship with Marlene.

"Yeah," Kelly added, "and they're mostly OK, except I didn't like that part where you said a lot of people don't know anything about us, that we're invisible."

"You are, to most people, including most gay people," Mimi said.

"But you made it sound like that's our fault, that we're to blame because we're invisible to people who don't want to see us in the first place."

Mimi snapped open her notebook and switched on her tape recorder and Kelly backed up a couple of steps. "I just want to be certain that I get your words exactly as you're saying them," Mimi said, trying to calm and relax the woman.

"But why you got to turn that on?" She pointed to the micro-recorder as if it were something potentially lethal.

"Because I won't remember it otherwise and what you're saying is too important for me to try and trust my memory to get it right."

"You gonna put it in the paper?"

Mimi nodded. "If that's all right with you."

Kelly shared a look with Tyra who nodded. Then she looked to Terry, and then to Baby Doll, who had recovered her balance and the smart mouth that went with it. "You might as well talk now, that way we don't have to listen to you talk later. You know how you like to express your opinion. About everything."

Kelly took a moment to gather her thoughts. "You asked us what we thought about the demonstration? Well, we thought it was something very special because of all the different kind of people who came together like that. Part of it was a tribute to Natasha Hilliard, but part of it was a tribute to all of us, you understand? And that part felt real good. Then we decided we wanted to go someplace and celebrate but there's no place for us to go— for me and Terry. Marlene and Tyra could go to the Bayou but not us. We'd have to go someplace rough and ugly. You have any idea how that makes me feel?"

"What do you mean, some place rough and ugly?" Mimi asked.

"Like the Pink Panther," Terry answered for her. "A dive, a dump, some place men hang out, the DL kind."

"Why can't you go to the Bayou?"

"They don't want us," Kelly said.

"They told you that?" Mimi asked.

"In so many words."

"It's the attitude you get," Terry added. "The way they look at us. It's fear and loathing. That's what we get from them, and it's worse in a straight place. So if we want to go out, we usually just go to The Snatch, even if maybe you just want to go someplace quiet or romantic for dinner. We're not acceptable looking enough for that."

"Some people find your appearance threatening—"

"Oh, bullshit!" Terry chopped the air with the side of her hand, cutting off Mimi's words. "That's just an excuse not to have to deal with us the way we are. Why is it everybody else can be dealt with the way they are, but we have to change, to conform, so people aren't afraid of us?"

"Everybody else like who? Give me an example," Mimi demanded.

"Muslims, Arabs, East Indians. They come here and they wear their native clothes and we're supposed to be accepting because that's who they are. We're told not to judge Middle Eastern people, not to assume they're all terrorists no matter how they look, but it's all right to assume that I'm some kind of gangster because of how I look."

"You make a good point—"

"Oh, thanks," Terry said, sarcasm thick as tar. "You ever think about making that good point to people who think I look threatening and treat me like shit on the bottom of their shoe because of it?"

"I still think it's demeaning." They were standing at Carolyn's desk and she had exchanged her editor hat for the feminist one and was reading Mimi chapter and verse on the illogic of a bar owned by women being called The Snatch and featuring nude dancers. "And they want respect? Gimme a break!"

"They don't deserve to be disrespected because of it. They're providing good quality entertainment for their customers in a safe, attractive environment, which they have a right to do. These are law abiding, taxpaying citizens."

"Oh, stop defending them, Mimi! I can't believe you!" Carolyn shoved a strand of strawberry blond hair out of her face, only to have it fall right back down.

Mimi laughed. "What don't you believe? That women shouldn't have the right to own a nightclub featuring nude women dancers, that women shouldn't be able to enjoy that kind of entertainment, or that I shouldn't support those rights? I haven't seen one sleazy, immoral or illegal thing associated with the club or its owners—"

"Strippers are sleazy!"

"— no drugs, no prostitution, no gambling—"

"Murder is sleazy."

"Which occurred outside the club and which had nothing to do with the club or its owners. Come on, Carolyn, that kind of petty bias and prejudice doesn't become you. That's the kind of talk I'd expect from the suits."

That did it for Carolyn. "Well, that's how you score a bull's eye, kiddo, consign me to the boys' club." She gave a self-deprecating laugh. "I guess I did sound a little like the Weasel." She looked rueful. "And I guess I lead a pretty sheltered life, too, huh?" She sank down into the chair, leaned back, and put her feet on the desk. As tiny as she was, she looked like a little kid playing grown-up.

"You're not the only one. I'd never heard of that place until Natasha Hilliard was murdered, and in death she's shed light on a way of life unknown to most people, including many in the lesbian and gay community."

"Maybe that's not such a good thing, Mimi," Carolyn said.

"Why not?"

"Because people who are that different are that vulnerable. Because people like O'Connell and Burgess and Bailey live to exploit that vulnerability."

"And people like me live to show the O'Connells and the Baileys and the Burgesses the error of the ways," Mimi replied.

Carolyn released a world-weary sigh. "Did you notice your odds as you spoke them, Patterson? Three against one. And look at their back-up: The police and the church."

"Not all police and not all religious organizations, and besides, what about my back-up? This newspaper is not exactly a powerless entity."

"This newspaper gets weaker and more spineless every day," Carolyn said, dropping her feet to the floor. "I sometimes think that every media outlet in this country is owned by a cousin or brother of some other close relative of O'Connell or Burgess, and don't tell me you don't share that concern. No thoughtful, honest journalist could look at what passes for journalism these days and not be concerned. Scared, even."

She was right. Mimi knew she was right. But what was she supposed to do? What were any of them supposed to do, those who still operated under the banner of journalistic ethics and the notion of freedom of the press? Roll over, bow down, give the O'Connells and Burgesses and Baileys a free pass? "No, I'm not scared. Pissed off is more like it. I met some people tonight, some women, some decent human beings, who are ridiculed and reviled— and maybe even raped and murdered because of how they look, how they dress—"

Carolyn raised her hands palms out forward in defeat. "OK, OK. You're right and I'm wrong and I apologize. Now, I'm going to leave you alone so you can get to work. Speaking now as your editor, you've got an hour to get me my story."

Mimi's phone was ringing when she got to her desk. She fully expected Gianna. It was Marlene, sounding more subdued and sober than Mimi had ever heard her. "Thank you for what you did, for what you said about us being friends."

"We are friends, Marlene, and I'm proud to call you my friend."

Silence for a long moment on the other end, then, "Can you meet us, me and Terry, at that Chinese place, and bring your...bring the Lieutenant? Terry has something to tell her. It's about...it's something Terry thinks she wants to know."

Mimi hesitated for only a brief second. "When, Marlene?"

"Terry's off Tuesday and Wednesday, so any one of those days is OK."

"I'll ask her tonight and let you know. Call me any time after eleven tomorrow morning."

That's assuming I talk to her again tonight, Mimi was thinking, when Baby dropped another surprise. "I'm gonna give you my phone number— our phone number— and you can call us, OK?"

Mimi wrote down the number, told Baby to expect to hear something soon, and called Gianna at home, leaving Baby's message and phone number. Then she called her office and left the same message. Baby wouldn't have asked to see Gianna on Terry's behalf if it weren't important. It's something she wants to know. But Mimi didn't have time to wonder what it was; she had a story to write.

Anna Maria's was a throwback and therefore one of the most popular restaurants in D.C. After more than thirty years in business in the same location— a tight, congested side street off Connecticut Avenue— owners Anna Maria and Antonio Penza needed to keep a reservation book and they didn't understand why. They still served the same Italian food and wine: Pasta, bread and sauce made daily; meat, fish, fowl and vegetables purchased fresh daily; menu established daily, based on what meat, fish, fowl and vegetables were available; wine from a private stock unavailable in any store; desserts to die for. So why, all of a sudden, the line to get in? Because the nouveau riche and the wanna be riche finally tired of paying outrageous prices for outrageous and unlikely culinary creations by celebrity chefs whose focus was on ever more outrageous presentation instead of taste. All over town the pricey eateries were returning to basics and the basic eateries were doing booming business. Anna Maria and Antonio didn't care about any of that. They cooked and served the best food they could and catered to those loyal customers who had sustained them over the years. Which is how Gianna, who'd been dining there since her training academy days, and Cassie, came to be ushered through the packed dining room to a choice, private corner table on a Sunday night when the line stretched down the street for most of the block.

"Looks like The Snatch line," Cassie had mused as they walked past the people and in the front door, where Anna Maria greeted Gianna with a big hug and kisses to both cheeks.

"Gianinna, cara! Come sta?"

"Buono serra, Anna." Gianna returned the hug and kisses, asked after Antonio and their children, all of whom, except for the eldest boy, worked in the restaurant, and thanked her for the table on such short notice.

"Dove Mimi?" Anna Maria asked, giving Cassie a wall-eyed look, causing Gianna to laugh out loud and explain not only where Mimi was, but who Cassie was. Placated, Anna Maria raised her hand and water, bread and a carafe of wine appeared, along with menus. Satisfied that Gianna was comfortable, Anna Maria bustled away, leaving them in the care of an elderly waiter who'd worked at the place since it opened. He bowed, wished them *buono serra* in a whispery, gravelly voice, poured their wine, and backed away. He'd waited on Gianna often enough to know that she'd signal when she was ready to order.

"I already like this place and I haven't tasted a bite," Cassie said.

"Then you'll love it after you do." Gianna perused the menu. It was a veal night: Parmigiana, scaloppini, pomodoro, and Antonio, which was a roasted and stewed shank with herbs, and one of Gianna's favorites.

Cassie covered her growing uneasiness by studying the menu for much longer than necessary. When she finally put it down, the waiter was there. They ordered, he poured more wine, and left them. There was nothing left but to deal with the issue at hand. "Are you mad at me, Boss? Did I do something wrong?"

Gianna shook her head. "Of course I'm not mad at you, Cassie, but I am concerned, and since it has nothing to do with your job performance, you have every right to tell me to butt out and mind my own business." Cassie was left with her wine glass mid-air and her mouth open. Like she could ever tell the Boss to butt out. "Ah, then what is it?"

"You've never been a night owl, a bar hopper, Cassie." Gianna knew she had to tread carefully, that Cassie's emotions still hung by precariously balanced and very thin threads. "And I stress that your job performance is, as always, excellent. I'm just wondering what's changed that you seem to be spending so much time in bars."

Cassie put her glass down. "You don't think I should have been at The Snatch that night? You don't think I should go there?"

"You can be anywhere you want to be, Cassie. Please, that's not my point. I'm concerned that you seem to have cut Tim out of your life, you don't seem to spend time with Bobby and Linda and Kenny any more, and you do seem to spend time in bars, here in D.C. and in Baltimore."

"Yeah. All that's true I guess." Cassie's eyes filled and the tears swam in them before she dried them with her napkin. She gulped some wine. "Ever since...I don't know where I fit in any more, Boss, you know? I never worried about that before because the job was the most important thing in my life, and it was OK for Tim to be my best friend because he had dates and I had dates and neither one of us was looking for anything permanent. But then, after the...after my eye...when I thought I was gonna lose the job...I wondered where I would fit in. I didn't have any more dates. I guess because I had to wear that ugly eye patch for so long and nobody wants to go out with a pirate, right?" She gulped some more wine and got a moment of relief when the waiter brought their salads. He grated cheese and ground pepper and poured more wine, then evaporated.

"I'm sorry I wasn't more in tune with what you were feeling, Cassie. I was focused on getting you back to work, not on how you were getting back to life. I'm sorry," Gianna said, and she was. She was so careful to keep on the right side of the line that separated the professional from the personal, yet she had personal feelings for all her team. Strong personal feelings that she never allowed herself to act on. "Is there anything I can do to help?"

"Yeah. You can tell me what woman would ever find a one-eyed woman attractive." Cassie's despair was almost too painful.

"You've got two eyes, Cassie. One of them just doesn't see a hundred percent, and unless you reveal that fact, nobody would know unless they got awfully close. And I'm guessing that if a woman gets that close to you, you've already got her interested in more than whether or not you have twenty-twenty vision in both eyes."

Cassie smiled slightly. "Maybe," she said. "But then it seemed that all of a sudden women want you define yourself. I've never done a butch, femme thing, you know? I mean, I just was who I was and I was attracted to who I was attracted to. Different kinds of women at different times in my life, you know? And I liked women for how they were more than how they looked. Do you know what I mean?"

"Yes, Cassie, I know what you mean, and I think that most people would agree that they respond that way if they're honest with themselves."

"You really think so?"

"Yes, I really think so. Whether we're responding to friends or to lovers, I think most of us care more about how and who a person is than what a person looks like or does for a living. Certainly there always will be superficial people. But in truth, Cassie, would you want a woman who cares more about your eye than about your heart and your spirit? I promise you that some extremely fortunate woman will love you because of your damaged eye, damaged because you were protecting another human being. Against orders from your boss, I might add."

Their food arrived then— the scaloppini and the shanks— and they ate in companionable silence for quite a few minutes, Gianna hoping she hadn't overstepped a boundary, Cassie so grateful for the concern of this woman she admired and respected—and maybe loved—that she couldn't find the words to express it. Both Anna Maria and Antonio came to inquire about their meals, Antonio giving Cassie a sideways look as he asked that Mimi come see him soon.

"What you said about who people are on the inside being more important than what they look like on the outside? I think I'm going to be friends with Darlene Phillips."

"From what I've seen, I think Darlene would make a good friend. Dee, too, for that matter, and I think you'd both be lucky to call the other friend."

Cassie ate and thought some more. "Somebody I met there, at The Snatch, told me she saw a guy driving a pick-up chase Tosh one night."

Gianna put down her fork. "Why am I just hearing about this?"

"She just told me. At the demonstration. We've seen each other a few times, but she didn't know until last weekend that I was a cop. That's not something I tell just anybody. Anyway, I hadn't seen or talked to her for a while until tonight."

"What did she say, exactly? When did this happen? Who is she?"

Cassie's friend's name was Lisa and she remembered the incident because it occurred on July 4th. Dee and Darlene had sponsored a barbecue that day in Rock Creek Park. A couple hundred women, including Tosh and Lili, had attended. A soccer game was in progress in the field adjacent to the barbecue, and some of the men from the game, noticing a crowd of women, drifted over. Most of them, realizing that they weren't exactly welcome, drifted immediately away; three, however, remained and became aggressive and hostile. They were largely ignored until one of them recognized Tosh and began heckling and harassing her, calling her names, among them, infidel. Alarm bells sounded. "This guy was a Muslim?"

"I asked the same thing and Lisa said he looked and sounded like an American-born Black, not somebody from the Middle East, but he did have a beard and he wore a kufi."

Gianna thought back through the Hilliard file: Nothing that she could recall suggested any connection to Islam or Muslims. "OK, go on."

According to Lisa, the hecklers were asked to leave and when they refused, several of the women surrounded them, blows were exchanged, and the guys took off, the one who knew Tosh shouting threats at her. That night, as Lisa was walking to the club from the Metro, Tosh passed by in her Benz. Lisa recognized her because she was driving slowly, looking for a parking space. Suddenly a pick-up pulled up beside her. The guy from earlier was driving. He blocked Tosh's car, got out, and began screaming at her, calling her an embarrassment, disgusting, a dyke and an infidel. The way he parked his truck, Tosh couldn't get out of her car but she put down her window and squirted pepper spray at him. He cursed her some more, got back in his truck, and drove away. Lisa gave no more thought to the matter until Tosh was killed and hesitated to tell the police what she'd seen until she learned that Cassie was a cop.

"At this picnic, this guy specifically singled out Natasha Hilliard for his verbal attack?"

"That's what Lisa said. That he walked up to her, got in her face."

"Get her in for a statement, find out who else was at that barbecue and get them in, and Cassie? Good work."

"Thanks, Boss."

"Not just the job, Cass, but in your life. Not many of us ever have to contend with what you have and you've done a remarkable job of keeping body and soul together. And sometimes, Cassie, it takes true love an awfully long time to find out where we live ring our doorbells, so don't worry if it hasn't happened yet. Your eye has nothing to do with it."

The Bayou boasted a respectable crowd for a Sunday night though most were in the restaurant or in the piano bar. Mimi wandered around looking for one of the owners, Marianne or Renee. She didn't really expect to find them both on a Sunday, but she knew that one of them always was present. In the spacious main room a few couples were on the dance floor, half a dozen people were at the bar that could seat five times that number, and perhaps another ten were at the tables that flanked the dance floor. The restaurant was packed. About half the patrons enjoying a late supper of authentic New Orleans Creole and Cajun food were straight and a third were male— the restaurant's reputation had spread far beyond the lesbian community. Inside the cozy piano bar it was mostly women, a few men, and it was all about Peggy Brown, chanteuse extraordinaire. Sixty-something, gorgeous, sexy, sassy Peggy Brown who played the piano and sang four nights a week. When Mimi slid in the door, trying for unobtrusive, Peggy, playing and singing If the Moon Turns Green, slid in a quick bar of "start spreading the news," so quickly that nobody but Marianne noticed. She came from behind the bar to give Mimi a hug. "You here on a Sunday night? Gianna must be working."

Gianna and Marianne had been good friends for many years and now Mimi considered her a friend, too. "She's not the only one," Mimi said, keeping her voice low as Marianne had done.

"Come back to the office after the set, say hello to Renee."

"You're both working tonight?"

Marianne rolled her eyes heavenward. "Don't ask me why," she said, and returned to her duties behind the bar while Mimi found a seat at it. She hesitated when Marianne held up a wine glass with a questioning look, then nodded. She definitely felt the need of a glass of wine. She turned to face Peggy and watch the crowd. It was overwhelmingly if not totally homosexual, mostly couples, ninety percent white, and every one of them what Terry called "acceptable looking." She sipped her wine and thought about Terry, about Darlene, about Kelly. What about those women was unacceptable? They were pleasant, attractive, intelligent women who dressed like men. That's what was unacceptable to the people who made the rules. And what about the rest of us, those of us who just follow the rules? Do we think they're unacceptable, too?

Peggy finished her set and, as expected, the clapping and whistling and cheering went on for a while until she re-seated herself at the piano and launched into her encore set: A Tisket, A Tasket, Ain't Nobody's Bizness, Swing Down, Chariot, and, finally her signature piece, Love Letters. When she finished this time, everybody knew she was finished. She accepted her ovation, blew kisses to the audience and stepped down off the bandstand, working her way through the crowd, shaking hands, receiving hugs. Mimi enjoyed watching her. She'd gotten to know Peggy under unusual and unpleasant circumstances the previous year. A trio of killers who lured wealthy older lesbians to D.C. had taken a woman Peggy cared for very much as one of their victims. Gianna was working the murders as hate crimes and Mimi had stumbled upon the case accidentally. Her investigation had put her in harm's way, but it also led to her meeting Peggy. Mimi gave Peggy and big hug and her seat at the bar, and bought her a drink. "You're quite stunning this evening, Miss Brown."

"I look stunning every evening, my love," Peggy said archly, accepting her glass of champagne. She was sheathed in shimmering turquoise satin and dripping jewels. "Where's that gorgeous lieutenant?"

"Working. Why, won't I do?"

Peggy gave her a slow up and down. "In a pinch, I suppose."

Mimi hooted and gave her another big hug. "When can we take you to dinner? Or better still, up to the mountains? Gianna's been promising to take a few days off and we've got a couple of months before it starts to snow up there."

"Will the boys be there, too?"

"The boys" were Mimi's best friend Freddy Schuyler and his partner Cedric Foster. Freddy, a former Washington Redskin and owner of popular night spot peopled by the young and trendy, had a cabin in the Cacoctin Mountains north of Washington in Garrett County, Maryland that was her and Gianna's de facto vacation home. They'd taken Peggy for a visit and she'd fallen in love with Freddy and Cedric and the cabin.

"If we give them enough advance notice," Mimi said.

"Can we go for Thanksgiving?" Peggy asked.

"That's an excellent idea," Mimi said. She'd mention it to Gianna tonight or tomorrow. "So, how's everything with you?"

Peggy gave and elaborate shrug and wiggled her hand in a side to side motion. "So, so. Can't complain. You?"

Mimi shrugged. "Same old, same old."

"Well, not exactly, is it?" Peggy arched an already raised left brow until it seemed to reach her scalp line. "I mean, this business with the Doms and Ags. I never heard of such! I sent my friend Earlene over there to that club to see what was what and oh, my dear! The things she told me! I'm thinking about going over there myself. I want to see those dancing girls. Earlene says they're quite lovely though they apparently do some quite nasty things on top of that bar. Have you seen them?"

Mimi was laughing so hard she could do no more than shake her head. When finally she could speak she allowed that no, she hadn't seen The Snatch Dancers yet but she planned to, and the name sent Peggy on another verbal tangent that caused Mimi to get up and leave. "I've got to go eat, I'm starving, and you're going to kill me, Miss Brown. Good night."

She made her way through the main room, around the bar and down the hall that ran between the restaurant and the bar, to the office. She knocked, heard a harried "come in," and opened the door to find both Marianne and Renee, one seated at each of the desks placed on adjacent walls. She hadn't seen Marianne leave the bar.

"I knew you'd show up tonight," Renee said, standing to give her hug. "I told Mare you'd show up. You always do when there's trouble."

Mimi backed away and looked to see if she was kidding. She wasn't. "Maybe I should leave, then," she said, and she wasn't kidding, either.

"Ignore, her, Mimi. You said you wanted dinner, didn't you?" Marianne started for the door. "Let's go do that and leave ol' sourpuss in here to grouse all by herself."

"What's she grousing about and what's it got to do with me?" Mimi really was pissed and she really wanted Renee to know it.

"Those stories you've done about that bar across town and about the super butches. Then that rally tonight all over TV, I knew we'd get spill-over and sure enough, we did. Half a dozen of 'em showed up here." Renee shook her head in disgust. "My Sunday night shot to shit."

"Nobody told you to come over here," Marianne said. "You could have stayed home. I didn't need you running over here."

"You'd have let 'em in," Renee said, belligerent and accusing.

"What 'them' are you talking about?" Mimi asked.

"Pay attention, Mimi," Renee said, as if talking to someone very young or very intellectually challenged. "The super butches. What've you been calling them, Doms and Ags? Such stupid shit! Where do they come up with these names?"

"You refused to let people in because you don't like how they look?"

"Don't take that tone with me, Mimi. I'm running a business here and yes, I make decisions about who comes in based on how they look."

"And I make decisions on where I go based on people's behavior and I don't like yours. Good night."

Marianne grabbed her arm. "Mimi! What are you doing? You can't just leave like that!"

"Sure I can. If I weren't with Gianna you probably wouldn't let me in, would you, Renee? You'd find something unacceptable about the way I look, like the color of my skin."

"That's a shitty thing to say!"

"What you just said about an entire group of people, none of whom you know, was pretty shitty, too. That's discrimination of the worst kind, Renee, the kind based on a stereotype. No difference between what you just said and those who say no Blacks, no Jews, no Hispanics allowed. No gays allowed."

"No, it is not the same thing!" Renee was as furious as Mimi. "My God, you've seen them. They look like gangster hoodlums, wearing those horrible baggy pants and shoes with the strings untied. They look—"

"Unacceptable?" Mimi offered.

Renee nodded emphatically. "Exactly. So since you understand what I'm talking about, why are you giving me such a hard time?"

Mimi shook her head. "I've got to go."

She left, feeling more unsettled than she had in a long time, because of what Renee said but also because of how shocked Marianne appeared to be. Was it possible that Marianne wasn't aware of Renee's thoughts and feelings on such matters? Mimi knew from Gianna, and from her own experience, that Marianne was a kind and generous woman, perhaps to a fault. Renee had been right about one thing: Marianne never would have refused admittance to somebody because of how they looked. Had they never discussed such things before opening the Bayou? Probably not. How would they have known to say, "By the way, what's going to be our policy on admitting Doms and Ags?"

Mimi's anger had carried her out into the night and half way to the parking lot where her car was before it receded enough to let her realize how hungry she was. Now what was she going to do? It was Sunday night in D.C. Where would she find anything worth eating...Chinatown! She reclaimed her car, put the top down, popped in a Donna Summer CD, and headed across town. At the first stop light she called Gianna to see if she'd gotten home yet, to see if she was hungry. When she got no answer she considered calling her cell phone, then decided against it. She might still be with Officer Ali and it wouldn't be prudent to interrupt whatever that was all about.

Traffic in Chinatown was as dense as if it were high noon on a week day. No place to park within four blocks of her favorite restaurant, and she was in no mood to walk that far just to eat, then to have to walk that far to get back to her car. In truth, she was too tired for it. She was exhausted. She'd planned to be asleep by now. Curled up next to Gianna, music playing softly, and deeply asleep. "She works hard for the money," Donna sang, and Mimi wondered if sometimes it wasn't too hard, or at least too many hours. How often were their lives put on hold because of the work they did? But how happy would they be, either of them, if they didn't do the work they did? She didn't have to say the answer to herself as she made a U turn in the middle of Seventh Street under the Pagoda Arch and headed home. She'd scramble some eggs, toast an English muffin, have another glass of wine— or two— and get in bed with a book. Poor substitute for Gianna but at least she'd get more sleep with the book for company.

Darkness Descending

CHAPTER NINE

HUNDREDS GATHER ON HARLEY STREET
TO MOURN SLAIN HISTORIAN
   By M. Mongtomery Patterson
   Staff Writer

   More than three hundred mourners gathered last
night at the litter-strewn vacant lot where 29-year old
Natasha Hilliard was murdered two weekends ago. The
occasion was notable not only because, for the first time
in recent memory, lesbians and gays of all ages and races
came together for a single purpose, but also because it
acknowledged the existence of a group of lesbians known
as Ags or Doms— shorthand for Aggressives or Dominants.
These are women, predominantly young and Black or
Latina, who are masculine in appearance and frequently
in behavior. "I suppose it's what used to be called 'butch,'"
said Caroline Silbert, executive director of the Metropolitan
Washington Gay and Lesbian Community Organization.
"Though I'm not entirely comfortable with having to
place labels on people," she added.
   The murdered woman was known to frequent The
Snatch, a bar on Harley Street that caters to Doms and
Ags. She had just left that establishment when she
was shot in the back on the night of September
19th, then stabbed repeatedly and left to bleed to death.
She apparently had kept that aspect of her life secret
from her friends and acquaintances in academia, as she
kept her academic life secret from her friends and
acquaintances at The Snatch. "I had no idea she
was a historian and university professor," said
Delores Phillips, co- owner of the Harley Street club.
"In fact, I knew very little about her at all, which
I now regret," Phillips said.

According to Phillips, Silbert and others, Doms and Ags are perceived negatively, and some even consider them dangerous, the assumption being that they have gang affiliations. Women who self-identify as Doms and Ags find those perceptions insulting as well as hurtful. "I don't like it that people think of us as some kind of freaks," said 27-year old Kelly Jones. "Either that or they don't see us at all." Jones, a mechanic for the city's transit authority, lost her job in Richmond, VA because of her appearance. "People ask me why I want a man's job. If I'm doing it, it's not a man's job, is it? And why shouldn't I earn $35 an hour? I'm a master mechanic. I trained long and hard to acquire the skills I have."

The women don't understand why anybody would find their appearance threatening. "I can understand why somebody wouldn't like what I wear. I don't like the clothes some other people wear, but I wouldn't hate them for it," said 28-year old Terry Carson, a big rig driver for a national grocery chain. "Why is it OK for all kinds of other people to be accepted for how they look, but not us? The government says don't fear Muslims and Middle Easterners because they're not all terrorists. But it's all right to fear me and think I'm a hoodlum because of how I look?"

And how they look also is a problem for some restaurant and nightclub owners who deny entrance to Doms and Ags, including some gay and lesbian-owned establishments. "Do you have any idea how that makes us feel?" asked 25-year old Tyra Simmons. "It's bad enough when straight people treat us like garbage, but it really hurts when our own people do it."

Several of those who attended the Hilliard memorial service saw it as a potential turning point for that kind of attitude. "It was a tribute to Tosh, definitely," one woman said, "but in a way, it was a tribute to all of us."

"Tell her she comes in voluntarily or she comes in under arrest, in cuffs," Gianna stated. "Same goes for the Hilliards and for Ray Washington. Do these people think we're inviting them to Sunday afternoon tea and they can either accept our invitation or decline it? Arrest every one of them if you have to, but no more kid gloves."

Gianna was up and pacing and borderline angry as she addressed her team that Monday morning. She understood that the Hilliards were grieving the loss of their daughter and that Lily Spenser was grieving the loss of her mother and that Lisa Last Name Unknown (because Cassie didn't remember it) had had bad experiences with cops in the past. But what they all needed to understand was that she had a murderer and three rapists to catch and that reality took precedence over their feelings.

"We really may have to charge that Washington character," Linda said. "He's giving us nothing but lies and bullshit."

"Then charge him," Gianna snapped. "Go to his home right now and get him, Linda, you and Tim. Bobby, I want you here to walk me through the deep and skinny on Mr. Washington, step by step. Kenny, sic the ABC Board and the Department of Licenses and Permits on him. If there's any way to shut him down, even if it's just for a day, do it. I want his full and undivided attention and I want it today."

Linda and Tim left. Kenny got on the telephone. Bobby corralled the thick stack of files on Ray Washington and the Pink Panther, ready to answer when his boss was ready to question. Gianna resumed her pacing. She stopped in front of the board where the crime scene photographs hung. She looked up at Natasha Hilliard's dead body, then across the room at Cassie. "This Lisa, would anybody else know her last name? Think, Cass! I can't believe all those people hang out in that club, that they all see each other at least once a week, and that nobody knows anybody's full name, telephone number or address. Didn't you ever call her?"

Cassie nodded. "But it was an answering service. She checks for messages several times a day, then returns calls, usually from her job."

"Dammit! What kind of people have we become? Eric, take that number and do whatever you need to do to ID that answering service, then subpoena their records and get this girl's name. And somebody else saw and heard that guy go after Tosh. Cassie, get me more names! You said this was a big event, right? People partying in the park. Somebody else saw that confrontation and can help us out with a description of the guy."

"Darlene's checking. She remembers the incident but she wasn't close enough to it hear or see anything. She did have her camcorder, though, and she's looking for the cassettes from that day."

"Go to her house and help her," Gianna snapped, and Cassie rushed out.

Gianna continued to prowl the room. She stopped at the artist's sketch of Joyce Harper's rapists and tapped each one of them. "Alice, you haven't seen anybody who even remotely resembles these sketches?"

Alice walked over to the board where the sketches were hanging. "To tell you the truth, Lieutenant, these sketches look like everybody and nobody. Poor Joyce. I think it's all running together in her mind. Any one of those bastards looked like the others 'cause they were doing the same thing to her, and I think these sketches represent pieces of all of 'em. Which isn't to say I'm through looking," she hastened to add.

"I know you're not, Alice. And while you're looking, make time for a little chat with the Mid-Town undercovers, find out if they ever got any official word from Command that they were to fail or refuse to provide aid to any patron of The Snatch or the Pink Panther, or to any homosexual."

"What?" Eric had been calm and quiet up to this point, listening and taking notes, keeping a list of those things he knew Gianna wanted expedited. "O'Connell couldn't have been stupid enough to issue an order like that! Could he?"

"That's what I'm trying to find out."

"You think that's possible, Lieutenant?" Alice asked.

"Yes, I do," Gianna answered. "And one more thing, Alice. If we succeed in closing the Pink Panther's doors for a few days, which I hope we do, I'd like you to show some interest in becoming a member of the Ark of the Covenant Tabernacle Church."

Alice's face lit up and she rubbed her hands gleefully together. "Oh, I'd love to! I give really good Church Sister, and after what I've read about the good Reverend Bailey in the newspaper, why I just can't wait to be in the presence of such a good Christian servant of the Lord."

Alice's Southern accent had gotten more pronounced with every word, and by the time she finished her sentence Gianna didn't understand a word of what she was saying, but she knew that Charles William Bailey was in for it.

*****

"It's really quite a simple request, Edgar," Mimi said between clinched teeth, which she hoped moderated the sarcasm. "Do you know whether there's a way to find out which of the non-denominational and super conservative churches preached the same sermon in support of Frank O'Connell yesterday? Either these guys are organized or they aren't, and I think they are. I need to find that organization, but if don't know anything about it, Edgar, just say you don't know. No harm in that—"

"I'm just asking why you want to know. Why can't you answer?"

"Because it's none of your business," Mimi snapped.

"I'm the Religion editor, it is my business. You're asking about religion, that makes it my business."

"I'm not asking about religion, I'm asking about an organization, if one exists. How would a group of ministers go about deciding to preach a sermon on the same topic if they don't have an official organization to facilitate that? How would men as different as Charles Bailey, with his raggedy little storefront church in the Black ghetto, and Elwood Burgess, with his suburban palace and its five thousand members in the white suburbs, ever even meet each other, to say nothing of agreeing to do something together, if there's no organization? And if there is an organization, that's not religion, Edgar, that's politics, and that's my business."

Mimi well understood that Edgar Whitfield had been a reporter for almost fifty years, all of them right here in this same newsroom, and that he harbored proprietary notions about what he did. He'd first got the job of Religion Editor way back when nobody else wanted it, back when religion in America was a simple matter of being Protestant, Catholic or Jewish: Mainstream Protestant, mainstream Catholic, mainstream Jewish. Now that there was nothing at all simple and very little mainstream about religion as practiced in America, or in the world, the paper didn't know what to do with a man who not only didn't know the difference between Buddhists, Hindus and Muslims but who didn't care to know, so Edgar remained Religion Editor in name only while the paper's bosses waited for him to retire or die. Meanwhile, a host of other reporters covered the many aspects and facets of religion and spirituality, from the ordination of homosexual priests in the Anglican Church to the abuse charges leveled against priests in the Catholic Church, from the increased interest in Eastern spiritual philosophies, to the increased interest in all manner of fundamentalism. Used to the politically correct way of doing things, Mimi had come to the person nominally responsible. Big mistake. And didn't the paper have a mandatory retirement age? Edgar must be at least seventy-five.

"Look, Edgar, just forget I asked." Frustrated, she stalked away to look for her pal Tyler Carson, to ask him which of the reporters who wrote about religion most likely would know the answer to her question.

"Elwood Burgess is no man of God."

Mimi walked back to Edgar's desk. "What did you say?"

"I said Elwood Burgess is no man of God."

"What do you mean by that?"

"He uses the pulpit for personal gain, not to preach the gospel."

"You mean so he can collect tax free money?"

"And so he can recruit for his so-called army. You're right about one thing," Edgar said, a bit grudgingly. "What Burgess does is definitely more politics than it is religion."

This is what Mimi was after and it had been right here in her own backyard the entire time. "I heard something about him having an army but I dismissed it as idle talk."

Whitfield shook his head so vehemently that blowsy white tufts of hair danced in the breeze. "That's what everybody thought and now it's too late to do anything about it."

Mimi continued to play her part. "Do anything about what, Edgar? Now I'm confused." She grabbed the chair from the adjacent desk, pulled it close to Edgar, sat down, and took her micro recorder from her pocket. Edgar glanced at it but didn't blink or hesitate. In fact he seemed relieved to be able to talk about what he knew.

"He used to be with the police, Burgess did. This was a long time ago, way before your time, back when police could do the kinds of things he did and get away with it. You can probably guess what kinds of things I mean, you being Black and all?" He made it a question and Mimi nodded her answer. She already knew all this but she was loathe to do anything that would take the wind from Edgar's sails now that he'd unfurled them. "Somebody finally put a stop to him. Nobody ever knew for certain who it was but at the time the speculation was that it was a Negro Vietnam veteran."

Mimi gave Edgar the surprise reaction he expected. "Why do you say that?"

For the first time the old guy displayed a trace of humor. "Because somebody was taking shots at Burgess with some kind of high-powered gun and the shots always got close to him. Too close, as if the shooter missed intentionally. The speculation was that he— the shooter— wanted Burgess to know that he could kill him at any time. Burgess got the message."

"He ceased his police brutality?"

"He left the police department," Edgar said with a satisfied nod. His blue eyes blazed. "But he was just getting started. He bought himself some divinity degrees— not real ones from recognized theological schools— and set himself up as a preacher, recruiting the worst elements from the police departments, and back then, the bad element pool was well stocked."

Mimi knew all this but she smiled enjoyment of the old man's well-turned phrases and their imagery.

"We've got to stop meeting this way, Edgar, your generation and mine, each thinking the other is hopelessly out of touch."

He emitted a surprised bark of laughter. "I'm pleased that you don't find it hopeless."

"Do you?"

He nodded sadly. "I'm afraid so. But! Let's return to Officer Burgess, shall we? And by the way, when you talk to him, which I'm assuming you will, call him that: Officer instead of Doctor. It'll turn him purple with apoplexy!" The old man almost giggled at the thought, then returned to his story, which was that Burgess initially built his church on cops and their families, preying on old style Southern racist sympathies of which there were plenty in D.C. and environs thirty-five years ago. As his congregation expanded to encompass and include the general population of the neighborhood, Burgess refined his message and his presentation. He stopped looking and sounding so much like the redneck he was. He used some of the many thousands of dollars he was raking in to establish programs for young people. He toned down his strident anti-government message and re-introduced it to his congregation as a tax assistance program. The church grew, and grew more prosperous as new congregants, more sophisticated than the coarse PG

County residents who had been bedrock of the church, realized that they had a forum not only for their religious beliefs, but for their political ones as well. Not only could Burgess now carry an anti-government, anti-Black message, he could preach against abortion, women's rights, homosexuality, and all those other religions that didn't interpret the Divine message the way he did. And those youth programs and taxpayer assistance programs became armies: cadres of trained "Christian soldiers" who carried out specific "missions" under Burgess's direction.

Mimi was still listening though Edgar had stopped talking. For a moment she couldn't think of anything to say. "What kind of missions," she finally managed.

"I've been reading your stories. I read the entire paper, cover to cover, each and every day, you know, and I read your stories very carefully. That Inspector Frank O'Connell. He's one of Burgess's soldiers. The dereliction of duty you alluded to would not have been an oversight on his part."

"How can I prove that, Edgar?"

He gave her a long, steady look, held her gaze as tightly as if he had a grip on her hands with his. "Come by at the end of the day. I'm here until six forty-five."

Mimi knew he was finished talking. She stood up and slid her chair back to the desk where it belonged. She didn't want to leave. "One more question, Edgar, please. Why would Burgess ally himself with Charles Bailey?"

"I don't know Bailey but I do know that many of the Black ministers are as pedagogic and pedantic as Burgess, and so blinded by their fundamentalist fervor that they don't understand they're nailing themselves to their own crosses, so to speak."

"You mean, for example, how the homophobia of the Black church contributes to the spread of AIDS?"

He gave her a beatific smile. "Perhaps not hopeless after all." Then he rattled off the names of half a dozen pastors of independent, non-denominational churches who likely would have shared the Burgess and Bailey message on Sunday.

Mimi returned to her desk on the other side of the football-field sized newsroom. She wasn't exactly sure what she was feeling, but her thoughts were all over the place. All the years she'd been at the paper she'd never spoken to Edgar Whitfield, and after what she'd just experienced, she realized that everything she thought she knew about him was incorrect. He might be old but he certainly wasn't out of touch.

She removed the cassette with the Whitfield interview and popped in the one with Burgess's Sunday service on it. She put on her headphones, leaned back in her chair propped her feet on the desk, and closed her eyes. The sound quality was as good as what she'd gotten recording Bailey's service—the little recorders were surprisingly reliable. She'd managed a seat in the second row of Bailey's church and the recorder picked up every word of his sermon as well as the plop-plop-plop of water into the almost full plastic containers situated in the four corners of the little church. The intern who'd attended Burgess's church must have sat directly beneath a speaker, bless his observant little heart. Every word was there with perfect clarity, the same words that Charles Bailey had uttered. She had fast forwarded through the sermon the first time, just to make certain that it was there. Now she listened carefully and closely, listening for the subliminal message as well as to the spoken words. If ever interred in a POW camp and forced to listen to this garbage on a regular basis, Mimi would opt for Bailey over Burgess. Bailey at least sounded like he believed what he was saying. Burgess oozed unctuousness. How could anybody take him seriously as a spiritual leader? Then again, perhaps nobody did. Perhaps that's not why five thousand people listened to him every Sunday morning.

"Shit!" She sat up straight and dropped her feet to the floor. She'd almost missed it, what with her thoughts drifting about like clouds. She backed up the tape then re-played the section following the end of the sermon. Both Bailey and Burgess had concluded by asking for a show of support for the wronged Frank O'Connell, but Burgess had something that Bailey did not: O'Connell in the flesh. He must have been up there with Burgess because Burgess said, "Here he is," and there was loud clapping and cheering that went on for a while. Then, during a break in the adulation, Mimi heard, "God hates fags." It was loud and strident and there was a moment of dead silence in the church, as if God had said, "Say what?" Then the words came again, louder and stronger: God hates faggots! And the clapping and cheering erupted and the organ began to play and a song started.

Mimi switched off the machine and sat there looking at it. Who had said, "God hates fags"? It wasn't Burgess, she was certain of that. O'Connell? Had he actually stood in front of a packed church on a Sunday morning and said that? She was half way across the newsroom before she remembered that Carolyn wasn't at work; she was off Mondays and Tuesdays. The intern! Who was the intern who'd attended Burgess's church service? She telescoped the huge room, looking for an intern-like face, then got control of herself. She wouldn't know him if she tripped over him.

"Shit," she said again, and dropped back down into her chair. God hates fags. If that was O'Connell, he was finished in the D.C. police department. Might not be enough to get him fired but certainly sufficient to guarantee that he never got another command, and perhaps not another promotion. Would the chief tell her if that was O'Connell's voice? Perhaps, but he'd probably also confiscate the tape. Inspector Davis? She didn't know him well enough. And the one cop she did know well enough... She made her decision. She grabbed her rucksack, tossed the necessary equipment into it, including her laptop, and started for the door.

"Patterson!" She heard her name yelled over the newsroom din.

Mimi looked for the source of the summons, saw the receptionist waving her arms, and headed for her. "What's up, Maggie?"

"Visitor in the lobby. Some guy wants to talk to you about the Hilliard person you've been writing about."

Maggie was newsroom legend. Nobody knew how old she was and she wasn't telling. She dressed like a hippie, talked like a Valley Girl, had a memory like an elephant, and the personality of Morticia.

All right. Tell security I'm on my way down. Thanks, Maggie."

"And Patterson? It'd be nice if you let me know when you're leaving the building, you know? That way I'm not, like, looking for you and you're not here."

Mimi nodded, told Maggie where she was going, and left, wondering whether she'd just lied. It was her intention to go to police headquarters to find Gianna and ask her to listen to the Burgess tape, ask her to identify Mr. God Hates Fags as O'Connell or not. Now she was wondering how Gianna would react. Mimi sometimes forgot that Gianna was a cop, all cop, with a cop's instincts and feelings, and as such, she'd be in no hurry to help Mimi nail O'Connell's hide to the nearest tree, even if she acknowledged that maybe he deserved it. So, if not Gianna, then who? Dare she call on Ernie Binion again so soon? She weighed the possibility, was turning it over, when the elevator doors opened and she was pushed out into the lobby by the tightly packed crowd. She was headed for the security desk when a neatly dressed man approached her. His hair was very short and he wore a full, neatly trimmed beard. He had on a knit skull cap and tiny wire-rimmed glasses. He looked about twenty-eight or twenty nine, maybe a couple of years older— about Natasha Hilliard's age, Mimi was thinking— when he got close enough for her to see his eyes. She backed up a step. He also looked crazy.

"You are M. Montgomery Patterson." It was an accusation, not a query.

"You have information about Natasha Hilliard?"

"Stop writing about her," he said in the same tone of voice. "You demean and disgust her family and her memory. Don't write anymore."

Anger rose up fast in Mimi. "Excuse me," she said instead of the 'Fuck you' she wanted to say, and started to walk around him.

"Don't you dare walk away from me," he said, his tone so menacing that Mimi stopped and turned back toward him.

"Who the hell do you think you're talking to?" The fury in her voice and eyes matched his and he wavered for just an instant.

"You are to write no more about the abomination that infiltrated Natasha and ruined her life. It is against Allah."

Mimi turned away from him again. Another religious zealot. Trying to engage in a rational conversation with him would be as big a waste of time as trying to talk to Charles Bailey. Give me Edgar Whitfield any day, she was thinking, when the blow to the middle of her back staggered her. She turned and the second blow caught her on the side of the head, sending her flying backward. "You stupid son of a bitch!"

Infuriated, he charged her. "You evil woman! You speak and act against the laws of Allah and you will be punished!"

Mimi swung her rucksack as hard as she could. It connected with the side of his head just as three security guards rushed him. They pushed her out of the way to get to him, sending her careening across the polished marble floor and into one of the center columns. One guard finished the job of knocking him to the ground and the other two each grabbed an arm. They had to work to hold on because he was kicking like a drunken mule and screaming about retribution and the will of Allah. The guard who'd knocked him down knelt on his legs and the two holding his arms managed to get handcuffs on him. The kicking and screaming continued, drawing a dangerously large crowd.

"Death to you and to all homosexuals!" he screamed as the guards worked to control him. "Death to all infidels! Homosexuality is an abomination!" Mimi struggled to her feet as four D.C. cops bounded into the lobby. In seconds, they had the kicking, screaming man out the door— two of the cops carrying the front end, two carrying the legs that Mimi wagered would be broken by the time he got to Central Lock-Up if he didn't settle down. She touched her face where it hurt and it hurt even more. Her rucksack had spilled open and its contents scattered across the floor. The micro recorder was in pieces and the laptop had popped open. She bent to begin retrieving things, felt dizzy, and swayed. One of the guards wrapped his arms around her, steadying her.

"I've got you, Miss Patterson," he said.

"And not a moment too soon," she replied, waiting for the wooziness to pass. "I think I'm going to have a pretty good headache."

"Not as good as the one he's gonna have," the guard said. He held her at arm's length and took a good look. "Think you oughta see a medic?"

She touched the sore place on her face again, looking for blood. It hurt like hell but that was all. She shook her head, regretted the action, then spoke the words. "I don't think so. Not unless I look a lot worse than I feel, and I'm trusting you to tell me the truth."

He gave her a sideways grin. "Like I said, you look a hell of a lot better than the other guy's gonna look. Who the hell is he, by the way?"

"No idea. Maggie said somebody in the lobby wanted to talk to me about one of my stories—"

"Yeah," the guard said, "I could tell, all the damn screaming about Allah and homosexuals and infidels. Crazy son of a bitch." He looked around at the cleared-out lobby and beckoned to another guard who trotted over. Mimi saw why: He had stripes on his arm and out-ranked her protector.

"You all right, Miss Patterson?" the sergeant asked, giving her a critical look. "He landed one on you, didn't he, little son of a bitch."

"Two, to be precise, but I'm fine and I appreciate your coming to the rescue, both of you. If I can just collect my belongings, I'll be on my way."

"Oh, no, Ma'am. We've got to do the paperwork now," the sergeant said.

"What paperwork?"

"Filing the charges. So far I count assault, battery and trespass. I'm sure the cops will have a few more by the time they get him to Central Lock-up."

"Oh, I don't know about that," Mimi said, wishing she was someplace else.

"Not up to you," the sergeant said, "the paper will press charges. That's policy. One of their employees was assaulted on their property, they're gonna throw the book at that guy. He'll wish he'd never seen a newspaper when they finish with him."

Mimi thought she could understand the sentiment.

The air was a little lighter in the Think Tank, due primarily to the better frame of mind the Boss was in, that change due to the fact that Ray Washington's Pink Panther was closed until further notice, the fact that Lisa Baker had provided a description of the man who had harassed Natasha Hilliard and of the pick-up truck he drove, and the fact that the Hate Crimes unit was in possession of three video tapes shot by Darlene Phillips's date at the July 4th barbecue in Rock Creek Park. Darlene hadn't realized that she'd zeroed in on the hecklers but she was an excellent photographer and Lisa Baker had excellent recall. Her description of the man who had hassled Natasha Hilliard was almost as perfect as a photograph, which they'd have by tomorrow morning— a still lifted from the video tape. Perhaps one of the dead woman's family members or friends knew the man— a likely supposition since he'd singled her out by name for his harangue.

"Too bad the parking lot's not in the shot," Eric said, "or we might be able to get the truck, too."

Kenny's eyes lit up. "I could try for that," he said, always game for a technical challenge of the computer sort.

A knock sounded. It was rare that they had visitors, even rarer that the occasional visitor knocked on the door, so they all looked up as a plain clothes detective entered. "Lieutenant Maglione?"

Gianna walked toward him. "What can I do for you?"

"Detective Schuster, Downtown Division. My boss wanted me to let you know about an incident we had this afternoon. Might not be anything, but the Chief made it clear that anything that gave any hint of being a hate crime was to be brought immediately to you," he said, and gave her a folder.

"I appreciate the heads up," Gianna said. "What happened?"

"Guy we're taking to be a Muslim attacked a reporter. He wanted her to stop writing stories about homosexuals—"

Everybody in the room stood up so suddenly that Schuster backed up in alarm. All eyes were on him. Schuster's eyes flicked from one to the other of them.

"What reporter, Detective Schuster?" Gianna asked so calmly that Schuster visibly relaxed.

"That Montgomery Patterson, the one who always writes about the corruption. She's been writing about homosexuals—"

"You said she was attacked, Detective. Does that mean she's injured?"

He shook his head. "No, Ma'am. At least not bad enough for the hospital. She wouldn't go. It's all in the report, Lieutenant. And the perp's in custody."

"Thank you, Detective, and thank your boss for me. Who is, that, by the way? Downtown Division, you said? Shirley McManus still in charge over there?"

"Yes, Ma'am, she is, and I'll tell her what you said."

Schuster left but nobody moved. Now all eyes were on Gianna. She was thinking— hoping—that if Mimi was seriously hurt she'd have called, but she knew for certain that if the injury was not serious, Mimi never would call her at work.

"Let's see what we have here," she said, overriding her emotions and opening the folder. She read the first page quickly, turned to the second page and couldn't stop the reaction. "Son of a bitch!" They all crowded around her and looked at the processing photograph of the perp. It was Natasha Hilliard's attacker.

"What's his name?"

"Michael Howard Nelson AKA Abdul Sharif. And the icing on the cake? They impounded his pick-up truck. He drove it to the paper and left it double parked when he went inside. We ought to see if Lisa Baker wants a job with us." She headed for the door. "I'm going to give Shirley McManus a call and tell her I want Mr. Nelson AKA Sharif. Eric, get warrants for his home, car and any other personal property he might have and Bobby, you and Cassie sit on his home until the warrant comes. Tim, you watch the truck. Kenny, get on the computer and find out anything you can about him. Linda and Alice, you two stand by. You'll be with me. I'll be back shortly." She barreled out of the room, leaving electrically charged air in her wake.

They all stood motionless. They knew that she'd gone to her office, not to call Captain McManus— she could have done that in the Think Tank— but to call Mimi Patterson. "Schuster said she was all right, she didn't have to go to the hospital," Bobby said. "If something was wrong, she'd be in the hospital, right?"

"Right," Cassie said.

"So probably nothing to worry about," Tim said, worry etched all over his face.

"We'll know in a minute," Alice said, concealing her own worry about the woman she'd still like to get to know a lot better. If only she had a different lover...

Mimi had a fierce headache, her butt and side hurt where she'd slammed into the hard marble column and then the floor, and her back hurt where Nelson had hit her, but her real pain was caused by the fact that both her micro recorder and her laptop were more seriously injured than she was. Her pride also sustained a bit hit. Here she was at home at five o'clock in the afternoon taking aspirin and drinking herbal tea. She wiggled around on the sofa trying to find a comfortable position, then gave up. Every movement caused some part of her body to hurt, even reaching for the remote control. She flicked on the TV and muted the sound while she flipped around looking for something inoffensive to watch. She settled on the early edition of BBC News and turned up the sound a bit, but found she couldn't concentrate. She cast a baleful glance at the little stack of cassettes and diskettes that represented her shattered tape recorder and battered laptop computer, and wondered what was happening with the SOB responsible. The phone rang and she almost fainted from the pain caused by reaching for it.

"You don't need to work, Mimi, you need to rest," was Gianna's response to her grousing about the busted equipment.

"You could be right," Mimi said, stifling a groan.

"Why? What's wrong?" Gianna said so quickly Mimi would have laughed had she not known instinctively not to.

"I'm just agreeing with you."

"That's what's wrong. I wish I had time to come look at you in person, to be certain that you're all right, instead of having to rely on a police report description of your injuries. Dammit, Mimi, that's what cell phones are for!"

Mimi winced. Gianna had been really angry that Mimi had left messages on her home and office phones instead of calling directly. "You know I don't like to disturb you when you're working, Gianna. And it wasn't an emergency."

"We'll discuss what disturbs me and what doesn't later. Right now, you rest. And, by the way, thanks."

Something about her tone of voice... "Thanks for what?"

"We've been looking for Mr. Nelson, only we didn't know what his name was or where to find him. All of which means I may not get home tonight but I'll call and check on you periodically."

"Don't worry about me, but I would appreciate it if you'd explain to Mr. Nelson why beating up on reporters isn't—" For some reason the image of Edgar Whitfield popped into her mind. "— isn't acceptable behavior," she said, ending her call with Gianna and placing one to the white-haired gentleman himself.

Acceptable behavior wasn't of particular interest to Michael Nelson. He spit at Gianna, tried to kick Bobby, and called Tim a devil. It was clear they'd get nothing useful out of him.

His truck and apartment, however, were proving much more forthcoming: A diary, half a dozen fat spiral notebooks filled with rambling anti-homosexual writings, a map of American University with the History Department circled, a city map with Lander Street marked, fishing gear and a tackle box with several knives, a set of carving knives with one knife missing, a huge cache of anti-homosexual literature, a Beretta semi-automatic, a photo album containing photographs of the entire Hilliard family, and a divorce decree, filed in D.C. Superior Court last year, ending the two-year marriage between himself and Felicia Hilliard.

"The man had threatened your daughter and it never occurred to you to mention that to us? Even after you knew that we were considering her death a hate crime, it never occurred to you to mention Michael Nelson?" Gianna was furious. "The first thought in your heads, the first words out of your mouths upon learning of Natasha's death, should have been 'Michael Nelson'."

The Hilliards were stunned. They sat side-by-side at a table in the Think Tank, gripping each other's hands, alternating between looking forlornly at Gianna, looking helplessly at each other, looking around the room, bewildered by their surroundings. They'd driven down to D.C. from Philadelphia in response to her summons and they looked a hundred years older than when she'd last seen them, the day after their middle daughter's murder. Then, less than three weeks ago, they were shocked, stunned, grief-stricken. They now looked...Gianna wasn't sure. It was more than shock and grief, though. Destroyed is the word that came to mind. They were a handsome couple— or should have been. Robert was a six-footer and looked like the scientist he was: Silver-haired, be-speckled, wearing a three-piece suit with a watch chain visible on the vest. Gianna wasn't sure what women ministers should look like, but the Reverend Doctor Christine Hilliard, in a long-sleeved cranberry knit dress, sheer black stockings, black high heels, and discreet gold jewelry at ears, neck, and hands, looked like one of those magazine ads for the perfect over-fifty woman. Only the gold cross on the long chain, resting against her breasts, gave hint to her calling.

"Nobody in the family ever took Mike seriously," Robert Hilliard said. "Of course we never wanted Felicia to marry him. They'd both just started graduate school—" He put his head in his hands and sobbed. Christine Hilliard put her arms around him and they sat that way for a long moment. Bobby poured them some water. They drank it down and seemed calmer.

"Believe me I'm sorry to have to put you through this," Gianna said more gently. "And I wouldn't if there were another way to get the information we need, but there isn't."

"Part of what we're feeling, Lieutenant, is guilt. Bob said we didn't take Mike seriously, but more than that, we...diminished him, I think."

Gianna pulled up a chair close to the Hilliards. "What does that mean, Mrs. Hilliard? I need facts here, not...psychology."

"We embraced Natasha as we embraced our other two daughters, and we made certain he understood that we expected him to embrace her, too. We also made certain that he understood that while we respected his choice of religion, he could never expect Felicia to be anything but a Christian. He felt we weren't taking him seriously."

"We weren't!" Bob Hillliard, composure regained, behaved like the father of a murdered daughter. "How do you take seriously a grown man in twenty-first century America who thinks his wife should defer to him?" Hilliard jumped up, fists balled at is sides. His wife pulled him back down. "It'd be different if he'd been born in the Middle East, been born a Muslin. But he was a Tennessee Baptist, converted to Islam four or five years! I thought he was full of crap and Christine told him he was!"

Gianna looked at Christine and she nodded sadly. "Though not in those exact words. I merely questioned his interpretation of some of the Koran's passages. He didn't seem really to know very much about Islam..."

"He was just using that as an excuse to be a bully," Bob Hilliard stated.

"Anyway," Christine said, "a year into the marriage, Felicia had had enough. She literally ran away from him." Christine Hilliard wiped her eyes and blew her nose. "And it didn't do any good. Didn't make any difference." The Hilliards drifted off into a grief-stricken silence. Gianna looked from one of them to the other, waiting for one of them to continue. It was Robert who eventually did.

"Because the rest of us were at home, in Philadelphia, it was Tasha who was there for Felicia. It was Tasha she called and who came running when Felicia and Mike had trouble. It was Tasha who always took her side and supported her, not necessarily against Mike, but that's how he read it: If Tasha was supporting Felicia, then she was against him. What he never really understood was our girls would have supported each other against Jesus Christ, and that's the truth, Lieutenant. Tasha didn't like or dislike Mike, she just adored her baby sister and the feeling was mutual."

Gianna eyed them closely. Something was wrong. She still wasn't getting the entire story. "Did Mike ever threaten Tasha in any way, verbally or physically?"

Both Hilliards hung their heads. Gianna waited. Christine finally looked up. "Most of the time his abuse was verbal, quoting from the Koran about the duties of wives, and spewing hatred about the evils of homosexuality and the penalties for offending God. But he started to get worse after the divorce. Felicia was living with Tasha while she finished her masters and Mike would come around, begging her to return, cursing her when she refused. One Saturday night Tasha was having a party. Nothing elegant, just a group of her friends. They were listening to music in one room and dancing, watching movies in another, popping corn. Casual."

"Were these professional friends, University friends?" Gianna asked, knowing the answer but needing to ask anyway.

It was Bob who answered this time. "Personal friends. All women. Felicia was there, too, laughing and enjoying herself. She knew Tasha's friends and they knew her. Mike went crazy. That night was the first time that he threatened to kill Tasha."

"The first time?"

Christine gave a weary nod. "He made so many threats after that we lost track, and we stopped paying attention to him. We'll never forgive ourselves."

"Did he kill Tasha? Did he tell you that he killed Tasha?"

"He told Felicia that he did."

"We need to talk to Felicia."

Christine Hilliard broke then, completely and totally. She screamed and beat off her husband when he tried to comfort her. "You can't! He's got her! He's got her!" The screams became wails became sobs as she dropped to the floor and curled into a ball.

Gianna processed the behavior and the words, fully understanding yet yielding to a moment of pure denial. The she got control of herself and tried to get control of Christine. She knelt down beside her. "Michael Nelson has Felicia? Against her will? He's kidnapped her?"

Christine moaned louder. Gianna jumped up and grabbed Bob and shook him. "Does Michael Nelson have Felicia?" He nodded. His head bobbed up and down like a bobble head doll on a car dashboard. "When?" Gianna asked, "and from where?"

"We think Friday, from her apartment—"

"Friday! That maniac has had your daughter since Friday and you haven't reported it? What is wrong with you people! He's taken one daughter and you give him another!"

"He said he'd kill her, too, if we told anybody!" Christine was hysterical now, pounding the floor, first with her fists, then with her head. Her husband grabbed her and held on. "He said he'd kill Felicia, then he'd go get Jill and kill her too!"

Gianna's fury propelled her out of the door. Eric and Cassie followed. It was Monday night. Felicia Hilliard had been gone for seventy-two hours, abducted from her Philadelphia apartment by a man arrested in Washington, D.C. just a few hours earlier. So where was Felicia? Still in Philly? In D.C.? Stashed in one of the hundreds of motels on the highways and toll roads between the two? Or dead like her sister?

Gianna had taken the stairs, two at a time, up to her private office. One hand held the phone to her ear, the other held her head. Her conversation was hurried and intense. Then she listened for what seemed like a long time, nodded, and ended the call. After a moment, she released her head and turned around. Eric and Cassie were there, waiting. "Special Ops and Hostage Negotiation are on their way here. We'll hand off to them."

Eric took a breath. "We're just going to turn it over to them?"

"They know better than we do how to find a girl who's been missing for three days. Anyway, our part in this is over. Michael Nelson killed Natasha Hillard."

"They'll just give it to the Feds," Cassie said, "and we all know they can't find their own asses with their own hands."

Gianna hadn't felt so dispirited since attacks on Mimi a couple of years earlier. "It's procedure. You know that. We follow the rules. We don't get a choice."

"She's ours, Boss," Eric said. "Felicia's ours."

"Because Tosh is ours," Cassie said.

"Joyce Harper is ours, too," Gianna said. She felt so weary she had to hold on to the desk or she felt she'd collapse.

"And we'll get who did her," Eric said. "You know we will."

"But we can't be finished with Michael Nelson. We can't be," Cassie said.

But they were finished with Michael Nelson. The Feds had him and the Hate Crimes Unit of the D.C. Police Department would be lucky to get back him back long enough to charge him with the murder of Natasha Hilliard.

CHAPTER TEN

MURDER SUSPECT IN CUSTODY;
SECOND SISTER KIDNAPPED
  By M. Montgomery Patterson
  Staff Writer

Michael Howard Nelson, a 26-year old graduate
student at Howard University, was arrested late
yesterday and charged with the September 19
 murder of Natasha Hillard. Nelson also is suspected
of having kidnapped Hilliard's younger sister, Felicia,
who is his ex-wife. A convert to Islam, Nelson, who
also goes by the name Abdul Sharif, reportedly
believed that Natasha, a lesbian, turned Felicia against
him. He allegedly murdered and mutilated her in
retaliation. He so far has refused to disclose Felicia's
whereabouts. Because kidnapping is a Federal offense,
the FBI has assumed jurisdiction over the kidnapping
case and Nelson is being held in U.S. custody without
 bond.
    The situation creates an unusual dilemma for D.C.
Police investigators. "It allows us to close a murder
investigation," said Lt. Giovanna Maglione, head of
the Hate Crimes Unit, "but we're obviously very
concerned about Felicia Hilliard's well-being."
    Maglione refused to comment on the nature
of the evidence against Nelson, except to say that
she's "confident that he is responsible for the death
of Natasha Hilliard."
    Nelson was arrested in the lobby of this newspaper
yesterday and charged with assaulting a reporter.
Items found on his person and in his vehicle tied him
to the Hilliard murder. Ironically, at the time of
his arrest, investigators in the Hate Crimes Unit
had identified him as a "person of interest" in their
investigation of the Hilliard, but had only a
description of him and his vehicle.
    "The arresting officers followed procedure," said
Police Chief Benjamin Jefferson. "The suspect used
hate language when he attacked the reporter so the

incident was reporter to HCU, which already was looking for him. This is the kind of cooperation I expect from officers in this Department."

Hilliard was killed after leaving The Snatch, a popular night club on Lander Street in the Mid-Town district that caters to lesbians. Sources say that Nelson had stalked Hilliard in the past, and may have followed her to the club. However, because he is in Federal custody, D.C. police have no access to Nelson and cannot question him further about the Natasha Hilliard homicide.

Nelson, a native of Nashville, Tennessee, has no prior criminal record. He is a graduate student in Philosophy and has, according to friends, studied Eastern religion and philosophy in the Middle East.

MURDER SUSPECT ATTACKS REPORTER
By R.J. Jones
Staff Writer

M. Montgomery Patterson, a reporter at this newspaper, was attacked yesterday afternoon by murder suspect Michael Nelson, in the lobby of the newspaper. Nelson had asked to see Patterson, claiming to have information about the murder of Natasha Hilliard, a story that Patterson has covered.

"I went down to the lobby to meet him. He told me to stop writing about Natasha," Patterson said. "He called homosexuality an abomination. I turned to walk away from him and he hit me in the back."

Patterson says she swung her briefcase at Nelson and he hit her again. At that point, building security guards and D.C. Police officers subdued Nelson, who was forcibly carried from the building, calling for "Death to infidels" and "Death to homosexuals."

Patterson's injuries were not serious, and, according to her editors, she will not stop writing about the Hilliard story. The paper has pressed charges against Nelson for the assault on of one of its employees on its property.

"There are fifteen messages from Ray Washington," Eric said as he hung up wrote down the date and time of the most recent one. "We'll never know if anybody else tried to call us last night because Ray used up all our message minutes."

Linda walked over to where Eric was sitting and he gave her the notepad. "He said nothing about giving up any names? All those calls are about him demanding that his business be re-opened?" Linda went to her desk, snatched up the receiver, and punched in a number. "This is Officer Lopez of the Hate Crimes Unit...no, you listen to me, Mr. Washington: The Police Department did not close your business, the Buildings and Permits Department did and that's who you should be calling. You only call us if you have information regarding the rape of Joyce Harper, and we'd appreciate your assistance in that matter. Thank you and have a good day."

Linda slammed the receiver into the cradle so hard that it bounced back out and skittered across the desk, the cord preventing it from landing on the floor. Tim retrieved the phone then wrapped Linda in a big, quick hug.

Cassie took Linda by the arms, guided her to her desk, sat her down, lifted the top off her cup of coffee and gave her the cup. "Drink, *mi hermana*. The caffeine'll calm you down, chill you out."

Bobby laughed. "Nobody but you, Cassandra, would give somebody a shot of caffeine to calm their nerves. Any more stimulation and Lopez'll go over to Lander Street and shoot the son of a bitch."

"I'll drive," Kenny said. "The least I can do for such a good cause. Let me know when you're ready to leave, Linda."

"I'll ride shotgun," Alice said, opening her own coffee and propping her long legs up on the corner of the desk.

Linda sipped her coffee. "Thanks, guys." Then she looked over at Gianna, seated behind her desk, watching, listening, not participating, as she often did, freeing them up to think and express freely. "Only reason I don't go shoot his ass, Boss, is it would get you in trouble."

"Hell, Linda, I haven't been in any trouble lately—"

The hoots and guffaws broke the tension. They all relaxed.
Gianna got up and began to pace, a good sign for her; it meant that she was ready to be back in action. "You think he lied to you about the men he was talking to the night Joyce was raped?"

"He did lie, the son of a bitch! Nobody by those names lived at any of the addresses he gave up, none of the other regulars ever heard of these guys, and we can't seem to get a good grip on Washington himself. All of his background checks are...what's that word you like, Bobby, the one that means not quite right?"

"Hinctey?"

"That's the one. Washington's background checks come up hinctey."
Kenny was rustling through his files and folders, ready to answer the
question the Boss was about to ask. She nodded at him. "The name on his
business license is Raymond Lee Washington. The name on his driver's
license is Ray L. Washington, Jr., DOB 25 March 1978. The name on his tax
return is Raymond L. Washington, DOB 20 September 1948. The home
address he gave us, the one on the drivers license, is on Harris Boulevard,
across the River in Anacostia, but the phone number he uses, the one Linda
just called, is a Northeast exchange, over in Brookland, and it's not a cell
phone. We haven't had a chance to check that address yet, Boss."

Gianna looked from Linda to Bobby. Linda answered the question. "The
man we know as Ray Washington looks a lot closer to the 1978 DOB than
the 1948 one."

"I've got a question." Bobby said. "Does somebody have to be gay to own
a gay bar?"

Tim fell into his Queen Routine. "Not if you're thinking of changing
professions, Big Boy."

Bobby actually blushed. "I've gotta learn to stop giving you these
openings—" He realized what he'd said and threw his hands up in surrender.
Linda came to his rescue.

"What Officer Gilliam keeps trying to convey is the fact that we don't
think that Ray Washington is gay. Not that he'd have to be to own a gay
bar—"

"But it sure would help," Cassie said. "What makes you think he's not?"

"No gay vibe," Kenny said.

"There's a such thing as a gay vibe?" Cassie's question was a challenge.
Kenny and Linda both looked sideways at Tim.

"Whatever do you mean to suggest?" he lisped.

Gianna got them under control, though not too tightly. She needed the
release as much as they did. The events of the previous evening had wrung
them all dry, especially the not knowing the fate of Felicia Hilliard, and not
being able to do a damn thing about it. Michael Nelson had sent for an Imam
and a minister and had refused to utter another word. Nothing they could do
about that: The man had a right not to talk, but every one of them wished
they'd pushed forward on second interviews much sooner than they had.
Especially Gianna.

"Tim notwithstanding, are you saying you can tell somebody's gay by
looking at him?" Gianna asked, making eye contact with each of them.

Alice answered before Kenny or Linda could. "I know what they're saying,
Lieutenant, and I agree with them. Bartenders, straight or gay, they establish
a rapport with their customers, whether they're first timers or regulars. This
Ray Washington guy, he just serves drinks. He's polite enough, but there's
no rapport, no connection to the people buying the drinks."

"How would you describe him, Alice?" Gianna asked.

She thought for a second. "Watchful. And careful."

"Pull all the paper on Washington, on the bar— who owns the building, by the way? Him?"

Linda shook her head. "A corporation."

"Find out who the corporation is, who the principals are. Run Washington through every system available. We have his tax returns so that means we have his Social. I want to know everything about this guy, down to the brands of toothpaste and deodorant he uses. And if there are two Ray Washingtons I want the same info on both, and if the son is fronting for the father, I want to know why. And folks? I want to know today. Pull out every stop, take short cuts, be demanding, be polite, kiss ass, kick ass— I don't care what you have to do. I don't want to be surprised or blindsided by this character."

"We're going to need you to input your WASIS access code," Eric said. The Washington Area Shared Information System or WASIS was a computerized data bank of information on crime and criminals that combined the law enforcement efforts of every agency in Metropolitan D.C., and there were lots of them. The system contained details from every report submitted during the investigation of every crime in D.C. and the Maryland and Virginia suburbs, details being the operative word: names, addresses, phone numbers, license plate numbers, driver's license numbers, and birth dates of every person charged with a crime, every victim of a crime, every person interviewed during the course of an investigation, and information on any other crimes a suspect was connected. Because the information was so invasive, a certain level of authority was required to access it. There were ten levels of authority. Gianna had eight levels of clearance. Whoever Ray Washington was, if he was suspect of pissing in the shrubbery in the D.C. metropolitan area, they'd find out about it.

"Anything else?" Gianna asked, when she finished inputting her code in the computer.

"There is one thing bothering me, Lieutenant."

Gianna looked directly at Alice. If there was something bothering her Gianna wanted to know about it. Alice was a seasoned cop, with experience on several details and extensive undercover placement.

"There's this one guy who hangs out in the Pink Panther, something about him is too familiar. Not like he's a perp I've made before, and it's not just that I think he's straight, which I do. It's that he feels, well, like a cop."

Kenny swiveled away from his computer and toward Alice so fast that his chair rolled halfway across the room. Gianna was still looking at Alice, who was so still she looked frozen. That was a hell of a thing for one cop to say about another one. Then Bobby jumped to his feet and was stalking up and down the room shaking a fist. Now all eyes were on him instead of on Alice. He was pointing a finger— jabbing the air with it— as if making a point. He finally got to it. "Yes!" he said, pumping the air with his fist. "Yes! That makes sense, Boss. It finally makes sense."

"Bobby, I have no idea what you're talking about. Relax and take it from the top." To help him calm down, Gianna sat at her desk, leaned forward, and folded her hands, waiting.

"That night we were at The Snatch, the first night. Miss Phillips— Darlene— described two cars that had cruised by threatening them. When we were cruising the block, Tim and me, we saw one of those cars and we scoped 'em out pretty good. One of 'em looked familiar to me, just like what Alice was saying: Not familiar like I'd busted him but familiar like...what she just said...that's it! I was at the Academy with that dude! He's a cop and if I look at my class photo I can tell you his name."

Gianna got up. She wasn't liking this at all. Alice and Bobby were as different externally as two people could be: She cool, calm and collected, he excitable and mercurial; but internally they were serious, dedicated cops who didn't make the kind of mistake this would be if they were wrong. But if they were right...

"And another thing, Boss," Bobby said. He was cracking his knuckles and both Gianna and Alice winced. He stopped. "As I'm thinking about this cop angle, the way Ray Washington's been treating us? We've thinking it was cop-hating hostility, right, Linda? But it's not! It's familiar, you know? Street punks don't talk to us the way this guy does. They know we'll feed 'em their fuckin' teeth, but this Washington character, he's not scared of us! He talks trash to us like he talks trash to cops all the time. Does that make sense?"

Gianna understood what he meant but it didn't make a damn bit of sense. "Get his name, Bobby, and find out if he's still on the job and where he's assigned. I'll check with Inspector Davis and make sure your guy isn't one of his. Alice—"

"He's not, Lieutenant. I made Mid-Town's undercovers and we've been checking out each other. No, this guy I'm talking about is in with Ray Washington."

Gianna didn't like the sound of this at all. She looked at her watch and slipped her jacket on. "I'm out of here for a couple of hours but I'll be close at hand if you need me, phone and beeper both on." She started for the door, then turned back. "Make sure we know where Mr. Washington is at all times, in case we need to... talk to him."

And she was out the door, glad for the time alone even though it would be short-lived. Lunch with Mimi, Baby Doll and Terry at the Chinese restaurant across the street from the paper. She didn't really have time for lunch but she needed to eat, she needed to see Mimi, and she really wanted to know what Terry had to tell her.

The restaurant wasn't that far from police headquarters in terms of miles, but downtown traffic could make it feel like the other side of the world. That's why they'd set the meet for the end of the lunch rush, so traffic wouldn't be too terrible and the place wouldn't be too crowded. She put her police ID in the windshield and parked in front of the place so she could leave quickly if that became necessary. Too bad she couldn't plan and arrange cases to work out so conveniently.

She was the last to arrive. The big dining room was full and waiters still served food, but the kitchen was closed to orders. Gianna could see all the cooks, seated at tables in the far back corner, having their own meals. And she spied Mimi's head full of curly ringlets in one of the semi-private alcoves. She surprised Baby with a hug and a comment on how good she looked, and Baby loved every second of it. Mimi, on the other hand, didn't look so good. An ugly bruise colored one side of her face, she held herself stiffly, and her eyes were dull, reflecting the pain she was in. Gianna wanted to hold her. That wasn't possible. She sat down in the booth next to her, touched her arm gently. "You should be home in bed."

Before Mimi could respond, their waiter arrived with a platter of steamed dumplings. Gianna's stomach rumbled. Not only did she need to eat, she was ravenous, unable to remember whether she'd eaten a meal yesterday.

"I ordered orange chicken for you," Mimi said.

"And what else?" Gianna helped herself to two dumplings.

"You can share my moo shu vegetables."

"I thought you said I could share that?" Baby almost whined.

"There's more than enough. Anyway Miss Jefferson, didn't you tell me you wouldn't eat anything that looked like that?"

"A girl can change her mind, you know." Baby dipped a dumpling into sauce, took a bite, smiled broadly as she chewed, and nodded her head appreciatively.

"Since you like those, we'll have pot stickers next time," Mimi said, and watched for Baby's face to wrinkle in displeasure. It did, but she smoothed out the wrinkles almost immediately. She was learning.

"It's really nice that Marlene has friends like you all," Terry said, trying for a smile. But her face wouldn't cooperate; a look of misery overtook her so quickly that she had to put her fork down. She clearly need to say what she'd come to say, to get the weight of it off her mind.

"What is it, Terry?" Gianna asked, her direct, calming gaze working its magic.

"I overheard these people...I think they know who raped Joyce Harper. I heard these dudes talking, right? They didn't know I was listening. I was hiding, tell you the truth." She looked around to make certain nobody was listening to her. She was breathing heavily. Her hands, resting on the table top, clenched into fists. "One of 'em doing the talking, he's a cop. Works out of Mid-Town."

Mimi and Gianna were shocked speechless. Marlene and Terry were frozen in fear: Suppose they'd made a big mistake in trusting a cop. They waited for Gianna to say something while Gianna waited for her brain to clear. Mimi knew better than to say anything—this wasn't her show—but the silence couldn't stretch much further without breaking something. The deus ex machina was the arrival of the waiter with the serving cart. He took the empty dumpling platter and loaded the table with heaping, steaming ones of chicken, vegetables, rice, fish. He refilled their water glasses, gave them a fresh pot of tea—Marlene had emptied the first one by herself—bowed, and left. By then, Gianna was ready to talk.

"Thank you, Terry. We need this help, and we appreciate it, and I promise you we'll try to develop a case without the need to bring you into it."

Terry's relief was so intense they all sensed it. She obviously very much wanted to do the right thing but no way did she want to be out in front of any action that could bring shit to her door, and anything that involved a dirty cop brought shit with it. "I appreciate that, Lieutenant. I want to help. If I can."

"You already have," Gianna said, and hesitated, forming her next words carefully. "I don't want to go into too much detail in a public place, but where did you overhear the conversation, and how do you know one of the men is a police officer?"

"'Cause he used to come around there in uniform, in the police car, with this other cop, a white dude, always preaching about how homosexuality is against God and how we're all going to hell and how he wasn't going to protect us no matter what the law said. God's law was the only law that mattered to him."

Mimi made a sudden movement, then groaned in pain. Gianna turned to her, concerned, but Mimi waved her off and Gianna turned back to Terry. "Come around where, Terry? Where did this happen?"

"At the Pink Panther, in the back room."

Gianna tensed. "What back room?" There was nothing in any of the reports about a back room at the Pink Panther.

Terry gave a sideways grin and the kind of head shake that suggests a feeling of pity. "That bastard thinks he's so cool. You get back there through the toilets. He has to tell you how to do it, and he doesn't tell everybody. It's supposed to make you feel special." She spat the word out.

"Ray Washington?"

Terry nodded, then looked at Baby. "Tell them, Marlene. You said we both could trust them, so you have to tell your part, too."

Baby looked like she'd rather eat worms than tell her part. "I know him from when I...from before, you know? He used to have a place off Columbia Road." She looked directly at Mimi. "You dropped me off there one night, remember? That night when I saw—"

"I remember," Mimi said quickly to spare the girl from the weight and pain of dredging up any more of her ugly past than was absolutely necessary. "That was the night you first maligned my old car."

Baby gave her a high wattage smile of gratitude and got on with her story. "He wasn't nothing but a pimp calling himself having a bar. But that's how you got to the trick rooms, through the bathrooms. Police tried lots of times to bust him 'cause they knew he was up to shit but they couldn't ever find anything."

Baby enjoyed that memory briefly, then continued with her story: When crack and AIDS and a serial killer negatively impacted the number of women on the street, she said, Washington just changed locations and his customer base but kept the same business. "Boys turn just as many tricks as girls and those DL's are so paranoid about somebody catching on to 'em, they keep that back room real busy."

"So the back of the Pink Panther is a brothel?"

"Not totally," Terry said. "There's a pool table and some pinball machines back there, and a slot machine he stole from one of the casinos on the Eastern Shore. That stuff's in the main room. The private rooms are back behind this main room."

"Will you come with me, both of you, to give statements? Nobody will know who you are and you won't have to see or talk to anyone but my people. You know who they are, you've met them, you know you can trust them."

"I won't talk to anybody but you," Terry declared.

Gianna nodded assent and looked at Baby. "Marlene?"

She looked from Gianna to Terry and back to Gianna and nodded. "I'll talk to whoever, I just can't miss no more work. I took today off to be here with Terry, so can we do it now?"

"After we eat," Gianna said, piling orange chicken on her plate.

Marlene Jefferson and Terry Carson spent the remainder of the afternoon and into the evening behind the closed and locked doors of the Think Tank. There was an initially tense but ultimately amusing moment when Terry spied Alice, whom she recognized from the Pink Panther. When she finally understood that Alice was working undercover, she had a good laugh. "I knew you didn't belong in that place," Terry said.

"I thought the same thing about you," Alice said, and Terry sobered and saddened and it took a few moments to get her back into the moment. Once back, though, she delivered.

Terry's memory of events was sharp and clear, her descriptions of people detailed, her speculations and opinions, when requested, well-founded and logical. She'd been a regular at the Pink Panther for the past year, almost always on the nights she worked the late shift because she liked to wind down after work and she didn't want to disturb Marlene, who had to rise early to be at her own job by seven o'clock. Terry's pattern was to sit at the bar and have one beer, then take a second one to the back and play the pinball machines for about an hour, then head for home. Yes, she said, she did this every week. No, Ray Washington didn't treat her any better or worse than any other customer, aside from giving her access to the back room. If she stopped frequenting the bar he wouldn't care, wouldn't ask if she were ill, wouldn't know whom to ask, probably didn't even know her name. The only people who interested him were the men who rented his back rooms by the hour, and his cop friends.

"Well," Linda said after Marlene and Terry were gone, "we knew there was something hinctey about Mr. Washington, but wow!"

"No shit, Sherlock," Cassie said.

"How do we handle this, Boss?" Eric asked.

"Use what we know to leverage information about Joyce Harper's rape, then turn the whole thing over to IAD and Vice," Gianna said.

"You gonna cut Washington a deal?" Kenny asked, frowning slightly. Gianna shook her head. "Lawyers make deals with criminals, we don't. We tell him what we know about him and his operation— what we can prove— we tell him what we want to know about who raped Joyce Harper, we tell him how much better it will be for him to cooperate, then his lawyer gets to play Let's Make a Deal with the government's lawyers. Now. About these low-life cops."

The thought sickened her. A dirty cop was bad enough— a cop on the take, a rogue cop stealing from the drug dealers, a vigilante cop dispensing his own brand of justice— but cops withholding protection from victims and leaving the door open for rape and murder...that was much too much. She considered, then rejected, the idea of talking to the Chief or to Inspector Davis before taking action against Ray Washington. If these cops were that bad she didn't want to leave them in place another day. If she could take them down today, tomorrow, that's what she'd do, and let the chips fall where they fell. After all, it wouldn't be her job to clean up the mess. But she was still smarting from losing Mike Nelson to the Feds. She wasn't about to lose Ray Washington to the Internal Affairs spooks, in many ways, worse than the Feebies.

Bobby had supplied the name of his former Training Academy classmate, Roger Holcomb, and the information that he indeed was assigned to Mid-Town. Alice had learned from the Mid-Town undercovers that the cop she'd seen at the Pink Panther, the one she thought was Ray Washington's friend, was named Thomas Murphy. He'd spied the undercovers coming in the door two nights ago and jumped off his bar stool and headed for the bathroom so fast that Washington was still talking to him after he'd gone. The undercovers had gotten a glimpse of him, though, enough to ID him, and she, in turn, had told the undercovers that they'd been made. Fortunately, it no longer mattered.

Roger Holcomb and Thomas Murphy. How many more were there, Gianna wondered, because if there were two, she was certain that there were more. What about Ferrell, the young Mid-Town Command cop who'd called her a dyke? Some situation, some set of circumstances must exist to allow him to feel comfortable enough to challenge her like that. That argued for telling the Chief first and letting him deal with it, or for telling Eddie Davis about the snakes crawling around in the grass in his field. No. She'd made her decision. She'd tell them after the fact. After Ray Washington was arrested and charged.

Her cell phone rang. She flipped it open and frowned at the caller identification info on the screen. Who would be calling her from George Washington University Hospital?

She put the phone to her ear. "Yes?" Then, "Don't let them do anything until I get there. Fifteen minutes."

She snapped the phone shut and looked at her team, all of whom were looking at her. "Miss Patterson— Mimi— apparently sustained a couple of cracked ribs and a possible concussion in the assault yesterday. She's at GW ER."

"I'll drive you," Cassie said, grabbing her briefcase and coat.

"I've got everything covered here, Boss," Eric said, "and Cassie can keep the lines open between us. You go."

And she left, for a moment feeling more grateful than worried; grateful that the people who worked for her cared about her life, grateful that she'd learned to trust them enough to let them care. Cassie drove so that Gianna could think about what Mimi had said and not about how she had sounded, because if she focused on that, she might start to unravel, for Mimi had barely been able to speak, so intense was the pain. Apparently a rib was poking something somewhere, and the pain was excruciating. She also was dizzy and beginning to sound incoherent. Thank goodness she'd called Beverly when she did, otherwise...no, don't go there. No need. Mimi had recognized that she was in trouble and she had called her best friend and she was at the hospital about to go into surgery, and she would be fine.

She'd told Mimi fifteen minutes but with lights and siren activated, Cassie made it in twelve. She pulled into the Emergency Room portico. "I'll park and find you inside," Cassie said.

Gianna rushed inside. She'd been in every emergency room in town during the course of her career and they all looked, felt and smelled pretty much the same, though renovations here at GW certainly improved the look of the place, and she imagined that changes in the way medical care was delivered these days accounted for the fact that the place wasn't overrun with the destitute and the indigent. No longer was patient care the first mission of the medical establishment. Securing a signature on the insurance form was. She walked directly to the intake desk then spied Beverly Connors, who saw her at the same time. She and her lover, Sylvia, rushed toward Gianna.

"God, I'm glad you're here," Bev said, hugging her tightly. "Of course they won't let us in or tell us anything."

"Why not?"

"We're not family," Sylvia said.

"Come on," Bev said, pulling Gianna toward the desk. "She wants to see you before they take her to surgery. She's got something crucial to tell you.

Her words, not mine," Bev hastened to add when she saw the look on Gianna's face.

"I need to see Marilyn Patterson," Gianna told the nurse at the desk.

"Are you a family member?" the nurse asked, not looking up from the chart she was writing in.

"I'm Lieutenant Maglione, Metropolitan Police Department," Gianna said, holding up her gold shield. The nurse raised her eyes long enough to get a good look. "Now where is Miss Patterson?"

The nurse sighed, got up, quick-stepped down a short hallway and swished through a curtain into a room full of beds, all of which were surrounded by the accouterments of modern day emergency medicine. Mimi was in one of the beds, hooked up to an intravenous line of some sort, and a heart monitor. Her eyes were closed and she looked small and frail. She wore a hospital gown, pale green with some kind of design pattern on it. The plastic identification strip encircled her wrist. Her too-long hair spread out over the pillow, its dark, mahogany color in stark contrast against the institutional white. Her breathing was shallow. Gianna reached out to touch her but couldn't. She felt paralyzed. Mimi must have sensed her presence because she opened her eyes and smiled. It was a weak smile, one that held pain dulled by the administration of narcotics, but it still was Mimi's smile. The one that always welcomed Gianna.

"You really came. You're really here."

"Of course I did. This is where I belong." Gianna leaned over the railing and kissed her forehead, smoothing back her hair. "You know that haircut you were going to get last week? And the week before?" Gianna whispered the words through tears that choked the back of her throat.

"You can't nag me, I'm sick. Besides, I've got something to tell you before I can't." And that would be soon; already her words were dragging and slurring.

Gianna leaned in closer, holding Mimi's hands in her own as she listened, understanding dawning about why Mimi's focus had been on O'Connell. He was worse than a dirty cop, he was a dangerous one. Mimi knew she had just the tip of the iceberg, just like Gianna did with Holcomb and Murphy, but it was clear that the problem was large and pervasive. She gave Gianna the passwords to her computers— the one at the paper, the one at home, and her laptop— and the codes she'd used to hide all the different files. And she told her where the cassettes and computer diskettes were, locked in her desk at home, and where to find the key. Gianna wrote it all down as Mimi instructed.

"You can do this yourself tomorrow, you know," Gianna told her.

"Just in case I can't," Mimi mumbled. Her eyes fluttered as she struggled to keep them open, to keep her brain functioning.

"You will," Gianna said, resting her face on Mimi's, on the side that had turned ugly shades of green and purple where Michael Nelson had hit her.

"I told them, at the admitting desk, that you're my domestic partner. It's on the form, so they have to tell you everything—"

"You'll have to leave now, Lieutenant." Two nurses and a doctor had appeared at the foot of Mimi's bed. "We've got to get her into surgery." The medical personnel moved in, clearly accustomed to being in charge, to getting their way, to having civilians move out of that way. Gianna stepped away from the bed.

"Is that safe? I thought she had a concussion."

"She's also got a piece of a rib poking into the side of her chest wall. We've got to put it back where it belongs before it pokes into something more dangerous," said the doctor, a young Asian woman with spiky hair, three earrings, all in the same ear, and a killer smile. "She's in no danger," the doctor said. "As long as we get that rib put back in place," she added. Gianna peered at her name tag: Ellen Chang, MD. She was about to ask another question when the two nurses, both Black women roughly her own age, started to push the bed, with Mimi in it, past her. The doctor followed. Gianna reached out to touch Mimi, touched hair, and watched the procession leave her standing there. "How long?" she called out.

Dr. Chang turned back but didn't stop walking. "If all goes well, she should be in recovery in a couple of hours."

"All better go well," Gianna muttered to herself, and returned to the waiting room. Cassie, Beverly and Sylvia were sitting together and she joined them, told them what she knew. She was about to sit down when Bev jumped up, grabbed her arm, and dragged her to the opposite side of the room.

"That business with the badge, Gianna, what was that all about?" Beverly was a therapist, the no-nonsense kind, the kind who took charge, not one of those who tiptoed all around issues and problems.

"I had to get in to see Mimi. That always does the trick."

"So does being the registered domestic partner of the patient do the trick," Beverly said, and waited. When Gianna had no response, Bev lit into her. "You two are unbelievable. You're ridiculous. This is insane. Neither of you has family here and even if you did, would you want Mimi's father or her brother making decisions about her life? And suppose something happened to you? Mimi doesn't have a badge to flash to get in to see you. Come on, Gianna! If you two are going to be together, then be together. You don't flash your badge to get in to see her, she's not a perp, she's your next of kin." Bev looked at her watch. "I've got to go, I've got late call at the clinic tonight, but Sylvia will be at home. Call us when you know something." She gave Gianna a hug and a kiss and left her standing beneath a wall-mounted television tuned to ESPN and a football game. She hugged Cassie, took Sylvia's hand, waved good-bye, and they were gone.

Cassie hurried over to her. "Everything OK, Boss?"

"They're taking her to surgery. You don't have to sit here, Cassie, though I appreciate it," Gianna said quickly when she saw Cassie's face about to change.

"I don't mind," Cassie said. "Besides, we can always work."

Work. Gianna actually had forgotten it for a few, brief minutes, and being reminded of what was hanging over her mind suddenly made her so tired she needed to sit down. Cassie had taken out her laptop and was pulling up the Hilliard and Brown case files. She gave Gianna the stack of Michael Nelson's diaries and notebooks. "You said you wanted to do these yourself."

"I do. Thanks." But first. She took out her cell phone. Cassie pointed to a sign on the wall prohibiting the use of cellular phones inside the hospital. "I'll be right back," she said, and headed for the door.

Outside felt good. It finally was cooler in D.C., summer fading into memory. She called Eric, told him what was happening, and told him to send everybody home for a good night's sleep and an eight a.m. report time. She started to call Mimi's father and brother but decided to wait until had something definitive to tell them. Until then, she'd sit in the waiting room with Cassie, trying not to think about what was going on in an operating theater somewhere inside the hospital, and trying, instead to understand what was going on in Michael Nelson's mind.

It felt funny being in Mimi's house without her, but it would have been even stranger being in her own home knowing that Mimi's house was empty, not because she was out of town, but across town in the hospital. She'd be home in twenty-four hours, Dr. Chang said, with her ribs tightly taped and very sore, woozy from the drugs, and on complete bed rest for another forty-eight hours. Gianna hoped they planned on sending enough drugs to keep her woozy, otherwise keeping her in bed for two days would be a real challenge. Especially since sex was out of the question.

Gianna turned on the lights in the living room, in the kitchen, in the bedroom, so the place would look like it looked when Mimi was here. She lit one of the presto logs in the fire place and a stick of Mimi's favorite incense, and she turned on the CD player and pushed the play button. She'd listen to whatever Mimi had listened to last, and have a glass of wine while she fixed something to eat and tried to calm her body and her mind. She was relieved that Mimi's surgery had gone well and that Mimi was, in hospital parlance, resting comfortably, though the truth was, she was too drugged for anyone to know whether or not she was comfortable. She'd made all the necessary phone calls— to Mimi's family, to her own mother, to Bev and Sylvia, to Freddie and Cedric, to Eric, who, along with Cassie, would inform the others. The refrigerator was a treasure trove of goodies and Gianna was surprised momentarily. Then she remembered that they were scheduled to have dinner here tonight. Scheduled. Like they were a business arrangement instead of a couple. And then she understood what was pressing so heavily on her mind and it wasn't the weight of the work she still had to do that night. It was Mimi's "You're really here, you really came." And it was Bev's "She's your next of kin." Those phrases, those words, rolled around in her head while she fixed a plate of roast chicken, Italian green beans and risotto and put it in the microwave. Mimi had found the time— and the energy— to brave the traffic of Georgetown and the always frantic pace of the Whole Foods Market to buy food Gianna liked, simply because Gianna liked it. And yet she'd been both surprised and relieved when Gianna showed up at her hospital bed. She's your next of kin.

Gianna took her plate, glass, and a half bottle of Chardonnay, to the dining room table, where Michael Nelson's writings were spread out in the order that she wanted to read them. Working notebooks first, filled with page after page of thoughts, ideas, plans, schemes, all written in the neat, orderly script more likely to be found in someone twice his age. The punctuation, grammar and spelling were those of an educated, literate man, not the usual idiotic garbage they got from crazed criminals. Then there were five year's worth of daily diaries, different from the notebooks in that they contained his thoughts and feelings about falling in love with Felicia Hilliard, courting and marrying her, and about the dissolution of their relationship. Here also were his thoughts and feelings about Natasha Hilliard. She read long after she'd finished the food and wine, long after the CD player had stopped, until the five-hour fake wood log crumbled into dying embers.

She made a chicken sandwich to take to work, cleaned the kitchen, and went upstairs to bed. Four or five hours' sleep would be better than none, she told herself, knowing it not to be true given her recent lack of sleep. She needed to sleep for ten or twelve hours, free of even the thought that a phone could ring, to say nothing of the possibility of such a thing. Well...soon, perhaps. For now, four or five hours would have to suffice. Maybe the phone wouldn't ring. The team meeting wasn't until eight.

There was enough coffee, muffins, Danish and doughnuts to satiate a work crew twice as large at the HCU because everybody had brought goodies, but it was Cassie's offering that captured their attention that morning. She'd stopped at Ma's Kitchen, the restaurant owned by the Phillips sisters and their family, and bought cheese and egg sandwiches for everybody. Gianna added a couple of gallons of orange juice and blood sugar, along with energy levels, soared. They talked while they ate. Instead of going home last night as Gianna directed, they'd all remained late and sifted through every file, every report, every bit and piece of evidence, and weren't surprised that Gianna had done the same thing with Nelson's papers. The surprise came when she told them what she'd found, and ordered the immediate arrest of the Ray Washingtons, both Jr. and Sr. While she was explaining why, Detective Schuster from Downtown Command arrived with the latest information on

Michael Nelson: He was on a seventy-two hour psychiatric hold at Howard University Hospital after trying to hang himself in his cell.

"That's what happens when you turn your cases over to the Feds," said Bobby said, disgust dripping off the words.

"Wasn't he under observation?" Gianna asked, feeling every bit as disgusted as Bobby sounded.

Schuster shrugged. "They say so."

"Don't let that son of bitch off himself until they find Felicia Hilliard," Eric snarled.

"I wish it was under our control," Schuster said, "but you know how the Feds operate. We wouldn't have known about the suicide attempt except we've got good contacts over at Howard Hopsital."

"Is there any word at all on the search for Felicia Hilliard?" Gianna asked.

Schuster shook his head. "Nada. My boss even called over there herself and they wouldn't tell her anything."

"And I suppose they're telling the parents even less?"

Before Schuster could answer, Eric jumped to his feet, waving the report Schuster had brought. "Look at this! You won't believe this shit!" They all crowded around him, Schuster included. He'd typed the report and obviously didn't remember anything in it worth jumping up and down about. But then, he didn't know what the Hate Crimes team knew: That the Reverend Doctor Ray L. Washington, who was listed as a spiritual advisor to Michael Nelson, was, at that moment, the subject of an arrest warrant.

"I gotta call my boss." Schuster sprinted for a phone and was dialing before he caught himself. "I'm sorry. Is it all right?"

Gianna waved off the apology. She was making her own phone call, to the Chief, to ask him to expedite getting the warrants for the Washingtons signed, and explaining to him why. And after that was taken care of, he demanded to know why she hadn't called him last night.

She didn't know what he was talking about. "Sir? Call you last night why?"

"Why!" he thundered. "I shouldn't have to read about it in the newspaper like every other Joe in town, Maglione!" Then his voice changed, softened. "Don't you think I'd have wanted to know?"

He of course was talking about Mimi. There must have been a story about her emergency surgery in the paper. "I'm sorry, Chief. She's doing well...may I call you later?"

His answer was a dial tone. She'd indeed call him later. In the meantime, there were arrests to be made. Schuster's boss, Shirley McManus, wanted a piece of it since Junior lived in her Command, and Gianna was only too happy to oblige; she could use the extra manpower as well as the relatively new facilities at Downtown Command, a four-cell lock-up and fully equipped interrogation rooms. Bobby, Linda, Tim and three of McManus's people headed over to Washington, Junior's Brookland apartment, while Kenny, Cassie, Alice, Schuster and two of McManus's people headed across the Anacostia River to sit on Reverend Doctor Washington. Eric and Cassie went to pick up the warrants and Gianna went to Downtown Command to wait, and to explain to Captain McManus why so many bodies were needed to arrest two men who had no reputation for violence. On the drive downtown, Gianna worked to come up with language that would convey the possibility that the Washington's might be the beneficiaries of the protection of the certain police officers without actually calling any cops dirty. She needn't have worried her brain.

"I've heard about them, Anna," Shirley McManus told her. "I think I've even got a couple of 'em in my Command. Arrogant, evil little pricks. One of 'em called me a dyke once. Thought he'd spoken low enough under his breath that I didn't hear him. When I got done wiping the floor with his ass he was ready to believe that his mother was a dyke."

Gianna couldn't believe what she was hearing. Shirley McManus looked like the grandmother she was: Maybe five-foot-five with a head full of untamable blond-going-to-silver hair. She had sparkly blue eyes surrounded by crinkly laugh lines, and with good reason: She laughed a lot, and when she wasn't laughing she was talking, still sounding like the Brooklyn she'd left as a teenager. She had the figure of a woman half her fifty-two years, and that figure and her personality had won her a legendary reputation as an undercover in her youth. These days she had a reputation as a crack administrator with her chief weapon being her mouth.

"You actually hit him?"

"Damn straight I hit him. Round house right to the jaw. He went down hard, got up quick and aimed one at me, but he's about a foot taller than I am so I went under his swing and caught him in the gut. Little bastard had the nerve to try to bring charges against me. When I got finished with him he was lucky to still have his badge."

"And he's still here in your house?"

Shirley gave an evil grin. "He keeps trying to transfer. I keep blocking him. He wants to go to Mid-Town in the worst way." She gave Gianna a steady, appraising look when she said that, and waited.

"I'm sure Inspector Davis'll be happy to have him," Gianna deadpanned.

Captain McManus was still chuckling when she led Gianna down the stairs to the cells and the interrogation rooms. She'd brought a telephone, which she plugged into the wall in one of the rooms. "I've got some stuff to finish up but I'll come down when they bring your perps in. I want to watch."

Gianna's first call was to the hospital. She talked to a still groggy Mimi who was feeling well enough to complain about having been awakened "at some truly ungodly hour to have my temperature taken," and about the doctor's intention "for me to get up and walk. I can barely breathe and she wants me to get up and walk."

Gianna felt so much better after the call that she actually found that her head was clear, that ordering her thoughts wasn't a struggle. She got out her notebook and began strategizing the interrogations of the Washingtons. Junior's warrant charged him with suspicion of rape, Senior's with conspiracy to commit murder. Her hope was that she could leverage information about Felicia Hilliard out of the elder Washington and information about Joyce Harper's rape out of Junior. It was heavy-handed and it was a gamble but it was all they had. She wished she had some statistics from Atlantic City on how often a good poker face won the pot, no matter what cards were in the hand.

Ray Junior strode into the interrogation room huffing and puffing and demanding a lawyer. He was wearing sweat pants, a tee shirt, a pair of expensive high top sneakers, and he looked ready for action of some kind. He refused to sit down, refused even to look at Gianna. He called Linda a Spic and Bobby an Uncle Tom. (And Gianna had thought she was old school.) Then Alice Long walked into the room, wearing a black suit and a white silk tee shirt, every article of clothing fitting her body as if painted on. The high heeled boots made her seem longer and taller than usual. Ray took one look at her and collapsed into his chair. Before they could ask the first question he was giving up information. Eric stopped him, switched on the recorder, Mirandized him, made him say that he understood the warning, then stood back and let him talk. He couldn't keep his eyes off Alice.

"Murph said there was something off about you." He said that three times, his eyes boring into her. "A cop." He shook his head, then rested it in his hands. "I should've let him have at you."

"What did you say?" Eric leaned over him. "Sit up, Mr. Washington, and repeat what you just said." Washington didn't move. Eric slapped at his hands and they fell away from his face. Washington was still looking at Alice. "What did you just say?" Eric repeated, and Washington slowly turned his gaze to Eric.

"Murph wanted to take her but I wouldn't let him."

"Take her. You mean rape her?"

Washington nodded. "I wouldn't let him. That other one— that never should 'a happened."

"Thomas Murphy raped Joyce Harper?"

"His buddies did."

Alice walked over close to him and he devoured her with his eyes, licking his lips. "Who are his buddies? What are their names?" Alice was killing him with her eyes and biting her lips to keep from killing him where he sat with her bare hands.

He ogled Alice the whole time he was giving up Patrol Officer Thomas Murphy and his three friends: Roger Holcomb, Slim Jim Johnson, and "some guy with a Wop name I can't pronounce. Dee-Chechy-something. Vinnie's his first name." He shook his head at Alice again. "I still can't believe you're a cop, and I know you're not a dyke. I told Murph you were no dyke but he didn't believe me. He's not gonna believe you're a cop, either."

"Just goes to show you how stupid Murph is," Alice drawled. She turned away from him, the effort to keep her face under control visible to everyone. She took a deep breath then turned back toward him. "How much was Murphy getting off the back room, Ray?"

Ray Washington's eyes bugged and his mouth dropped open. He couldn't speak. Alice crossed her arms over her chest and stood looking at him, waiting for an answer to her question. He finally got his mouth and his brain on the same page. "How do you know about that?"

"Same way we know about the club you used to have up on Columbia Road. Same way we know everything about you. See, the cops we hang out with aren't stupid like your pal Murph. Whatever you were giving him, it was too much."

"Five hundred a week," Washington mumbled. "That's what he was getting from me. I don't know how much he was getting on the side."

Eric moved to stand beside Alice. "What's on the side, Ray?"

Washington shook his head. They thought he was done talking, but then he threw his head back and let go a scream. It was primal and it was a major release of something that he'd kept inside for a long, long time. He looked at Eric, then at Alice, and it was to her that he spoke. "He was shaking down the DL guys. They'd come in, do their thing in the back, then leave, and he'd follow them, get their license plate numbers, find out where they lived, worked. It was a pretty good hustle 'cause he knew they'd never complain. Who're they gonna tell?"

"You hate homosexuals that much, Ray?" Alice asked.

"I hate all freaks that much," Ray said.

In the room next door, Ray, Senior was considerably less forthcoming. He had all but dismissed his Miranda warning with a flick of his hand, claiming that as a minister of God he didn't need it because God's law took precedence over man's. Gianna made him listen to, and made him say, in those exact words, on tape, that he waived his right to have a lawyer present.

"You are aware that Michael Nelson is in serious trouble," Gianna said. Washington looked down at his manicured nails, then up at the ceiling, and said nothing. Neither did Gianna, and she proved that she could outwait him.

"If you're waiting for me to talk about anything that Mr. Michael Nelson has said to me, you've got a long wait," he said, explaining, as if to the intellectually challenged, that any conversation with Michael Nelson was sacred communication. The muscles in his jaws worked when Gianna told him that his mail order degrees didn't hold the same weight as divinity degrees from legitimate institutions of higher learning or ordination into a legitimate and recognized religious institution. but otherwise, he showed no reaction. Still, Gianna knew she'd touched a nerve.

"Ray, you're just another wanna-be with some mail order degrees and nothing Michael Nelson said to you is privileged. At this point, you'd do well to forget about protecting him and start worrying about taking care of yourself."

"I've done nothing wrong."

It was clear to see where Ray Jr. had gotten his arrogant, imperious manner. Ray Sr. was a tall, thin man. His close-cut hair bore no traces of gray though his thin mustache did. He wore thin, gold-rimmed glasses that added to his distinguished look. The well-cut gray pin-striped suit completed the picture. Or it would have had he been allowed time to add a tie to the white shirt or socks to the black wingtips. As it was, the arresting officers thought they'd been more than generous to allow him to dress at all. He sat with his long legs crossed at the knee, his bare ankles a humorous distraction from the proceedings. Unlike his son, he refused to look at the woman questioning him. Perhaps because he could believe all too well that she was a cop.

"Oh, but you have, Ray," Gianna said in her most condescending tone. "You told Mike Nelson to kill Natasha and you helped him kidnap Felicia. If she's dead now, too—"

He was on his feet, eyes blazing. "That's a lie."

"Well," Gianna said, borrowing a bit of a drawl from Alice, "if it is, it's one a lot of people are willing to believe. You see, even though Mike has real degrees from real universities, it's clear that he's, well, not the most stable person in this situation. Or the smartest, to tell you the truth. You, on the other hand, are the picture of stability, and more than capable of conceiving and executing a plan to—"

"I conceived and executed nothing." Spittle formed in the corners of his mouth and anger radiated from him. "I am that boy's spiritual advisor and that is all."

"Mike's a Muslim. What does he need with you? He's got an Imam."

"I help out with certain...matters. I interpret certain points of Christianity for him, clear up things he's heard from other...ministers."

"You mean like his former mother-in-law, who really does have a Doctor of Divinity degree from a real university and who really is ordained and who really and legitimately can be called Reverend Doctor?" Gianna was goading, baiting, praying to put a crack in his steely facade. "What points of hers can you possibly clear up? You don't know half of what she knows."

"I know more than she'll ever know! She produced a pervert! From her loins sprung the hated of God and for her there will be no redemption! She blasphemes! She calls herself a preacher of the Gospel! I call her Jezebel! Mary Magdalene! No woman can be ordained of God to preach the Gospel and no perversion can go unpunished. Draw nigh and hear the word of God, the only true word of the only true God: There is no mercy for the evil doers, there is only justice, and that justice shall be meted out with the sword of righteousness! They shall die that they shall be born again into truth. She shall no more preach evil. Her mouth is silenced."

What the hell was he saying! "Ray, you've just proved my point." Gianna stood directly in front of him, forcing him to look at her, forcing him to climb down off the bully pulpit and return to the hard chair in the interrogation room. "What you've just said, Ray, proves what I said about Mike not being quite up to speed. He might have killed the wrong woman, Ray. The mother is fine, Ray. Reverend Doctor Christine Hilliard is at this moment in a suite at the Radisson DuPont Circle. Felicia is who Mike kidnapped— his ex-wife, Natasha's sister. He killed Natasha like you told him to, but not the mother, Ray. He messed up, and now he's messed it up for you, too. Reverend Dr. Hilliard will be sermonizing about you for years."

Anger replaced fervor in Washington's face. "He is an obedient servant of God. He would not transgress as you suggest."

"He got the reporter, Ray. You know, the one writing all those stories about homosexuals and about Natasha? He went to the paper to tell her to stop, but of course she won't. People like her don't take orders from people like Mike Nelson. Or you."

"It is the word of God that should be read daily, not that trash."

"But what about the other thing, Ray? What do you want Michael to do about the other thing? He's got the sister, not the mother. The mother will be in her pulpit Sunday morning preaching the Gospel, just like always."

"Harlot! Whore! No woman can preach the word of God. The Imam knows." Washington brought his palms together, then raised them, looked up, and said something nobody could understand. Then he dropped to his knees, leaned forward and touched his head to the floor.

Gianna rushed to the door and opened it. Shirley McManus was standing there. "A warrant for the Imam," Shirley said without Gianna having to utter a word, then rushed away, not waiting to hear the answer. Gianna turned back to Washington and waited for him to finish praying.

"I was wrong about you, Ray," she said when he stood up. "Or should I call you Imam? You've been studying Islam, I see."

"The one true religion."

"Maybe Mike told the real Imam where Felicia is, maybe he didn't think you'd understand enough of what he was feeling. After all, Felicia and Natasha were very close. Maybe he thought that Natasha had perverted Felicia, his wife."

Ray Washington smiled. Then he nodded. "We work together, the old religion and the oldest religion. The God of Abraham and the God of Mohammed."

"Maybe you don't know this, Ray, but Christianity is older than Islam. You should've studied more, I guess."

He looked at Gianna as if seeing her for the first time. The look turned to a hate-filled glare. She held his gaze, again able to outwait him. The effort seemed to cost him. He deflated like a balloon. Then he sat down hard and inhaled deeply. "She is where whores go. You know where that is, I'm sure, for all women are whores."

"If that's the case, then I need to be where Felicia is. Tell me where to go, Ray, and I'll go there. I'll go be with Felicia."

"The back room," Ray said. "Whores belong in the back room"

When Gianna rushed out of the interrogation room, Bobby and Kenny were already half way up the stairs. She heard Eric yelling instructions to the others. Shirley McManus was yelling orders at her people. They already had search warrants for the Pink Panther. All they needed now—all any of them wanted—was to find Felicia Hilliard alive.

CHAPTER ELEVEN

FELICIA HILLIARD FOUND ALIVE
IN MIDTOWN NIGHTCLUB
By R.J. Jones
Staff Writer

Felicia Hilliard, a 26-year old Philadelphia resident believed kidnapped last Friday by murder suspect Michael Howard Nelson, was found alive last night in a secret back room of the Pink Panther nightclub, the scene of another recent violent crime. Even though the Federal Bureau of Investigation had assumed authority over the case, it was the D.C. Police Department's Hate Crimes Unit investigators who discovered the victim handcuffed to a bed in a locked room at the rear of the downtown nightclub, which is located on Harley Street.

"We got lucky," said Police Chief Benjamin Jefferson. "Our officers were executing a search warrant at that location in connection with another crime and happened upon Miss Hilliard." Chief Jefferson dismissed as "preposterous" charges that his officers interfered with a Federal investigation.

"Besides, I'm sure Miss Hilliard and her family don't care who broke down the door and freed her."

Felicia Hilliard is the sister of Natasha Hilliard, the American University history professor who was murdered September 19th after leaving a nightclub on Lander Street. The suspect in that case is Michael Nelson, who happens to be Felicia Hilliard's ex-husband. One theory police are pursuing is that Nelson, a graduate student at Howard University, blamed Natasha Hilliard for the break-up of his marriage. Natasha was a lesbian and Nelson is a convert to Islam.

Nelson also is charged with assault and battery, among other things, for

his attack on M. Montgomery
Patterson, a reporter at this newspaper,
who is recuperating from emergency
surgery to repair injuries sustained
during Nelson's attack.

Gianna folded the paper and poured herself another cup of coffee. She'd
read enough. Besides, it wasn't the same reading Mimi's story written by
another reporter. Yes, the facts were there, and correct as far as they went,
but she could see the gaps in the reporter's knowledge. It wasn't R.J.'s fault,
whoever he or she was. Just as it was difficult for Gianna's team to play
catch-up on a case other cops had worked, it was difficult for a reporter to
step into a story, especially one as murky as the Hilliard/Nelson/Harper/Pink
Panther/Snatch story. She did think it was a nice touch, however, for R.J. to
quote the chief as having said "preposterous" to the FBI claim that D.C. cops
poached their case. What the chief had said, loudly and clearly, was
"bullshit," followed by the suggestion that the FBI couldn't find flowers in
spring. There'd never been any love lost between D.C.'s finest and the
myriad Federal forces that exercised authority over the various outposts and
agencies of the U.S. Government, but things had worsened after the 2001
terrorist attacks. Federal officials behaved as if D.C. was their personal turf,
under their control, and the people who lived in and were responsible for the
city, didn't like it. The District of Columbia was not just the nation's capital,
it was home to half a million people.

She looked at the clock when the phone rang and willed it not to be
anything to do with the case. She'd given her team the morning off and she
herself was taking her time about getting downtown. Still, she was showered
and dressed and if it was absolutely necessary, she could head into work.

"Come get me right now!" the phone demanded.

"You're obviously feeling better," she said to Mimi.

"I feel like shit! Did you see that crappy story?"

Gianna was glad Mimi couldn't see the grin on her face. "I thought it was a
very good story."

"Come get me out of here or I'll take a taxi home. I swear I will."

"What's the rush? You're supposed to spend the next two days in bed
recuperating."

"Calling the taxi company!"

*****

"I'm not saying don't run the story, Mimi," the Chief growled. "I'm just
asking that you hold it for a few weeks, give me time to identify all the rotten
apples. Once I've got 'em all lined up in a row, you can start picking 'em
off."

Mimi shook her head. "I've got to do my job, Chief, you know that. I can't hold a story this important."

"It's because it is so important that I'm asking you. You know I'm no censor, no subverter of the Freedom of the Press Amendment."

The chief was up on his toes, pacing up and down his office. Mimi had faxed him a copy of the story she'd written detailing Inspector Frank O'Connell's long term relationship with Edgar Burgess, and detailing Burgess's management of a clandestine organization that funded, endorsed, and instigated acts of violence against Blacks and other racial minorities, homosexuals, and women. The story identified by name half a dozen D.C. police officers who either belonged to Burgess's church or worked for O'Connell and participated in illegal acts against homosexuals, hiding behind the protection of a badge, and implied that there were other officers involved. The chief wanted to find those other officers before Mimi's story ran. "You'll drive 'em under and we'll never find 'em," he said, and she didn't doubt that. She just doubted that it was her problem.

"Tell you what, Chief. Call my boss. Tell him what I've got and tell him what you want. I'll abide by whatever the decision is." The big bosses were vetting this story now, though Carolyn still was the editor of record, the editor to whom Mimi turned in her story. But Carolyn couldn't refuse or agree to hold a story. That was a decision for the top editor, one Mimi wasn't going to ask him to make. If the chief wanted the story held, he'd have to ask for that.

He stopped pacing and looked down at her. It was still too painful for her to turn her torso so she didn't try to look up at him. Besides, she knew what he looked like when he was mad, and she knew he was mad. He wanted her to agree to his terms, not have her boss order her to. "That's a cop out," he said.

"No, it's not, Chief, it's me bending my own rules to find a way to give in to you. Don't you see that?"

He saw it. He didn't like it but he saw it. They both were pretty certain that the editors would tell Mimi to hold her story for a couple of weeks, given the guarantee that the story wouldn't leak to another news organization. All the top brass were involved and Mimi had to be extra vigilant to prevent them from closing Carolyn out altogether. Mimi still would get her story and the chief still would gather up the bad apples in his department and try his best to hang felony charges on all of them. That's after he fired them and took their pensions. He nodded as his phone buzzed. He crossed to the door and opened it. Gianna stepped in, controlled a look of surprise at seeing Mimi sitting there, and kept her eyes on the chief.

"Sit down, Maglione, make yourself comfortable."

She sat next to Mimi in the other wing chair opposite the chief's massive desk but didn't know what to say to her, didn't know what was going on between her and the chief. Mimi told her.

"Sounds reasonable," Gianna said.

"Cops," Mimi snorted derisively.

"You know what the story says?" the chief asked, and Gianna shook her head. He didn't believe her. "You really don't know what she's got?" He grabbed the copy from his desk and tossed it into her lap. "Read this and weep."

Gianna read and almost did weep. It was worse than she thought. Roger Holcomb and Thomas Murphy and Farrell and O'Connell and McGillicuddy weren't even the half of it, nor were ministers Bailey and Washington. Disgust rose up in her like bile when she read about Burgess and his connection to the Department. She gave the papers back to the chief and looked over at Mimi. "That's incredible stuff."

"You two really don't swap stories?" The chief looked from one to the other of them, his expression both skeptical and incredulous. "You take principles and ethics to new levels."

When Mimi had arrived home from the hospital she'd asked Gianna whether she'd read the files in the computers.

"But that's why I gave you the pass codes," Mimi said, when Gianna told her that she hadn't accessed her files. "I knew I had information that could help you."

"Your information is your information," Gianna had said. "Besides," she'd added, "I have to be able to go to court on my information, and I'm not sure I'd be able to do that on yours. Where do you get this stuff?" Then, when it looked as if Mimi were going to answer, she raised her hand to stop her. "Never mind. I don't want to know."

Now she told the chief what she'd told Mimi about being able to testify in court about her investigations and he actually blanched.

"Mimi, go home. I'll call your editor and yell and complain and jump up and down about yellow journalism. He'll agree to hold the story for a couple of weeks, which is all the time I need..." He turned to Gianna, "to collect court-worthy dirt on these low-life bastards."

Mimi struggled to heave herself up from the chair. Gianna jumped up to help her. Because of the pain, she no longer carried her purse or rucksack. She also didn't need them since she was spending no more than two or three hours a day at the paper, and that in meetings with editors. She'd done all the writing at home. She had money and a cell phone in her pocket. She'd take a taxi to the paper, meet with the editors, and, like the chief said, go home.

He walked her to the door. "This is damn good stuff, Mimi. The department owes you a debt of gratitude. But in case you're wondering, I won't be saying those exact words to that smarmy little editor of yours. I don't like that guy."

"You know the Weasel?" Mimi said, surprised.

"I know everybody," he said, closing the door behind her.

Gianna started to talk before the chief could. "I hope your plan doesn't include holding off on announcing arrests in Joyce Harper's rape."

"What difference does a few weeks make?"

"A big difference to Joyce," Gianna said. "She wants to go back to work, to get on with her life, and she'll do that a lot easier knowing that Thomas Murphy, Jim Johnson and Vinnie DeCecchio are where they belong. We can leave Holcomb out it if you want, since he didn't actually participate in the rape."

"He's going to be charged as an accessory."

"I just want to be able to tell Joyce and the Phillips sisters and all those women who thought they didn't matter to us that they do. I messed up, Chief, and I want to clean up my mess."

"Not a word about the connections between Murphy and the Washington men and Nelson, beyond the fact of his arrest for Natasha's murder. Agreed?"

"Agreed."

"And no more talk about O'Connell."

"OK," she said.

"And beyond the fact of her rescue, you're to say nothing about Felicia Hilliard. Not a word, Maglione, and I mean it."

Gianna started to balk, then changed her mind. Two of the men who had raped Joyce Harper had also raped Felicia Hilliard, and Roger Holcomb also had participated. She nodded. "Yes, sir," she said.

He came over and stood beside her. "I watched you interrogate that Washington creep. Damn fine work, Maglione, but I gotta tell you, I thought for sure you were gonna punch him."

"I for sure wanted to."

"We're going to have to make you a captain pretty soon, give you a Command. You saw how much fun Shirley McManus is having."

Gianna stood up quickly. "I like where I am just fine, sir."

"I know you do but that's not the point. If the mayor gets re-elected and I get re-appointed I may need you in another role. But don't worry about that now. For now, Maglione, focus on a job well done."

"Thank you, Chief." She headed for the door, almost got there, then turned back to him. He was still looking at her. "There's something you should know, Chief, and I'm only telling you in case it should become public knowledge, though there's no reason that it should. I just don't want you caught off guard."

"What are you talking about, Maglione? You sound like one of the PR flacks issuing one of those statements that means nobody's to blame for whatever it was that officially didn't happen."

"I've registered with the city as Mimi's domestic partner, and that'll be reflected in my personnel file as well sometime soon."

He looked at her over the tops of the reading glasses he'd just recently begun wearing. "Took you long enough," he said, and waved her out of his office.

END

Other books by Penny Mickelbury

In the Mimi Patterson/Gianna Maglione Mystery Series:
KEEPING SECRETS—First in the Series
NIGHT SONGS—Second in the Series
LOVE NOTES—Third in the Series
DEATH'S ECHOES—Fifth in the Series (Summer 2017)

In the Carole Ann Gibson Mystery Series:
ONE MUST WAIT
WHERE TO CHOOSE
THE STEP BETWEEN
PARADISE INTERRUPTED
ONE RED SHOE (Winter 2017)

In the Phil Rodriquez Mystery Series:
TWO GRAVES DUG
A MURDER TOO CLOSE

A Novel of Historical Fiction:
BELLE CITY

Short Stories:
THAT PART OF MY FACE

Penny Mickelbury is a novelist, playwright and journalist who
lives in Atlanta, GA and Los Angeles, CA

Visit her website: www.pennymickelbury.com
Write to her at mysteries at pennymickelbury.com

An excerpt from DEATH'S ECHOES, Mimi/Gianna #5
Coming Summer 2015

Mimi was more out of sorts than she recalled being in a very long time, and that realization depressed her as much as it angered her. In fact, the more she allowed herself to fully feel what was happening inside her, the more depressed and angry she became. What the hell had happened?! Here she'd been looking forward to spending a quiet, private five days alone with Gianna at Freddie's mountain cabin, and now here she was at Freddie's mountain cabin angry, depressed—and alone. Well, it certainly would be quiet and private. Freddie and Cedric were in Europe on a real vacation and the summertime hikers and bikers and boaters and swimmers who thronged to Western Maryland were long gone by the end of October, though now, as far as Mimi was concerned, was the most magnificent time of the year up here in the Allegheny Mountains. The foliage colors almost defied description so brilliant were the reds and golds and oranges, and Deep Creek Lake shimmered dark aquamarine, deceptively and dangerously placid. This was Mimi's vista from every window in the A-frame hillside cabin.

Inside, a fire blazed in the hearth, Keith Jarrett simmered on the CD player, and Mimi seethed as she paced up and down. A lousy five days. It was not too much to ask, especially considered that two of the days already were days off for both of them, and Gianna had enough accumulated vacation that she could take off until next year this time. Could take off but never would. She had returned more vacation time to the city than many people earned in a year. Mimi, on the other hand, used every second of her earned vacation every year. She worked as hard as Gianna did, often going two or three months without taking a day off. She understood dedication and commitment to work as well as Gianna. She just refused to allow the job to own her.

"The job doesn't own me, Mimi," Gianna had said, sounding both weary and angry. She was tired of their argument and she was getting angry.

Mimi, already angry, had shot back, "Bullshit, Gianna! We've had these plans for almost a month, but your boss, selfish bastard that he is, snaps his fingers and nothing else matters to you,"

"What's bullshit, Mimi, is what just came out of your mouth," Gianna had said as she walked out the door, which she closed gently and quietly behind her instead of slamming it, as Mimi knew she would have done.

That was yesterday, the day before they were to drive up to the cabin for the five-day hiatus that Mimi refused to call a vacation for the simple reason that a vacation was away—was someplace else and involved air travel and hotels and, preferably, passports. And this was today. Mimi had made the two-hour drive alone, not enjoying the scenery or the workout her new Audi convertible was getting on the mountain roads. She had brought the food, drink, books, movies and music that would have sustained the two of them for five days and got pissed off all over again as she unloaded the car. She knew that Gianna was hurting, that the chief was hurting—that they all were mourning the loss of one of their own. But wallowing in their hurt and pain and cutting their loved ones out of their lives was not a solution.

Mimi switched off the CD and switched on the TV. Something stupid and mindless to watch instead of listening to Keith Jarrett's moody, provocative chords that made her think and feel. And watching TV at Freddie's always was fund because it was like being at a movie theater: The screen occupied an entire wall. That's why she and Gianna had brought with them all the movies they'd missed—which was most of them given their respective work schedules. But for now: What was on television on a Frida afternoon? Freddie had every available channel in the universe and Mimi flicked through them until she saw Morgan Freeman and Denzel Washington on the screen. "Glory." She's seen the film half a dozen times and never tired of it.

She awakened to darkness and momentary disorientation. Then it all came back to here, where she was and why. She shivered, sat up, yawned, and almost choked to death. She jumped to her feet, not believing in ghosts but not believing her either, either.

"What are you doing here?"

Gianna hesitated briefly before answering, clearly weighing her words. "Would you rather I went back to Washington?"

"Don't be a jerk," Mimi snapped.

"Then don't ask me a question like that," Gianna snapped right back. "You know very well what I'm doing here."

Mimi turned from her, crossed the room to close the draperies and turn on a light, and then to add more logs to the fire, which had burned down to embers. Then she turned back to Gianna. "What changed your mind?"

"You could have told me you were coming up here," Gianna said, her calm tone of voice belying the anger she felt.

As usual, Mimi let hers hang out. "I shouldn't have had to tell you anything, Gianna. We planned for almost a month to come up here today. Then you change your mind and I'm supposed to, what? Sit home and sulk?"

"So instead you come up here and sulk," Gianna said, picking up the almost empty wine bottle. "And get drunk."

"I am not drunk!"

Giana gave a slight smile, then quickly stood and strode over to Mimi, reaching her in a couple of steps. Mimi turned away to face the fire. Gianna spun her back around, grabbed her arms and pulled her in close. She started twice to say something and twice stopped herself. Instead, she kissed Mimi, hard and fierce and demanding. Her hands dug into Mimi's arms, her tongue probed Mimi's mouth.

Shock froze Mimi momentarily, then passion ignited her. She returned the kiss with equal ferocity. She plunged her hands into Gianna's hair, seeking leverage and control of the kiss. Gianna wouldn't give it. Her hands moved from Mimi's arms to her breasts and, a nipple in each hand, she began to squeeze and massage, at first gently and then not, and the sound Mimi made deep in her throat startled them both. They took their mouths from each other but kept their faces close, their eyes locked. They had never been really angry with each other before and therefore didn't have a protocol for being really and truly pissed off. So they did the next best thing: Since passion fuels anger and they knew a lot about passion, they gave in to it. Together they sank to the floor, eyes still locked together. Gianna took control of Mimi's arms again as they eased into a reclining position and she pushed them above her head as simultaneously she pushed Mimi flat on the floor and positioned herself above, knees on either side of Mimi's body.

"You," she started to say, but couldn't finish because Mimi raised her head and re-started the kiss.

Gianna stretched out full length on Mimi, pinning her to the floor. Then she slid one leg forward and, knee bent, pried open Mimi's legs. She released one of Mimi's arms and a hand followed the knee. She could feel Mimi get hard through the material of her pants and, as she reacted, Mimi took advantage of the situation. She quickly flipped Gianna over, pinning her the same way she'd been immobilized just a moment earlier.

"Don't every walk out on me again," Mimi whispered, leaning over Gianna and holding her gaze in a piercing eye-lock.

"Don't ever give me a reason to," Gianna whispered back defiantly. Mimi held the eye-lock for a long moment before releasing it and dropping her head to Gianna's breast. She took an erect and hardened nipple in her mouth, first nuzzling it with her lips before taking it between her teeth. Gianna knew what was coming.

From DEATH'S ECHOES, Summer 2017

CPSIA information can be obtained
at www.ICGtesting.com
Printed in the USA
LVHW031527240121
677344LV00004B/642